DEATH WRITES ITSELF

CONNIE FROMAN DAVIS

** Trigger Warning | Sensitive Content **
Sex Trafficking and Sexual Assault

This material contains references to sex trafficking and sexual assault, which may be distressing or triggering for some individuals. Reader discretion is advised. If these topics are triggering for you, please proceed with caution or consider refraining from engaging with this content.

Copyright © 2024, Connie Froman Davis
Blue Bear Books
All rights reserved.

ISBN: 979-8-9903543-1-9

Produced by Publish Pros | publishpros.com

This book is a work of fiction. Any references to historical events, real people, or real places are used fictitiously. Other names, characters and events are products of the author's imagination and any resemblance to actual events or places or persons, living or dead, is entirely coincidental.

For Dad, Mom, and Curt

CHAPTER 1

JOE

Do you know when a woman is most vulnerable? Not when she's walking deserted, dark streets at two in the morning, not when she's alone pumping gas at a convenience store in a sketchy part of town, not even when she's inebriated and by herself in a seedy bar. No, a woman is most vulnerable in the presumed safety and confines of her own shower, reveling in the gloriousness of that cascading, comforting water, thoughts far away on a distant shore, maybe lost touching herself in those places where a woman's passion runs deep. Sounds buffered by the flow of streaming water, she doesn't hear the eager sighs of the bogeyman coming toward her.

Those thoughts flowed through Lieutenant Joe Morgan's mind as he looked at the dead woman lying over the track of her shower door. Water puddled on and around a daisy-patterned rug. As plain in death as she had been in life, Roxanne Richardson appeared to have been dead for several hours, but the coroner would have the final say as to exactly when her last breath floated through those pale lips.

The thirty-five-year-old had been brutally raped, likely multiple times. Bruises covered her breasts, upper arms, forearms, hip bones. He must have gripped her hard, held her fast; he must have been strong. She fought him for a while. The bruises were crowned by a large contusion on her left temple, smaller but darker ones on her left cheek. Defensive wounds marred her arms from wrist to elbow. The techs would probably find skin samples of her attacker under those clipped, unpolished nails. Bruise marks also encircled her throat, a gruesome necklace left from the brute strangling the air from her body.

Joe sighed and turned away. This was the fourth rape and murder in the last six months in his hometown, a grim record for St. Samuel. Their small city usually only averaged one murder a year, and before this string of atrocities, a stranger rape hadn't occurred in over a decade. Progress, Joe mused, as the town had grown exponentially in the last few years and remained small only in Joe's childhood memory.

All four women had been single. All four had been in the shower. The lingerie drawer of all four had been rifled through. How had the bastard known they would be in the shower? What was he looking for in the drawer? How had he gotten in? How did he come and go with minimal trace? Did he stalk them? Did he know them? Had he dated them? Joe was an experienced detective with instincts usually right on target, but neither he nor anyone in his unit had come up with the answer to even one of those questions yet.

This one would cause his chief to convince the Georgia Bureau of Investigation to finally put together a task force instead of just loaning them the single agent who had been working with the unit for the last few months. After the second shower rape and murder, Joe had had a feeling more dead bodies would be coming, his gut telling him so loudly and clearly, a phenomenon his paternal grandmother identified as the spirit eye in him. For as long as he could remember, Joe had lived with what some would call a second sight, although he preferred the more professional label of keen intuition. According to his granny, he came from a long line of spirit eyes, all of whom could sense any variety of things, and all of whom had died young. But no matter how accurate his gut might be, Joe's new police chief was a strict by-the-book gal, and Joe wasn't about to let her in on the secret of his inherited spirit eye. She would ship him back to patrol in a skinny minute. Joe hoped his mystical orb wouldn't call him to his grave any sooner than necessary, especially not before he found the murdering SOB who was wreaking havoc in his town. He was also hoping the spiritual presence would give him some serious clues, because right now he and his partner were stumped, the homicide unit was stumped, and a blazing aspirin-proof headache was centered just above his left eye.

Dodging a crime scene tech as he edged out of the bathroom, Joe beckoned one of the uniforms and asked if they'd found a kitten. The officer looked at him like he'd lost his mind but respectfully said, "No, sir, not that I know of. I did see some pet bowls in the kitchen, but I'm not sure if they're for a cat or dog. No sign of either, so far."

Joe thanked the young officer, told him to keep an eye out for a small feline, then went looking for his partner and best friend, Terry Hampton. He and Terry had grown up in St. Samuel together, reluctantly parted ways after high school to attend different colleges, then entered separate branches of the service—Joe to the Marine Corps to fly helicopters and Terry to the Coast Guard to enforce the law on the high seas. Eight years later they'd found themselves back together, no longer neighborhood boys, but grown men on the police force in their hometown. Picking up right where they left off, they had rapidly re-established their close friendship. They had been assigned as partners about four years earlier after Terry returned from a short stint with the Atlanta Police Department.

Terry's wife had begged him to give city living a try, claiming her career choices were too limited in their town. Although he had no desire to work law enforcement in a city the size of Atlanta, Terry had loved his wife and wanted to make her happy, so he talked to St. Samuel's police chief about a temporary exchange program. St. Samuel would send him to Atlanta for a year, and the Atlanta PD would send one of their officers to St. Samuel. The chief at the time had been college roommates at the University of Georgia with the Atlanta police chief, and Terry had served with their chief of detectives during his six years in the Coast Guard. The deal sealed, Terry, Penelope, and their three kids moved.

Eight months later, just as Terry and the kids were beginning to get used to big city life, Penelope announced she had filed for divorce, having planned for one all along. The conniving woman had wanted to be established in Atlanta before she ditched Terry. She demanded he move out. Immediately.

Recovering from that shock took Terry a long time. Penelope had gotten pregnant in high school; she and Terry married the day after graduation. They had been married for sixteen years of what Terry thought was happily ever after, so when he finally came back home to St. Samuel, he was one sad, disillusioned puppy. Fate was on his side, though. About a year after Penelope decided she didn't want to be a wife, she determined she no longer wanted to be a mother either, so the three kids returned to live with Terry in St. Samuel. A hands-on, loving father, Terry had missed his children terribly and was thrilled to be a full-time dad again.

He was a little surprised to see how quickly life with the kids became good without the perfidious Penelope. Love being blind and all that, he'd never realized how toxic his wife could be, although Joe could have told him. Joe's wife, Diane, had always called Penelope "Poison Pen" behind her back. Diane and Terry were close, had been since the moment Joe introduced them, but Diane and Penelope had only tolerated each other for their husbands' sakes. Diane considered Terry to be her "brother by another mother," but Penelope was nowhere on Diane's family or friend tree.

Terry's kids were now doing well, despite not hearing from their mom often. Caleb, the oldest, was a junior in high school, hoping to go to Valdosta State on a baseball scholarship. Ellen, a shy teen sandwiched between two gregarious brothers, was an academically gifted sophomore. The youngest of the trio was thirteen-year-old Devlin, a practical joker who terrorized his siblings so regularly they sometimes blocked the door to his room so he couldn't come out. Poison Pen had departed Atlanta for parts unknown with a two-bit salesman and occasionally reached out to her children, but never to Terry, which suited him just fine.

✧ ✧ ✧

"Any sign of a kitten?" asked Terry, coming up behind Joe in the hallway.

"No, but I'm sure one is here somewhere. Damn things can hide better than a 1920s bootlegger running from the law. We had a full-grown cat once that hid in that little triangle space behind the toaster oven on the counter. Don't know how she scrunched herself up back there. Didn't come out for the longest time; we had no idea where she was. Diane was frantic until the little cretin finally popped her head up and looked at us like, 'What? I'm trying to nap back here.'"

Joe was married, more or less, although when he thought about it these days, he figured his marital status was a lot less than more. His once loving and adoring wife was a fellow law enforcement officer who worked patrol in the Saddle County Sheriff's Office two counties over. Happiness had engulfed them like blissful fog for the first five years of their married life. But then they decided to make a baby and the fog dissipated, slowly and painfully. After a series of miscarriages, multiple failed fertility treatments, and a final diagnosis rendering them perpetually childless, their marriage went into a state of what seemed to Joe suspended animation.

Both Joe and Diane were physically present, living in the same house, doing the same things, speaking the same language, taking the same vacations. But they were no longer connected. Joe tried to make up for the loss, but nothing could erase the hurt or the failure for Diane. She was a shell of the woman she'd been before, and Joe was unsure how to help her. Apparently, so was their marriage counselor.

One miserably muggy night, after Diane was the first patrol unit to respond to a particularly horrific crime scene involving a brute of an ex-boyfriend, a four-year-old girl, and a weighted lead pipe, Diane disappeared. She walked away from the wooded scene into the dark Georgia night, drove off in her Saddle County Sheriff's Office vehicle, and had not been seen or heard from in five months. Saddle County, along with Joe and the St. Samuel Police Department, had put all their considerable detective skills to use, calling in favors, sucking their contacts dry, using every law enforcement tool available, all to no avail.

Diane's credit card had been used at a gas station and a diner, both in South Georgia, then she had literally fallen off the grid.

No one at either of those locations could say whether she'd been there or not, which left no way to determine if she was acting on her own volition, had been abducted, or if a stranger had stolen her card. Of the two security cameras available, one didn't record, and the other was in a permanent state of malfunction. Her marked county vehicle had never been found, a circumstance almost as puzzling as Diane's disappearance. The scent of her trail died just as surely as the hope of them ever producing a baby.

Joe carried on in slow motion, afraid if he crossed the line back into full living he would shatter into a million pieces. He kept fantasizing Diane would turn up at the farmhouse one day, perfectly fine, with a reasonable explanation on loving lips. But as time continued to march on, his hope faded.

Joe was a large man, bigger than most, but not as big as some. At six-foot-two, he'd been a star fullback on the high school football team and over the years had added to the muscle he sported as a teen. He hadn't yet gained any fat layers, a fact for which he was grateful, especially given his work schedule and late-night eating habits. Joe had often been told he looked like Tommy Lee Jones when the actor was young. He didn't see the resemblance himself, and he didn't think ol' Tommy was all that good-looking, even in his prime, so he wasn't sure he liked the comparison. Joe had to admit though, the man had something that made him a powerful presence on the big screen, so he always accepted the compliment, figuring a Tommy Lee Jones comparison was better than being compared to Tommy Lee from Motley Crue. Plus, he'd always liked the *U. S. Marshals* movie the Academy Award winning actor had starred in.

Shortly after Joe and Diane had purchased their new home, the town had invested a huge amount of taxpayer dollars into turning the old railroad tracks into running and walking trails through town and around the lake in a five-mile loop. The main trailhead was a short drive from their property. The trails were safe and well-lit, except for a couple of curvy spots, but the parks and rec department wisely closed the track every evening at dusk. In their almost ten years of marriage, Joe and Diane had enjoyed running the trails together, which helped keep them both in shape. After a five-mile run and laughing race to the finish, the sweaty couple would stop for breakfast at the Main Street Diner, where the loser was required to buy. Joe was a solo jogger now; no egg and waffle breakfast after a morning run unless he made the meal for himself at home. A swarm of good memories kept him out of the diner.

✳ ✳ ✳

"Hey, Lieutenant?" Crime scene tech Kelli Cochella, a new hire to the unit, called out from the bathroom. "Come take a look at this."

Joe and Terry squeezed into the room, bending over the kneeled tech's back. She had turned the dead woman over, fully exposing the corpse's front side. Kelli pointed to a series of jagged marks spaced about an inch apart on the right side of the victim's torso.

"I'm not sure exactly, sir, but it looks like the killer cut and sewed five buttonhole shapes into her skin using some type of heavy-duty thread. The coroner will know more, but I've never seen anything like this before."

Joe and Terry looked at each other. Up until six months ago, they'd never seen buttonholes sewn into a murder victim either. Now they were looking at their fourth set.

CHAPTER 2

PHOEBE

I threw down my pen, accidentally knocking the blank yellow legal pad into the napkin holder, frustrated. Trying to become a bestselling novelist is difficult. And aggravating. And sometimes not fun. And now I have to pick up a hundred outdated Christmas napkins strewn all over the floor. If I could just come up with an intriguing plot, a few interesting characters, heck, even an inviting title, I'd be well on my way to writing fame!

My name, which I hope will one day be a household word, like David Baldacci or J. K. Rowling, is Phoebe Evans. I'm divorced, still several years on the friendly side of forty, part-time librarian, part-time gym rat, and part-time writer. Although I suppose not much of that statement is technically true. I'm not actually a librarian, I just work at a library. I'm only in the gym an hour or so three days a week, which makes me more of a mouse than a rat. And while I am a wannabe author, I rarely write anything but thank you notes.

I fantasize about scripting amazing, unable-to-put-down fiction, but somehow I can't capture on paper any of the colorful characters who periodically pop into my brain. I've been unable to nab them on the laptop either, my frontal cortex not being inspired by technology.

Since beginning this writing adventure, I've been incapable of latching onto any characters I like or could build a story around. Maybe the problem is interesting characters don't like me. Hmm, what a disturbing thought. Surely that can't be the case. I'll have to talk over that troubling conjecture with Jack, Josie, and Jilly, my four-legged dream team. Those three occasionally inspire a story concept, but without cool characters as anchors, every idea drifts around in my skull like the debris floating in outer space, useless and irretrievable. I really don't understand how Stephen King does it, but I'd give my eyeteeth to have just one moment inside that man's head.

If I'm being completely honest, I do have one character stuck in my brain—a dreamboat detective I've named Joe Morgan. But every time I try to capture Joe and put him in cool crime scenes on the page, he floats right out of my head. I think about Joe so much, some days I'm concerned I'm head-over-heels in love with my imaginary man. Every date I've been on lately I find myself comparing the male across the table to my Lieutenant Joe, and the real man comes out the loser every time. Probably don't need to point this out, but my love life is pretty much at a standstill. Even my Lieutenant Joe doesn't come around that often, and I should be able to summon him at will.

That whole divorce thing was a real kick in the teeth. I'm not sure how most people feel about ending a marriage, but I hated the idea of being divorced. Never, ever, ever thought I wouldn't stay married until death actually did part us. I came out of my wedded years sad and lonely, but deep down I was secretly excited about a new start.

Paul and I were married for six years. No sob story about betrayal, no domestic abuse, in fact rarely even fights at all. Sweethearts since fifth grade, we muddled through high school and hormones as teenagers, stuck together through college. Sometimes I think we got married because we were so used to each other a different option never came to mind. We were supposed to get married after all that time together, right? Didn't everybody graduate, get a job, get married, have kids, get fat, retire into couch-potato-hood, and then die? Isn't that how life goes? Apparently I thought so, right up until the moment I didn't. Because then I thought, *huh, what am I doing? I have a life to live, books to write, a rock band to start, airplanes to fly.* Paul knew about my love of flying, but not about any of those other passions, and wouldn't have been interested if he had known.

When I finally poured enough liquid courage down my gullet to tell Paul what I was thinking, he shocked the ever-loving pee out of me when he said, "Ya know, the moment I walked into that church I knew we shouldn't get married."

Well, Paul, you would have saved us six years if you had thought to mention that little tidbit before I sashayed down the aisle to you in my three-inch ankle-turning heels. So much for open and honest communication between long-time partners. Paul moved on to greener pastures out West, found himself a sweet little rodeo gal, and now they raise horses on a small ranch. Finding myself divorced at the tender age of twenty-eight in the big city of Atlanta, and having only dated one person in my life, I promptly went a little crazy, bar-hopping and man-hopping and job-hopping until I finally heeded my Aunt Lucy's sage advice: "Don't do anything unnecessary." An oft-repeated phrase I had ignored multiple times.

DEATH WRITES ITSELF

My part-time library job is fun and helps pay the bills, which leaves me plenty of time to despair about my non-existent stories and would allow me plenty of time to write them if I could figure out how. Fortunately, my mildly eccentric ninety-seven-year-old aunt, the previously mentioned sage, died four years back and left me a large chunk of change (two years after my divorce, in case you are interested), which is why I can get away with working a fun job part-time instead of grinding away sixty-plus hours a week in a high-powered job or a dead-end job or any kind of real job. That large chunk has been chinked down to a much smaller lump though, so this writing gig better start coming to fruition soon.

Not so fortunately, Aunt Lucy also left me six of her fourteen cats which Jack—the handsomest German Shepherd you've ever seen—and I thought was outrageous, given Aunt Lucy knew full well Jack reigns over any domain we occupy. However, the aforementioned monetary bonanza was attached to those six felines—accept no kitties, receive no kitty chow. So, we grudgingly brought the little buggers into our cottage by the sea, hoping they would all magically disappear without us having to do something horrible. Care for a dip in the ocean, my furry friends? Hee hee. No, Jack and I didn't do that, but some days we were mighty tempted.

Jack stoically accepted the cats into his kingdom. He did not chase them, bark at them, or even raise an eyebrow when they drank from his water bowl. He did, however, put his paw down, literally, when one of the two kittens tried to latch on to his magnificent tail. Jack whirled around, put his front paw squarely on the kitten's head, and gave her a glare fierce enough to fry bacon. Likely goes without saying, but the kitten, whose name is Josie, never tried that maneuver again.

Since most of the cats were as old as Aunt Lucy, four of them ended up crossing the Rainbow Bridge to hook up with her within six months. We tried to be sad, Jack and I, but truthfully, six sets of litter boxes had been more than a bit much. We managed to hide our glee, but that kindness turned out to be unnecessary as the two remaining kittens didn't seem to mind the loss of their elder stepsiblings either. They are mostly interested in treats and keeping an eye on Jack's tail. Jilly in particular eyeballs Jack's tail, probably because she doesn't have one of her own, hers having been bobbed to a nub after she kept attacking it, drawing enough blood to fill a crime scene. The vet finally chopped it off, and Jilly has been much happier without that particular temptation. Jilly is a beautiful tan tabby, with pearly luminescent fur and dark lemur-like rings around all four legs, the complete opposite of her completely black, long-haired sister.

So now Josie, Jilly, Jack, and I enjoy a comfy life in our small house on the Georgia seashore, in a not-so-little-anymore town called St. Samuel. I used a sizeable amount of Aunt Lucy's largesse to pay cash for the run-down cottage, which came complete with an amazing ocean view, 1960s linoleum, and complimentary black mold in almost every corner. The view and the short walk to the ocean make the décor worth it. I battle the mold every day with a spray bottle of bleach and a sponge. So far, the mold is winning, but I have hope for the home team.

One of Jack's requirements while we were castle hunting was a yard free of thorns and stickers, full of lush grass, and plenty of trees with squirrels. We searched until we found this little cottage with a small back yard that Jimmy—who I'll talk more about shortly—fenced in immediately. He built us a five-foot-high fence with staggered bricks. Brick for low maintenance in the humid ocean air, staggered so Jack can peer out and keep an eye on the neighborhood. Jack is in charge of home security, and he takes his role quite seriously, going out each night to secure the perimeter, checking each morning to ensure no breaches. I pity any fool who would try to come into our kingdom with Jack on patrol twenty-four seven.

Our small abode has three bedrooms, one of which is so tiny everyone except a real estate agent would call it a closet, two bathrooms, one half and one full, a living area that opens to the dining nook and the kitchen, a wraparound front porch with amazing ocean views from every spot, and a screened-in back porch. Since I leave the porch door open to the yard for Jack's instant access to his grassy domain, the screening doesn't help ward off Georgia's state bird, the mighty mosquito. Jack seems to be immune to their bites, but I swear, one of these days those beastly insects are going to carry me off to Mosquito Land.

The outdated linoleum is going the way of the dodo bird next week when my buddy Jimmy and I replace it with beautiful knotty pine re-purposed from the old barn on the former Hemingway property. The Hemingways, supposedly distant relatives of famous author Ernie, were the richest folks in town for centuries, until technology outpaced people and orders stopped coming to their family-owned mill. After the mill closed, the youngest generation turned the family mansion into a southern-themed bed and breakfast, complete with handmade quilts on the beds, creamy grits for breakfast, a library full of their purported ancestor's books, and several six-toed cats roaming the property. The inn was never successful, though. Town gossipmongers said the youngest daughter drank up most of the profits and the oldest son thought he was a better accountant than actually proved to be the case. Once the Internal Revenue Service started sniffing around, the gig was up. All I know for sure is they sold off the wood from the horse barn and Jimmy scarfed some up for me when he helped the last generation of Hemingways tear down the crumbling structure.

Jimmy is the maintenance guy at the library. Besides building the fence and adding a new storm door to the front, he's updated and remodeled the cottage's master bathroom, which I'm happy to report is modern and mold-free. When I say Jimmy is going to help me replace the linoleum, that's really a euphemism for me standing around holding a glass of wine and handing him the occasional tool while he does all the work. My construction skills are limited, and my enthusiasm for the work even more so. Luckily, besides Jimmy being super-skilled and one of the nicest guys in the universe, I suspect he has a huge crush on me. I try not to take advantage since he's not really my type, nor does he come close to measuring up to my Lieutenant Joe. Well, not too much advantage, anyway. A girl does need a good handyman.

CHAPTER 3

JOE

There's a fine line between one and one too many, Joe reminded himself as he watched a morose man at the end of the polished oak bar pick up his third whiskey of the night and take a soulful swallow. Since Diane had disappeared, he worried he was getting close to one too many more often than he should, so he was sticking with club soda tonight. Glimpsing movement in the antique mirror gracing the back of the bar, he watched Terry approach and turned as his best friend plopped down on the stool beside him. Terry signaled the bartender for a draft and reached for the peanut bowl at the same time.

Pushing the goobers closer to Terry, Joe asked, "So what do you think is missing? Underwear? He could be taking a pair as a memento. Or maybe a bra. Why else would the victims' lingerie drawers be standing open if the killer didn't take something?"

"Aww, are we going to talk about work? Can't we at least spend a little time discussing football or women, or heck, even the latest men's fashion first?" Terry threw peanuts in his mouth while he talked, more interested in discussing his faltering love life than their serial killer. His brain was exhausted from non-stop thinking about the case. He knew Joe's was too.

"Men's fashion? What the hell do we know about men's fashion?" Joe arched an eyebrow at his partner.

"Not a damn thing, but I do hate that man-bun look, and we've been working the case non-stop for the last six months. Can we give it a rest through the first round at least?" Mixing a murder case with cold beer always gave Terry a case of the crankies.

"Don't know why those drawers would be rifled through if not to collect a souvenir. Panties are easy to hide, but would stand out in a man's dresser drawers or closet. Which would be good for us if we ever find a suspect," Joe mused, only half under his breath.

Terry sighed and gave the bartender a come-hither sign for another round. They were at one of St. Samuel's three local sports bars, a family-owned establishment that had been open since the early 1930s. The Daisy Lady, one of the first bars to open after Prohibition ended, had developed a loyal following over the decades. Built well in her day, the place still showed the fine craftmanship common to that era. Third-generation owners John and Mary Callahan kept the oak bar polished, the woodwork oiled, and the brass hardware shined. Joe liked the atmosphere, the crowd being a little older and law-enforcement friendly. These days, not all bars were. Plus, John stocked several excellent brands of bourbon, Joe's favored alcoholic beverage.

"Okay, let's review what we've got," Terry said resignedly. Reluctantly taking his eyes off the bar's attractive guitar player who had just started her first set, he gave Joe his full attention. "Maybe the booze will inspire some creative next steps."

Being the good detective he was, Joe noted Terry's admiration for the talented young woman on the stage. She had a lovely voice and was singing an Alanis Morissette number, something about irony. On the sidewalk outside the bar's front door, a sandwich-style chalkboard had welcomed "Sally Wren" as tonight's special entertainment. Joe made a mental note to talk with Mary about the bar's entertainer. If Mary gave her a seal of approval, he would ensure several return visits to the Daisy Lady and encourage Terry to ask the singer out. Terry had dated since divorcing Poison Pen, but not a lot and nobody sane. No one his age, either. Sally looked to be about thirty, which was close enough to Terry's thirty-six. Although not an experienced matchmaker, and an unwilling one at that, Joe wanted his buddy to find someone to enjoy life with before he became too settled in his ways. Joe's dad had frequently proclaimed a man living without a good woman was destined to eat too much, drink too much, and grow old before his time. Or become a workaholic, the path Joe was currently marching down.

CHAPTER 4

PHOEBE

If I was clever enough, I could write stories about some of the characters here in my hometown; many of them are quite colorful. Take Danny Taylor the tailor, for example. Funny word play, huh? Now, he's a quirky guy I'd like to put in a story. He does alterations for most of the folks in the area, not surprising since he operates the only sewing shop within forty miles. His alteration skills are excellent, and he creates perfectly symmetrical buttonholes by hand, a manual skill unheard of in these high-tech times.

Besides his sewing talents, the most interesting thing about Danny is hardly anyone I know has ever seen him. He is phobically shy and doesn't much like people. Also, he lives in the closet. Well, technically he doesn't live in a closet, nor is he gay, as far as the town gossips know. But he keeps his industrial-size sewing machine in an industrial-size closet and rarely pokes his head out for any reason. His niece handles the customers; Danny handles the sewing. Whenever I go to his shop, I can hear the hum of the sewing machine methodically buzzing along. Danny will come out on occasion and talk to me briefly, but only if Jack is with me. Danny makes eye contact with Jack and carries on a short conversation with my charming canine before drifting back into his closet.

When I think of Danny, I picture him as a small, slight man, but I'm consistently puzzled as to why recalling his physical appearance is such a challenge. Even when he's standing right in front of me, his debilitating shyness so overwhelms his physical attributes, I could barely tell you what he looks like five minutes after I've seen him. Possibly I need to improve my observational skills. Anyway, Danny would be a great character for a book if I could just figure out how to develop him. Maybe a story that involves sewing up corpses? Hmm, must give that one some thought.

Danny isn't originally from St. Samuel. He just showed up one day with his niece in tow and opened up shop. Town council members were ecstatic to finally have the retail space he chose rented; that half of the old water company building had sat empty for a few years. Once the Taylors got settled in and Danny proved to be so reclusive, no one asked many questions about where they came from. The niece was chatty but vague on their background. Ultimately folks were just happy to have a tailor in town, and eventually curiosity waned.

In case you're wondering about my physical appearance (you definitely wouldn't misjudge my physique), I'm five-foot-eleven. Yes, tall for a girl, and no, I didn't play basketball or volleyball, thank you kindly for asking. I did, however, play fastpitch softball in high school, until the day I dropped three fly balls to right field one after another. Coach sat me on the bench for an inning but couldn't keep me there. I was batting .425 that year, so he put me back in as the extra hitter. My fastpitch career was over after that season, partly because of my abysmal fielding abilities and partly because it was my senior year. These days I play softball in the women's community league in town, but our team's record is as bad as my fielding still is. I can hit the ball over the back fence, though, so my Pink Panther teammates love me. I think the pitchers get confused because of my height. My torso and legs are so long they have a hard time finding the strike zone, so they almost always pitch right to my sweet spot.

My hair, like my torso, is also long. We are all blessed with good hair in my family. Mine is a lovely auburn color, if I do say so myself, thick and wavy. When short, my locks are poodle curly, which is one of the reasons I keep the length past my shoulder blades. The auburn color complements my eyes, which are usually green. I've never seen it myself, but friends tell me when I get angry, my eyes go gray. Usually I don't get angry, so green eyes for me it is.

The town of St. Samuel is in Frances County, Georgia, nestled between Brunswick and St. Mary's. Unfortunately, like many coastal towns, St. Samuel has been discovered by Northern invaders seeking warmer temps and lower taxes. Our formerly little township has managed to retain her small-town charm in the revived buildings and independently owned businesses on Main Street. The surrounding historic district, a half-mile swath comprised of beautiful homes dating back to the 1800s, also offers an alluring glimpse into the past. Most of the original buildings in town still stand, but instead of offering feed and grain, they boast expensive boutiques and antique stores.

We used to be a town of about four thousand, but I think the population is up to seventeen thousand or so now. Summer visitors swell the normal population by several thousand each year, but thankfully, most of them go home by Labor Day. Even though business is booming in the downtown stores, our former oasis is larger now than I'd like it to be. We've gotten too big to know everyone anymore, and news doesn't get around like it used to. I suppose the town council likes raking in all the new property taxes, though.

The town dates to the early 1700s when some guy named Samuel stumbled off a boat from England and claimed for himself the first plot of land his legs could stand on without wobbling. Samuel never got on a boat again as far as we know, not even after his wife and two daughters were carried away by Indians and his sons were killed fighting off the righteous natives. Samuel is supposedly buried under the old well in the town square, but really, how does anyone know those whitewashed bones are actually him? Maybe if he'd been killed trying to save his family or if he'd really been a saint, he'd have been buried properly with a fancy headstone in the First Baptist Church cemetery. Right now, the town council is in the middle of a fundraising campaign to build a fountain on top of the old well. If they ever raise enough funds and install the fountain, maybe the disturbance will cause Samuel to rise and tell us his story.

Besides the reclusive tailor, another colorful character in our town is Henry DeSantos, the oddball manager of the local animal shelter. Henry is a good enough guy, but he has a peculiar habit of dropping kittens off unannounced, and usually unwelcome, at unsuspecting people's houses. He has employed this unusual adoption method regularly throughout the years. Like Danny Taylor, Henry dislikes being around people, preferring the company of the four-footed friends he makes at the shelter. A big, brawny man (no trouble remembering what he looks like), Henry was a professional tattoo artist prior to discovering his true calling at the animal rescue. He still creates the occasional tattoo for shelter employees but is officially retired from inking. I've always wondered if he ever paid taxes on his tattoo parlor earnings but suspect not.

I have no idea why I'm curious about that fact, but the question always pops into my head when I see him. Possibly my interest has something to do with the Boston Tea Party tattoo brightly inked on his left forearm.

Henry was already here when my family arrived many years ago. We went through grade school and high school together, then he disappeared from St. Samuel for about five years. He reappeared when he was twenty-three, but he's never told anyone where he went or what he did while he was gone. One day he returned with all his needles and inks, rented a small shop not too far from St. Samuel's bones, and opened Rat Tail Tattoos. I know, right? An unpleasant name. Who wants to be reminded of hairy rats?

Tattoo lovers apparently didn't mind the image of rodents because business was brisk for the first few years, until one of Henry's most frequent customers, a lifelong Bruce Springsteen fan, developed an infection after Henry tattooed The Boss's face on his client's forearm. The infection itself didn't bother Bob, but the resultant scarring turned Bruce into a creepy-looking clown, a travesty Bob could not live with. No amount of additional tattooing could turn the clown back into Bruce. Bob sued Henry for the little he was worth, forcing Henry to close up shop pronto. Next career move for Henry? The shelter. Henry truly loves animals, and thus far, none of the cats or dogs at the shelter have had the wherewithal to sue him.

Henry's ventures in placing unasked-for pets in homes has led to an approximate fifty-percent forever home success rate. Given the shelter's official placement rate runs about thirty percent, maybe Henry is on to something. When families elect to keep Henry's proffering, he is so happy he offers them free tattoos—if they will sign an agreement not to sue him. If the family rejects the little feline, Henry has been known to flex his muscles and scowl. With his big bulk looming over them, the would-be owners often relent and adopt the poor creature. But when the bluster doesn't work, I've been told Henry cradles the tiny purr machine in his arms and stomps off. He's never hurt anyone, at least not that anybody in town is aware of. But he can be plenty scary when he's riled up.

A third possible character for my future bestseller is Kurt Von Schuster, the town cobbler and rumored town drunk. Kurt has also been a tattoo artist, but his experience and training are limited to his two stints in prison. Kurt has a good heart, but when he's over-imbibed, he has a penchant for stealing women's underwear, sometimes still in the package at the local department store, sometimes off a backyard clothesline, and a few times while breaking into a single woman's home. These misadventures have twice landed him in the pokey. However, since his latest release eighteen months ago, no underwear has been reported missing, so maybe Kurt has turned over a new leaf. Local gossip at the library also says Kurt hasn't been seen as regularly at his favorite bar, The Dug Out. Maybe less drinking has led to less panty stealing. The old-timers in town hope Kurt has reformed, as the talented cobbler's repair prices are much lower than the cost of a new pair of shoes. Also, his shoe repair skills are remarkable; he can breathe life back into the most damaged footwear.

Kurt has lived in St. Samuel all his life, so no one who knows him holds the panty stealing or the occasional public drunk against him. What they do hold against him is the pass he dropped the night of St. Samuel's only foray into the state high school football championships. The St. Samuel Spartans were down by six with fifteen seconds left in the fourth quarter. The Spartan quarterback threw a Hail Mary pass to his favorite receiver and the crowd held its collective breath, envisioning the team in the Spartan history books. The ball spiraled through the air, landing perfectly in

Kurt's gloved hands. He turned toward the end zone, a clear field ahead, no defenders in sight, running hard until, inexplicably, he dropped the ball at his cleated feet and watched in disbelief as the pigskin rolled all on its own into the end zone. The crowd groaned in horror and dismay as their state championship dreams dissolved in the crisp fall air. Kurt never recovered from that fall from grace. As everyone knows, when football is the topic, Southerners have extremely long memories.

None of these potential characters are married in real life, so if I were to base a story on them, I would have to fabricate their love interests. Danny is a widower (I overheard him tell Jack this one day), Henry has yet to find his one special gal, and Kurt's wives divorced him, one per prison stint. Kurt has dated one of the local honeypots on and off, but if either Danny or Henry has dated anyone, neither of them has kissed and told. Of course, Danny is so shy, he'll probably die a widower. I wonder how he ever found the courage to court his first wife. And Henry, well, I suppose he could find a woman who loves animals and tattoos as much as he does, but such a romance seems highly doubtful.

People in St. Samuel accept the men's various quirks, but unless a clothing alteration, a new four-footed family member, or a shoe repair is required, the townsfolk generally ignore them. The trio always brings to mind a piece of Aunt Lucy's wise advice, offered each time I left the house: "Watch out for the weirdos." While I wouldn't necessarily classify the men as weirdos, I do keep an eye on them, hoping they'll spark inspiration so my great writing adventure can finally begin.

CHAPTER 5

JOE

"What about those crazy buttonholes? What do they mean? You didn't button your mouth about something, so I buttoned it permanently for you? But if that was the deal, wouldn't he have sewn the lips shut? And remind me what we know about connections between the women." Talking as he pulled out his credit card to pay the tab, Joe waved to Terry to put his wallet away. "You bought last time, I'll get this one."

Watching Sally return to the stage after her break, Terry replied, "Well, we haven't unearthed any personal connection between the vics yet. The only things they all seem to have in common so far are being single, living alone, over five feet, seven inches tall, and between the ages of thirty and thirty-five. A dresser drawer was left standing open in each of the victim's bedrooms, with the contents messed up as if they'd been gone through.

"Oh, and each of the first three owned a kitten. The shelter took possession of an orange kitten, a Maine coon, and a grey tabby, all about twelve weeks old at the time of their owner's death. No sign of the pet in the last vic's home yet, although food and water bowls were present, along with a few cat toys. And an overflowing litterbox the crime scene techs didn't want to touch."

Terry concluded his rundown. "All four women were raped, beaten, and strangled to death while in the shower. Each body had five knife cuts on the abdomen, loosely stitched around the edges with dark red thread like buttonholes. Or possibly some other design we haven't figured out yet. Coroner says the cuts and stitching were done prior to final strangulation, so the victims were still alive for the mutilation. Finally, two of the women played in the St. Samuel community softball league. Still have to check to see if they played on different teams or the same one."

Joe considered Terry's summary, remembering the orange kitten had run through her owner's blood, leaving a trail of miniature pawprints leading to the little feline's hiding spot behind the washing machine. The Maine coon had been sitting beside her owner when the first patrol unit arrived, meowing pitifully. And at Eleanor Connelly's home, while searching through the closet, the uniforms had found the tiny tabby buried under a layer of dirty clothes in the laundry basket. Not for the first time, Joe wished he could speak cat.

"So, where did this guy come from? Where has he been? And why did he choose these women? For that matter, why did he choose our town? We've got to find some of these answers before another body shows up. The chief thinks we need to release additional details to the public, too, along with more safety tips and warnings." Joe rubbed a hand over his face in frustration as they walked toward the door. "I see her point but I'm not sure what to tell the citizens. We have no idea how this guy chooses his victims or how he gets in their houses. Plus, the chief hasn't had any luck bringing in the Feds, although she does think we'll get more help from the GBI eventually. And she told me today reporters have started asking a lot more questions. I guess with the drama in the governor's office calming down, the press is hungry for a new headline. All that said, we need to come up with some answers soon."

Joe suddenly stopped talking, disturbed by a familiar feeling in his psyche he knew never to ignore. Focusing his mind inward, he opened the pub door for Terry, then followed his partner to the maroon unmarked car in the parking lot. As tall men, Terry being six foot to Joe's six-foot-two, the partners appreciated the extra room afforded by the matriarch of police cars, the Ford Crown Victoria. The large four-door sedan was one of the last in the department's inventory. Like most law enforcement agencies, several years ago St. Samuel's police department had begun transitioning to the Dodge Charger Pursuit, a line designed specifically for law enforcement. Though the Charger was a much cooler looking vehicle for studly cops, Joe knew he and Terry would miss the extra leg room when their Crown Vic finally succumbed to the ravages of time and irreplaceable parts.

Joe's spirit eye had woken up as they left the bar, but he couldn't figure out what message it was trying to convey. Knowing something must be stirring in the night air, he scrutinized the parking lot quickly, his dark brown cop eyes scanning for trouble. All he saw was a lot full of cars and the back of a tall woman, beautiful auburn hair streaming past her shoulders, as she stepped into a dark blue BMW. Hair the exact color and length of Diane's.

CHAPTER 6

PHOEBE

An ancient, ramshackle house covered in vines and overhanging branches barely stands on the corner of my street, a one-story skeleton of what once was a beautiful wood-framed summer home. Through the missing front door, I can see a crumbling chimney constructed to warm three rooms at a time. The decaying structure sits on two-foot-high brick piers, the red rectangles a tribute to Georgia's ubiquitous red clay. Every time I pass the house, I wonder what those walls would say if they came alive one day and spoke. Who lived there? What did the people do for a living? Who died there? Did children live in the rooms and play in the yard, climb the trees, swing on a tire, keep a pony? Are the family pets buried in the back yard? What did the family argue and laugh about?

The house is owned by some long-gone heirs who live up north. Lord knows what they are holding on to the property for. Maybe each year they pray for a hurricane to sweep the place away. Land prices are at a peak right now, especially by the water, so even with the dilapidated old cottage, the spacious lot would bring a premium price. This house could be a character in my thus far nonexistent book, but the words I need to describe the imaginary lives lived within the walls lie frustratingly beyond the ink in my pen.

In my mind's eye I can see twin ten-year-old girls setting up a tea party on the front porch. The girls have white-blonde curls and are dressed in ragged overalls. When their mom calls, they run into the house, chattering loudly about the chocolate chip cookies the young mother has just pulled out of the oven. Turning the corner, the back yard comes into full view, and my brain conjures up a young black boy and a younger black girl, siblings definitely, swinging on a tire hanging from one of the big live oaks. An old hound dog watches them from the corner of the yard; an elderly woman pins laundry to the clothesline. But after the cookie-eating twins run into the house and the swinging siblings jump from the rubber tire, my imagination comes to a complete halt. What they do next is beyond me.

I so want to write a best-selling crime novel, not too full of violence, as I dislike graphic assault scenes, but just enough to let the reader know something awful has occurred. I figure fiction lovers have plenty of imagination; I wouldn't have to spell out each minute detail of a gruesome murder. I only need to imply what happens, like in those old black-and-white movies from the thirties and forties. The moment Humphrey Bogart pulled out his Saturday Night Special, you knew someone was going headfirst into the river with a hole in his forehead even though the camera cut away to the next scene as the gun fired. Those old movie directors knew the audience would get the point without having to show a closeup of blood spurting out of an artery or brain matter splattered all over the wall.

Of course, my novel must include a handsome detective who falls in love with the heart-sore heroine of the story. What sensibly romantic woman doesn't want a good-looking, kind, professional man in her life? I certainly do, and the sooner the better! One exactly like my fictional Lieutenant Joe will fill the bill nicely, thank you. My Joe is tall, at least six feet, looks like Hugh Jackman (or George Clooney, I can never quite decide), or maybe the craggy but sexy Tommy Lee Jones, muscles galore, a true chivalrous gentleman, tops in his profession, with a broken heart only the heroine can mend. Oh, look at that! I thought of some worthy words! Quick, quick, pen and paper before I forget them!

CHAPTER 7

JOE

Joe stopped in his tracks. Terry ambled on toward the Crown Vic and was halfway through the passenger door before he realized his buddy was still a hundred feet away, staring like a statue at the far side of the parking lot. Terry followed Joe's sightline but didn't see anything except a blue Beamer pulling out of the lot.

"Hey, Joe, what's up? Having a brainstorm about our murderer?"

Jolted out of his trance, Joe ran to the car and slung open the door, hollering, "Get in, get in!"

Terry slid in quickly, hooking his seatbelt and looking at his partner with concern. "What did you see? What, what? Talk to me, Joe."

"Diane, that was Diane in that car, that blue BMW."

Terry thought back to the bar. Joe had drunk club soda with lime, so he couldn't be inebriated or blurry-eyed, which only left hallucinating or lovesick. Personally, Terry thought Diane was dead, likely by her own hand, but if his best friend thought he saw her, then by heaven, Terry was up for a car chase. He'd like to find Diane himself and, despite their close friendship, tell her just what a miserable excuse for a human she was, leaving Joe with no explanation and a heartache the size of Texas. Terry had never seen Joe down about much of anything, but ever since Diane disappeared, his friend exuded a sadness as visible as the dust surrounding Charlie Brown's friend, Pigpen.

Joe screeched to a stop at the parking lot entrance, scanning left and right. Seeing taillights headed south, Joe turned, the Ford's powerful V8 engine burning up the road. As he pulled up behind the lone vehicle, Joe cursed as he realized he was following a black Hyundai, not a blue BMW. Stopping in the middle of the road, Joe got out and searched the roadway as the Hyundai's taillights faded from view. No other vehicle lights were in sight.

"Where the hell did she go? We couldn't have been that far behind her."

Terry popped out for a look up and down the road too, then glanced at Joe, concern for his friend etched on his face. "Not sure, but if she's in town, we'll see her again. Let's head home; it's been a long day. If that was her, maybe she'll be waiting for you at your house."

CHAPTER 8

PHOEBE

Now, depending on how old you are, you may wonder why I think Tommy Lee Jones is so sexy, since he's not nearly as physically appealing these days as he was in his youth. The camera still loves him, but that craggy look hasn't aged so well (sorry, Tommy Lee). Seeing him on screen in any role, at any age, though, reminds me of times spent with Aunt Lucy, who always let me watch movies my parents thought I was too young to see and who introduced me to a young, sexy Tommy Lee.

I saw my first TLJ movie when I was about eleven, much too young for war and romance, according to my parents, but not Aunt Lucy. The movie was *Heaven and Earth*, an amazing story in which Tommy Lee plays an American soldier in love with a haunted Vietnamese woman. So sweet. And Tommy Lee was nominated for an Oscar for his performance! Then, when I saw Tommy Lee play Woodrow F. Call in *Lonesome Dove*, my heart was forever in lockstep with that man. I also discovered then that I really liked Westerns. With horses, cows, cowboys, great scenery, and the good guys always winning, what's not to love? Even at the immature age of thirteen, Mr. Jones' portrayal of Woodrow Call's hardhearted, shy cowboy stole my heart. I've seen every Tommy Lee Jones movie ever made and am thrilled he continues to act. He still makes my heart throb.

On a completely different subject, I've been ciphering on something unusual lately. Have you ever considered how vulnerable a person is when they're taking a bath? I was in the shower this morning trying to conjure up interesting story lines and got to thinking about that after I heard a crash come from the kitchen. I listened carefully for a few more minutes, but hearing no other unusual noises and not really wanting to go investigate naked and dripping wet, I assumed Jack would eat anyone who was breaking in and returned to my creative musing.

Being nude, I suppose, is what creates such a sensation of vulnerability. You literally have no cover, nowhere to hide, no weapons to defend yourself with. Doesn't take much to imagine what an easy place the shower is to be murdered. Just ask Janet Leigh. Think about it. The murderer breaks in quietly, or maybe he's already in the house, hiding somewhere, waiting for you to come home. The running water shields the sound of his approach, and the next thing you know, *stab, stab, stab,* blood spurting out of your arteries. Or *bang, bang, bang,* gunshots reverberating against the tile. Or a silent garrote slips around your wet, soapy neck while your eyes are closed, head tipped back to rinse out the shampoo.

I went through a period in my younger years where each time I showered, I'd constantly peek around the curtain looking for Norman Bates, or I'd turn the water off to listen, thinking I heard an intruder's footsteps. I never actually watched *Psycho* in its entirety. The promo featuring Anthony Perkins standing outside the shower curtain holding his giant knife, with Janet Leigh blissfully unaware she's about to get a nasty surprise and will never get the suds out of her hair, was enough to keep me away. Creeped me out and I didn't even see the whole movie.

Thanks to Jimmy and my newly renovated bathroom, I now have a lovely walk-in shower, so no curtain to block any knife-wielding psychos from view. Clean line of sight or no, people are still in a vulnerable place when they step under that hot spray. If such a scenario happened in my Lieutenant Joe's world, I suppose he would find the victims grotesquely displayed over the track of the shower door, the water running cold, the condensation faded from the mirrors. Maybe I should put that scenario in a book: Water conservationist goes crazy, killing every member of local climate change denier group while they shower. Hmm, that storyline just might have some potential.

I contemplated this plot while I dried my hair, slapped on mascara, and threw on work clothes. Jack, Jilly, and Josie were all anxious for breakfast, getting underfoot, meowing and barking in concert in case I didn't understand JUST HOW HUNGRY THEY WERE! When I finally walked into the kitchen, I discovered the crashing sound had been Jack tipping over his bowl, probably to check for crumbs hiding beneath the metal. Luckily no axe murderer was in sight.

Welcoming the silence as they chowed down, I poured a bowl of cereal, pulled the blueberries out of the fridge, and enjoyed my own breakfast, all the while thinking about ways a water conservationist could pop off people in their own bathrooms. Not much came to mind, so I wrapped up my kitchen routine, let Jack out to run security while I brushed my teeth, let Jack back in with an unnecessary reminder to take care of his sisters and our castle, then headed off to work. As I got into my lovely dark blue BMW—another luxury courtesy of Aunt Lucy—I noticed a young woman standing on the beach staring at the house. She looked sort of like Danny Taylor's niece, but I couldn't tell for sure from this distance. She didn't wave or seem to recognize me, so I figured the woman must be a tourist enjoying the early morning ocean air. I needed to get going or I was going to be late for the morning staff meeting, so I left the visitor to her solitude and backed out of the drive.

CHAPTER 9

JOE

Belle greeted Joe with a loving bark when he opened the kitchen door, his mind still on the auburn-haired woman, Belle's mind focused intently on supper. Throwing his keys on the counter, he scratched behind the black giant schnauzer's ears, saying, "I know, sweetie, I'll fill your bowl in a second. Did you go out recently?"

Joe had installed a doggy door just after they adopted Belle. With the hours he and Diane worked, a puppy would have needed an industrial-sized bladder to make it through their shifts without having an accident. After filling Belle's bowl with grain-free dog chow, Joe watched the food quickly disappear. Belle always ate like a starved orphan, vacuuming up her kibble in about two seconds. Joe couldn't understand how the canine digestive system functioned with so little chewing and so much inhaling.

Thinking of the blue BMW, he poured a large glass of water, drank it down in one long swallow, then measured out his allotted two inches of bourbon for the evening. He pulled a fork from the drawer, dumped his carryout fried chicken salad on a plate, and dropped onto the couch. Since Diane had disappeared, Joe ate in front of the television, something they had never done in their married life. He'd discovered eating could be a lonely business, so he allowed the evening news or some mindless show to keep him company while he consumed his meal. Belle was good company, but she had terrible table manners, not being able to prevent the saliva dripping from her mouth at the smell of something delicious. The TV didn't drool over his evening entree.

Initially, Joe and Diane had disagreed about the type of dog to get. Joe wanted to rescue a plain old mutt. Diane had argued for a giant schnauzer, having seen one on the previous year's National Dog Show and becoming enthralled. Joe lost the argument, although in truth he didn't care that much. Generally, he was happy if Diane was happy.

Diane did her usual methodical research, telling Joe that the giant schnauzer was originally bred in seventeenth-century Germany to be a farm dog. Knowing her husband well, Diane was clever enough to point out one of the breed's many duties in those days was safeguarding the family's farm. When his canny wife further informed Joe the large canines also guarded not just farms, but breweries, factories, stockyards, and butcher shops, Joe was sold, amused by the thought that pay for guarding a butcher shop would have been excellent for a dog, with all those meat scraps continuously falling to the floor. Belle's genealogy included the German pinscher, the Great Dane, and the Bouvier des Flandres, all breeds with impressive histories of being guard dogs. Joe correctly surmised with that much genetic background as canine law enforcers, plus being military working dogs during the two Great

Wars, a giant schnauzer would fit in their own law enforcement household perfectly.

Belle had earned Joe's respect early on when she was still just a puppy. They had been getting ready for bed about ten one evening when Belle alerted at the bedroom window, ears and stubby tail high, soft growls rumbling in her throat, nose quivering and thrusting behind the dark green curtains. Even though not yet full grown, Belle was tall enough to look out the windows. Joe had taken one look at her, retrieved his nine mil from the nightstand, and quickly walked to the back door, Belle woofing softly by his side. As he stepped quietly onto the back deck, Belle streaked by him silent as a bird's wings, solid black body blending immediately into the dark night. The next thing Joe heard was a thud, soft growls, and a cry for help. Turning on the porch light, he saw Belle standing on top of a young male, holding her mouth around the nape of his neck. Following her training perfectly, she was not hurting the boy, just strongly suggesting he lay still if he wanted his jugular to remain intact. Joe ambled over, called Belle off, and hauled the intruder to his feet.

"Care to explain what you're doing in my back yard at ten o'clock at night?"

"I was just taking a shortcut home," came the mumbled reply, as the interloping teenager stared at the ground, inching away from Belle, who was industriously trying to sniff his crotch.

"A shortcut? Out here in the country? More like you were scoping out the house for a burglary. Or were you peeping in the windows? Are you some kind of pervert?"

The kid was visibly sweating, shaking his head no, and mumbling under his breath. Joe was considering the options when Diane came out to see what was going on, her duty weapon held by her side. When she saw the boy she said, "Don Daley, what the hell are you doing in my back yard?"

Turned out the boy had run across Diane's path a few times in Saddle County. No major crimes, just some impressive graffiti by a kid whose parents didn't pay enough attention. He had spiced up some of the abandoned buildings in the neighboring county, thinking fewer people would recognize him if he used his considerable artistic talent farther from home. Diane had been trying without success to get him to attend art classes at St. Samuel's teen center. Joe left her to do the scolding and went inside to finish his bedtime ritual. Belle, however, did not budge from the trespasser's feet until Diane sent the kid on his way and came inside. Since then, Belle had proved herself to be an almost perfect dog and an excellent companion.

※ ※ ※

The TV sat silent as Joe munched his salad. He couldn't get the auburn-haired woman off his mind. Was that really Diane? He was positive that hair could belong to no one else. Could she be in town and not reach out to him? Where did she go, and where did the Beamer come from? No, that woman couldn't have been her. Thousands of women have long, wavy auburn hair. And Diane wasn't that tall. The parking lot was dark. He could have easily mistaken the hair color. Besides, Diane wasn't cruel enough to return and not reach out to him. Then again, she was cruel enough to walk away without a word to begin with, so maybe he didn't know his wife as well as he thought he did. He had learned quickly in the police business that folks have all kinds of crazy secrets, and spouses are often the last to discover them.

Joe sighed, took his plate to the kitchen, washed up the dishes, and went to the bedroom to read for a while. His brain needed to focus on something else or he would never get to sleep, and he still had a serial killer to catch. He was currently reading a beautifully written novel about the connectivity between trees and humans for which the author won a Pulitzer Prize. Joe thought Richard Powers should also win the Nobel Peace Prize for the simple way he presented how humans and the ancient forests should live in peaceful harmony for the betterment of the world. The world could certainly use some peace, starting with his own tiny piece of the globe.

After a fitful night's dreams of blue cars and long-haired women, Joe woke to find Belle scrunched under his left arm and his right arm hanging off the bed. Belle always cuddled him to the smallest section of bed possible. Joe didn't complain since canine loving was all the affection he received these days.

Stepping into the shower after a meticulous shave, Joe tried to shake off the image of auburn-haired beauties so he could focus on his murder cases. The most recent victim, Roxanne Richardson, had been an accountant at a small but thriving tax firm in St. Samuel. According to her friends and work colleagues, she had led a quiet life outside of work and, having recently adopted a kitten from the local shelter, spent a lot of time at home. Her only hobby was square dancing. She was a teetotaler, regularly attending the First Baptist Church on Main Street in town. Neither Joe nor Terry had found anyone who could be considered an enemy, or for that matter, anyone who even mildly disliked her.

One of Roxanne's fellow square dancers had been in obvious distress over the news of her death. Teary-eyed, he admitted to having a giant crush on her, but he'd never had the guts to act on his feelings. Joe had wanted to give him the whole "life is short, and you never know so act when you can" speech but figured the timid admirer had just learned that lesson the hard way. As an unfulfilled lover, the dancer was easily a potential candidate for Roxanne's killer, but the detectives had quickly ruled him out. The night Roxanne was killed, the unrequited Romeo had been at a dance with their square dancing group waiting for her to show up, an alibi confirmed by several members of the Swing Your Partner Club.

After Joe and Terry left the Richardson scene, a fuzzy black-and-white kitten had finally presented himself to the crime scene techs, which tallied one kitten for each of the four victims. The little guy had scampered out from under the dresser, meowing hungrily.

"If those felines could only talk," Joe mused out loud as he stepped out of the shower. Belle, who always waited on the rug outside the shower door, cocked her head at him as if to say, "Well, even if they could talk, Dad, they're cats, they aren't going to tell you anything."

CHAPTER 10

PHOEBE

I'd had a good life, mostly, back in Atlanta. I had finally job-hopped to a paralegal position downtown on one of the many Peachtree Streets and stopped hopping. I've never understood why so many streets are named Peachtree in the Atlanta area. Though it may make sense to the street-naming people with Georgia being nicknamed the Peach State, more than one road named "Peachtree" is just confusing.

As for my paralegal job, I enjoyed the work quite a lot and was rather good at researching and deciphering legalese. I was even contemplating going to law school and becoming the next F. Lee Bailey instead of the next Jane Austen. But as I was filling out law school applications, two life-altering events happened within a few months of each other, and my potential legal career went down in flames before the first match was struck.

The second game-changing event was Aunt Lucy's advancement to the great beyond, leaving me with that heaven-sent financial windfall. And while I may sound flippant about her generous bequest, I am sincerely grateful for her and miss the old gal dearly. She was my favorite aunt. Of course, she was my only aunt, but still, she was my champion even when my parents weren't. We always had fun together, and I loved her with my whole heart.

Aunt Lucy was larger-than-life, with loads of personality, and would be a great character in one of my stories. She showed me how to become my own person, usually by example, but often through the old-fashioned sayings for which she was famous. For instance, when I was a teenager and wishing I could be anyone in the world except myself, she would frequently remind me, "Phoebe, in this world, you can be anybody. Best to be yourself."

One of her many other sayings was, "I always wanted to be somebody; I see now I should have been more specific." She used that line on me after I declared at fourteen my goal in life was to become the head cashier at the local grocery store. The woman in charge of all the cashiers sat in an office with a window about eight feet above the checkout lanes, a setup my teenaged self thought was totally cool. When I returned to the same store as an adult, the raised cubicle with a view of the whole store wasn't nearly so amazing. And if I'm being completely honest, neither was the idea of being a professional head cashier.

One of my favorite Aunt Lucy expressions is, "If I wanted any shit out of you, I would have pinched your head." Always makes me laugh. I've never used that one because it's so impolite, but occasionally I'm tempted by library members who get wound up over a ten-cent late fine.

Because of her wealth, Aunt Lucy also had a couple of witticisms about money, although she thought discussing the size of one's bank account was in poor taste. Regarding charitable donations, she told me, "Lead with your heart, not with your money." I was about ten the first time I heard her say this. Took me a while to figure out she meant to choose charities close to both your heart and your community's need, then contribute as many dollars as possible. Now I try to follow her example. Just ask Henry DeSantos who the shelter's biggest donor is. Besides allowing me to be extra-charitable, Aunt Lucy's inheritance money also put me in a position to buy almost anything I wanted. Within reason, of course. No multi-million dollar yachts for me, but I could pay cash for a nice sailboat. So far, Jilly and Jack have vetoed that idea, but Josie and I often dream about a pirate life at sea.

But back to my life-changing events. The first one almost sent me sliding out of Atlanta on a slippery slope straight for the closest psych ward. If Aunt Lucy hadn't been so present for me, I might well have pulled a Van Gogh, doing my best work from an insane asylum. I couldn't talk about that day for a long time, but after I lost my job, my current man, and most of my friends, Aunt Lucy insisted I find a good therapist.

Under duress, I went shrink shopping and found an older counselor who didn't irritate me like the younger ones did. After finally understanding I was incapable of speaking about this major life event, said counselor suggested I write down the story instead. Wouldn't you think the first thing a wannabe novelist would do is write down words too horrific to be spoken, a story too awful to tell out loud? But no, I just tucked all the details into a closed compartment in my brain, slammed the door, and double-sealed it with brain matter so I would never access those thoughts again. Of course, as every psychologist will tell you, memories sealed in one's brain never stay buried. The worst parts have a way of seeping out of the seams and cracks until eventually you fall flat on your face on the dance floor from exhaustion, pain, and running too long in the fast lane.

I suppose you're curious now, so I'll make my counselor proud and share the story.

Jack and I were out walking in our Atlanta neighborhood on a humid August morning. We lived in a cookie-cutter townhouse neighborhood with typical residential streets, but we had veered off into an older area without sidewalks, a two-lane street with no line down the center, the kind of road your grandmother may have lived on in the fifties. The road was plenty wide enough for us and any vehicle that might pass.

We were about a mile into our three-mile walk when I heard a loud engine coming up behind us. I looked around. The sound turned out to be a tractor pulling a trailer with two riding lawn-mowers on it. The driver and I exchanged a smile and a wave, polite and friendly, just like my momma taught me. Another hundred steps or so, and I heard what sounded like the tractor coming around again, which couldn't have been the case because I could still see him ahead of me. I didn't look back this time. Jack was busy sniffing under a wilting azalea bush, and I was trying to keep him from eating something disgusting. When the vehicle reached my peripheral vision, I saw a white truck moving fast, pulling a trailer with another riding lawn mower aboard. Must have been the morning for lawn care in that neighborhood.

Another friendly wave, another friendly smile. And then. And then.

I heard a thump like a mortar exploding, a squeal of brakes. I saw something flying in the air over the hood of the truck and at first I thought, *Wow, that's the biggest doll I've ever seen.* Then I realized the doll was not a doll but a child, flying. But children don't fly, and I comprehended the child had been hit by the truck and she was going to land in front of me.

But she can't, she can't do that because if she does, she'll hit hard on the pavement, so I have to run and catch her. So I do. I drop Jack's leash and hustle up, with my arms outstretched, my eyes never leaving her, knowing this can't end like a fly ball in the outfield, and I'm running, but my legs are like lead, and I'm reaching, reaching, I've got her, I've got her, but she's a dead weight, and we fall, we fall to the ground, my arms underneath her. But I can't keep her head from bouncing off the asphalt, once, twice, no three times. As her little head thuds against the pavement, I hear a cracking sound and then a pop, and all I can think is, *I got her, but I didn't get her, now what, now what?*

Like many people, I've taken basic first aid and CPR. Don't ask me to set a compound fracture, but I can handle spurting blood or a sucking chest wound. But the stillness emanating from that wounded child was something the Red Cross doesn't teach in any first aid class. A red puddle spread underneath the little girl's black curls, her face was a misshapen mass, and a large gash gaped open across her chest. Jack was to my left, barking and barking. I saw movement out of the corner of my right eye and looked up to find the driver and another man staring down at us in horror. A woman was screaming hysterically in Spanish, also to my right, but I couldn't see her.

As I ripped my t-shirt over my head, I shouted "Call 911!" I couldn't think of anything to do except try to stop the bleeding from the chest wound. I didn't want to lift her head to staunch that blood flow in case she had a neck injury. I pressed my t-shirt firmly against the large gash, then realized the two men hadn't moved.

I yelled again as loudly as I could, needing them to act. "911, NOW!"

They moved then. They jumped into the truck and hauled ass. I don't know if they called for help or not. The screaming woman finally ran over, crying, "Mi bebe, mi bebe, Anna, Anna." I could see the outline of the woman's phone in her pocket, so I tried again, less loudly but firmly, "Ma'am. Call 911. Now."

After that, after an endless amount of time pressing my t-shirt to Anna's chest and talking, talking, talking to her, asking her to stay with me, begging her to stay with me, listening to Anna's mother wail and Jack bark, finally the firefighters came, and the police came, and the ambulance came. They took Anna's lifeless little body away from me.

I had stayed calm in the moment of crisis. I've always been good in emergencies. When a softball smacked our catcher, LuAnn Lovett, in the face behind home plate one night, I was the one to hold her hand, put an ice bag on her nose, and staunch the bleeding until the medics came. But that day with Anna, I lost my composure when I had to tell the responding patrol officer what happened, then had to repeat the story to the police detective who showed up later. He was a compassionate guy and let me hold on to Jack's ruff while I talked, but by that time, I was shaking in the ninety-degree heat and could barely get my breath while Jack whined and anxiously licked my face.

The detective's name was Terry something; I've never been able to recall his last name. In attempting to coax me to speak, he chit-chatted at first about normal things like the weather, then told me a little about himself, his wife, his kids. Said he was from a small town on the coast and was just in Atlanta temporarily. Oddly, I recall he talked about his partner back home. While I contemplated Anna's blood on my hands, I remember thinking, "Why do I care about this?" as he said something about his old partner being in the Marines, flying helicopters, something, something, his words muted and virtually unintelligible in my ears.

After my statement to the detective, I never spoke about Anna again until I wrecked my life and found a shrink with the brains to suggest I write. Even now, I've never verbally retold the story, only written about it in my journal.

CHAPTER 11

JOE

Saturday morning at the station while he waited for the rest of the team to file in, Joe contemplated the case files of the four women murdered in his town over the last six months. Detectives from the Saddle County Sheriff's Office had called to get further details about the most recent case because a woman had been raped and murdered in a similar manner three years ago in Saddle County's jurisdiction. At the time, Joe and Terry were busy investigating a string of arsons around St. Samuel. One of the fires had killed the ninety-two-year-old well-loved town baker, so neither partner had followed the Saddle County case closely. By the time their arson cases closed, the sherriff's office was winding down their murder investigation. With no additional victims and all leads exhausted, the investigators eventually filed the case with the department's other cold cases.

DEATH WRITES ITSELF

The two homicide units had been exchanging information since St. Samuel's second rape and murder, but Joe had asked for a full copy of the Saddle County case file, which was being sent by courier that morning. One of Joe's junior detectives would return the favor with the St. Samuel files, then begin an intense review of Saddle County's case. Meanwhile, Joe, Terry, and Jeremy Dalton, the on-loan GBI agent, were scheduled to meet the Saddle County detectives for lunch at noon.

Joe was waiting to hear back from one of his detectives about the results from the National Incident Based Reporting System and Violent Criminal Apprehension Program databases. The rookie was checking to see if similar crimes had occurred anywhere else in the nation. They had checked NIBRS and ViCAP after the first three murders, but nothing had popped except the one potential match in Saddle County. However, some agencies weren't quick to input their case data into the systems, and not all were accurate with the information they did enter, so in Joe's view, periodic re-checks were always worth the effort.

This morning Joe, Terry, and Jeremy were going back through each file line by line to see what they may have missed. Terry had volunteered to stop on the way in to pick up a couple of good coffees; the station's coffee bar wasn't terrible, but wasn't great, either. With luck Terry would bring a big bag of ham biscuits, too. Joe hadn't taken time for breakfast this morning. He was running on limited sleep, extra caffeine, and a growling stomach.

Just as Joe picked up the first victim's file—May Ellen Landon, a pretty receptionist in an orthodontist's office who also played in the women's community softball league—he was interrupted by a sharp rap on the door. Joe looked up to see Chief Teresa Paris looking ragged with an unpleasant scowl on her face.

"What's the latest? Any leads on this guy yet?"

Joe shook his head. "No, nothing. We're going back through the files this morning to see if we can unearth anything new. Saddle County's full file should be here shortly, so maybe something will shake loose when we compare ours to theirs. We're also meeting with them today. No updates yet from NIBRS or ViCAP."

"I've got a press conference set for ten Monday morning. Shake something loose before then, will you? The press is going to eat us alive, followed rapidly by the citizenry, the mayor, and the town council. I can't keep a lid on the details of these murders much longer." The chief stepped away from the door, then turned back. "By the way, you'll be there, you and Terry both. And Jeremy. I'll ask Saddle County if they want to join."

Joe opened his mouth to protest but caught the look in the chief's eyes and clamped his jaws shut. He hated press conferences.

CHAPTER 12

PHOEBE

At Jack's "I'm hungry" bark, my head snaps up, and I peer through slit eyes around my dining nook. I feel like I've been in a trance. What the heck? I had been sitting here, trying to write but instead daydreaming about handsome detectives, sipping a glass of white wine, and what, did I fall asleep? The wine glass is empty, Jack's food bowl is empty, the cats are on the table eyeballing me, and oh my gosh, several pages of handwritten manuscript are laid out in front of me.

"'Genius burns,' as Jo's family would say," I murmur to myself as my brain takes in page after page of my handwriting on yellow lined paper. Jo, or rather Miss Josephine March, is my favorite heroine in all of literature from my all-time favorite book, *Little Women*. Louisa May Alcott knew what she was doing when she created headstrong, lovable Jo and her three sisters. I always wanted to be Jo; she was creative, determined, stubborn, kind, adventuresome, loyal, and hard-working, all the things I aspired to in my teens. When Jo would go up to her tiny garret and write her plays and stories, her sisters would call her creative process "genius burning." That's how I feel now for the first time ever. My genius burned! Ten whole pages!!

The thing is, a reason not to write always exists, at least for me. Other writers may not procrastinate, but in my world the cats need food, the dog needs food, the cats need to be played with, the dog needs walking, the cats need water, the poop must be scooped, the litter needs changing, the lawn needs mowing, groceries need buying, the toilets need cleaning, I need to wash my hair, I need to wash the car, I need to wash the dog, I need to . . . well, you get the idea.

The list is endless when you don't want to sit down to do the one thing in the world you most wish to do. Why would a wannabe writer not want to sit down to write? Good question. Fear, I suppose. Fear of having no ideas, fear of failing, fear of hearing the criticism bound to come. Maybe even fear of success. Plain stupid fear. Aunt Lucy used to quote an old inspirational speaker, George Addair, who once said, "Everything you've ever wanted is sitting on the other side of fear." Well, that's exactly where my dream man and my dream career reside . . . on a big ol' comfortable couch on the other side of my fear.

I get up and stretch, yawning hugely. Man, this writing business is tough. Let's see, what did I write here? Wait. Maybe I should have a fresh glass of wine to fortify myself in case the whole thing is garbage. Going into the kitchen, I see Jack is right, six thirty is way past his supper time. I fill his bowl with kibble, and by the time I've pulled a chilled wine glass from the freezer, the nuggets have disappeared. He must have been starving because Jack is usually a two-pieces-of-food-at-a-time eater. Don't tell him I said this, but he eats more like a cat than a big, tough dog. His breakfast always lasts until at least noon and his supper until after I go to bed.

I take a deep breath and sit down in front of my legal pad pages again. With a generously poured glass of unoaked chardonnay at hand to bolster my courage, I'm prepared to see what I've got. Okay, looks like my Lieutenant Joe showed up. Be still, my beating heart. Wow, he has his hands full trying to find a serial murderer in his town. And yes, there's a dead woman in the shower. The third victim so far. She's a member of an aggressive climate change denier group in the town, just like the first two. Not a bad plot, not a bad plot at all! Then there's a couple who were high school sweethearts who reconnect after forty years of separation. Sweet but ho-hum. And, oh brother! A flying saucer shooting laser-light beams at the couple? Where did that come from? From genius to ridiculous in ten short pages!

CHAPTER 13

JOE

Two hours after Terry arrived, life-saving biscuits and extra-large coffees in hand, he snorted, an always unpleasant sound, but usually one meaning he'd found something useful.

Joe looked up from the stack of paperwork on his desk. "What is it?" he asked, when Terry's snort wasn't followed up with an observation, astute or otherwise.

Terry snapped the community magazine he'd been reading shut. "You remember that shoe repair guy in town? Guy with the German name?"

"Vaguely. What about him?"

"Hang on a sec." Terry's fingers fumbled over the keyboard. When he finally looked up, he looked like the cat that swallowed the canary. "Yep, that's it! Our European friend has spent time in the pen for stealing women's underwear. I just saw an ad for his shop in this week's circular. That reminded me he was a previous con, but I couldn't remember for what. Says here he went to prison twice, once for taking women's underwear off a clothesline and once for breaking into a house and stealing the owner's undies right from her dresser drawer."

Joe grabbed the keys and tossed them to Terry. "In that case, let's go pay the man a visit."

Terry pulled up in front of Von Schuster's Shoe Repair, grabbing a spot just beyond the front door. Joe stepped out of the Crown and looked around. St. Samuel's historic downtown district was thriving, with a variety of shops and farm-to-table restaurants. Kurt Von Schuster's small business was on Main Street, sandwiched between an excellent pizzeria and a dusty antique store. "Shoe Repair Here" signs covered the left window. A smaller sign to the right of the door with some of the wording obscured offered hand-sewn custom buttonholes "to make a garment uniquely yours." Why a cobbler would also be adept at creating garment buttonholes Joe had no idea, but given the state of his four corpses, he planned to nail down that line of inquiry soonest. Joe nodded his head toward the sign as Terry came up beside him. Terry whistled low, raising bushy eyebrows at his partner.

An old-fashioned bell attached to the door rang as the two detectives stepped inside. The room was brightly lit, every available space filled with shoes, boots, and associated footwear accoutrements. The cobbler's store was neat and orderly with a place for everything. A glance revealed all items in their appointed spot. Two different types of filtration systems kept the dust to a minimum, and a modern air purifier hung from the wall. Joe recognized a sewing machine and an awl. Beyond those two tools, the rest of the equipment was foreign to him. Apparently repairing shoes was more complex than he had imagined. Joe had never been inside the repairman's shop before. When his shoes needed to be fixed, he just bought new ones.

The air smelled like good leather and old barns, reminding Joe of his family's farm, twenty-five acres about ten miles west of town. Though his dad had been a full-time electrician and a part-time firefighter, the senior Morgan had also muddled around with a few milk cows and a couple of horses. Joe's mom had worked part-time at the high school. When she wasn't working or keeping up with her two rambunctious sons, she kept the household supplied with fresh eggs from the chickens and loads of vegetables from her large garden.

Joe missed the serenity of those days at home, especially when, as now, a case was extra-complicated and frustrating. He wished his dad was still around. They had always been close, even through Joe's turbulent teenage years. When Joe first wanted to join the local Teen Deputy Cadet program at the Frances County Sheriff's Office, his dad encouraged him in the public service sector. Less thrilled by Joe's decision to commission into the Marine Corps after college, the senior Morgan still came to visit Joe at each duty station. In Joe's early days of law enforcement in St. Samuel, his father had proved to be an excellent sounding board for problems Joe encountered on patrol or with his fellow officers. Law enforcement culture was similar to military culture, but different enough that Joe had a little difficulty adapting at first. After taking some of his dad's advice, giving one or two colleagues another chance, and putting one toxic bully in his place, Joe settled in and eventually became a station favorite. Joe's fellow officers considered him to be a good cop, a mentor, and a friend. His superiors felt the same way, which was why Joe was now chief of the homicide unit.

Except for Diane disappearing, the worst day of Joe's life was a rainy day six years earlier when he unknowingly responded to the scene of his parents' death. Called out to a multiple car accident on a wet two-lane back road, Joe immediately recognized the canary yellow automobile in the ditch as his mother's Thunderbird convertible. A Volkswagen backing out of a driveway had hit a Suburban speeding by. Unaware of the accident, his parents had come around the curve at the same time a Ford F-350 came from the other direction. When Joe's mom swung to the left to avoid the Volkswagen and Suburban, she turned straight into the path of the F-350, which was carrying a full load of bricks in the bed. The Thunderbird crashed into the ditch. Joe's dad was pushed so far into the driver's seat, the couple appeared to be spooning, which is how Joe found them when he arrived.

At first Joe froze, unable to move or think, knowing from years of patrol experience that this much torn metal, shattered glass, and blood could mean only one thing. Blaring sirens from a second patrol unit arriving on scene finally broke Joe's trance. He scrambled down the embankment, shouting. When he got close and saw the insult done to his parents' bodies by the twisted metal, he closed their eyes and then his own, weeping silently as the rain poured down.

Joe had known for years that fate is a fickle beast, a lesson reinforced during his parents' accident investigation. Life can change in a moment, turning completely on one simple decision, insignificant choices made multiple times every single day by every human. Consider the elevator and the stairs in a hotel. Take the stairs? A person could trip, fall, break an ankle, meet an attractive emergency room doctor, fall in love, marry, have five kids, and live happily ever after. Take the elevator? That same person could get stuck on the fifth floor, stay trapped six hours, miss an important job interview, end up working as a car hop at a drive-in, and die penniless and alone. Or, as in his parents' case, take a new, shorter route the

GPS offers, avoid a car crash only to get hit by a large brick-laden truck, and die in the rain on a little-used back road.

Despite seeing indiscriminate chaos at work daily in his professional life, Joe had found the randomness of his parents' death hard to deal with. Afterwards, he gave Chaos Theory—the belief that one small movement, such as a butterfly flapping its wings somewhere, could effect huge change somewhere else—a lot more credence. Joe realized if his parents hadn't taken the new route, they would not have encountered the back road accident and not ended up dead in that ditch. Then again, maybe a truck backing out of a different drive on their usual route through the county would have hit his parents and they would have still died. Butterfly wings, timing, small decisions, disappearing wives. Joe had learned life was arbitrary and chaotic.

Joe didn't need further proof of fate's fickleness, but if he had, he only had to consider his murder victims. Jillian Finn, a teacher at the local high school who coached the girls' fastpitch team and played in St. Samuel's community softball league, shouldn't even have been home the night the murderer came to call. Jillian had planned to go out for a much needed girls' night with friends but had contracted a bad cold from a student and cancelled, electing to stay home instead with a bowl of homemade chicken noodle soup and her new kitten. Had Jillian gone to dinner with the girls, she might have escaped the killer's garrote.

The third victim had been equally unlucky. Eleanor Connelly, a student at Jackson Community College who waitressed at the Daisy Lady three nights a week, should have been attending, ironically, an evening forensic science class. Her professor was a retired GBI detective who sometimes moonlighted as a consultant for St. Samuel's Crime Scene Unit. He had been called to the station to help sort through forensic evidence collected at the two murder scenes, so he had cancelled class. Instead of being in a classroom learning about forensics, Eleanor had become her own forensics lab. Talk about random twists of fate.

When Joe thought about the day he was dispatched to his parents' accident on Old Blue Highway, he recalled his spirit eye had been pulsing all morning. Joe had assumed something bad would happen during his workday. A domestic going wrong, a major bar brawl he'd have to get in the middle of, something physical and unpleasant, but within the daily grind of the job. Never did he dream his intuition was forewarning him about the death of his own folks.

After the accident, Joe's family consisted of himself and his little brother. Although they'd been close when they were young, Joe didn't see much of Trey these days. Trey had followed Joe into the Marine Corps, deploying four times to Afghanistan. On his last tour, his team's Humvee rolled over a buried mine. The turret gunner was killed instantly, and Trey was trapped beneath the vehicle. By the time his squad mates hauled the machine off him, he was unconscious and close to death. The Bagram Air Base hospital surgeons worked a miracle saving Trey's life, but the price he paid was the loss of his left arm just above the elbow and his right leg just below the knee. Although his little brother never voiced the thought, Joe suspected Trey would have preferred the doctors not to have had such excellent life-saving skills.

Growing up, Trey was naturally athletic, a constant blur of motion, a gregarious comic. After his release from the hospital, he retreated to the mountains of North Carolina to adjust to a new way of life. His high school girlfriend stuck with him through the long recovery period, driving back and forth between Walter Reed Medical Center in Bethesda, Maryland, and St. Samuel several times a month, then eventually moving with him to Asheville.

Although Joe and his mom also spent a huge amount of time with Trey at the hospital, Emily was the one who nursed him through the most difficult emotional times and was by his side for rehab five days out of seven.

In the early days after Trey and Emily moved to the mountains, Emily confided to Joe that Trey often talked to her about suicide. As the years passed, though, Trey adjusted to his lesser-limbed body and was now at the point he could even make jokes about his high-tech prosthetics. He named his artificial arm Joe and his leg Terry, saying the two partners set such a good example of a team that worked well together, he wanted his titanium leg and arm to do the same. Joe had punched Trey in his real arm, relieved his brother had finally reached the place where he could joke about his injuries. Trey and Emily waited to get married until Trey was stable enough to stand without assistance. All the guests attending the tiny wedding teared up as Trey walked in a slow but steady gait to the front of the church to stand tall beside the preacher.

When Trey came home for their parents' funerals, he and Joe had a long talk, Trey finally telling Joe every detail about the explosion, his injuries, and the toll the accident had taken on him physically and emotionally. Joe listened in whiskey-sipping silence, letting his brother relay the story without interruption, then held Trey in a strong embrace while the younger man shook with long-withheld sobs. Two nights later Trey returned the favor, listening while Joe described the trauma of working their parents' accident, delving into emotions he had been unable to share with anyone else.

Since then, the brothers had re-established more frequent contact through phone calls and texts, but had only managed visits about once a year. Joe had been in the midst of planning a second trip to Trey's right before Diane disappeared. When he called

Trey to tell him about Diane and cancel their get-together, Trey surprised him by coming down to Georgia for a few days, simply to be present for his brother. A further surprise was the revelation that Trey had just acquired a license to be a private investigator in the state of North Carolina. During his visit, he helped Joe work through possible scenarios for the missing Diane, drawing the brothers closer together than ever.

✵ ✵ ✵

Joe pulled on his running shoes, prepping for his daily morning run. The weather was perfect for a long jog, seventy-two degrees and partly cloudy. Popping a treat up in the air for Belle, he headed out the door saying, "I'll be back in a while. Guard the house." His best friend snatched the treat mid-air, gobbled it down, sniffed the floor for crumbs, then padded back to their warm bed.

Joe stretched for a few minutes at the trailhead, then began a slow jog. About a half mile down the trail, he was just starting to sweat through his t-shirt when he glanced up and saw a long, auburn-colored ponytail bouncing a hundred yards ahead of him. The woman seemed too tall to be Diane, but still, that ponytail, that was Diane all over. Joe sped up, but when he rounded the curve, the woman was nowhere in sight. He jogged faster, scanning rapidly left and right, but the woman had disappeared.

Running as fast as he could, Joe finally came up behind the lively ponytail. Taking a gigantic leap, he tackled the woman, rolling over with her into the bushes. As he raised up on top of her, he saw she was not Diane, but a prettier woman with frightened green eyes and trembling dark lashes. As the stranger opened her mouth to scream, Joe woke up, sweating and cursing. Belle was tugging at the covers, whining anxiously.

CHAPTER 14

PHOEBE

The library has been quiet this afternoon, not much foot traffic. I just reshelved a couple of books from one of my favorite authors and now have no tasks until a customer comes in, so I'm putting on my best library assistant manners to ask: "Any chance you need a good book to read?" If so, I highly recommend the Pike Logan series by Brad Taylor. I really love those stories with Pike, Jennifer, and the rest of the Taskforce crew. Kurt Hale was my favorite character, but regrettably, Brad brought him to an untimely end. I was so mad about Kurt's demise I emailed Brad about the storyline. His response? "Well, Kurt had to go sometime, he was aging out." Not satisfying at all. I suppose if I ever become a best-selling author, I'll have to get used to people not liking parts of my storylines, too. Or maybe the whole story! Anyway, I picked a new favorite character, and while I love Pike, Knuckles is now my guy. Read the series if you like action-packed thrillers. You'll be hooked, too.

DEATH WRITES ITSELF

The Taskforce stories are about a secret United States government group taking down terrorists around the world. One of Taylor's best stories is *Exit Fee,* which is a novella about sex trafficking. I reread it recently, which I think is what caused the one other instance of inspirational writing in my life. Just after we settled into this house, early one morning I scribbled down the shortest short story ever about a young girl who ran away from home and found herself trapped in a human trafficking ring.

I had woken up about three-thirty that morning with these half-sentences repeating over and over in my head about a teenager trapped somewhere. I tried to go back to sleep but couldn't, so I finally got up and grouchily wrote down all the phrases circling in my brain. At that moment in the pre-dawn hours, I was much more interested in sleep than in becoming a bestselling author. After I got all the words written down on the legal pad I keep in the nightstand for just such inspirations (so why am I grumpy when they actually happen?), I turned out the light and fell back asleep for about ten minutes, only to wake up with more words knocking on my brain. So again, I turned on the light, I retrieved the notepad, I scribbled down the thoughts, and laid back down. A few minutes of sleep and more ideas were insistently waking me up. I finally gave up, got up, made coffee, and wrote for a couple of hours. I couldn't believe it. Nothing like that had ever happened before and nothing like it has happened since . . . until last week at the kitchen table.

Later that day, when I finally swilled enough coffee to get my brain functioning, I fleshed the words out into a fourteen-page, extremely short, short story. The human trafficking storyline was gruesome, not what I really want to write, but I knew the details were accurate from my days as a paralegal at the Bennett Harrison Law Firm in Atlanta. We had two attorneys on staff who specialized in human trafficking cases, doing most of the work pro bono. I interviewed eleven women who had been forced into prostitution in organized sex trafficking rings. I know the specific number because I remember each one's name and face. Their stories of abuse and being forced to work as sex slaves were horrendous and not something I'm likely to forget.

Despite the harsh topic, I did think my writing was decent. For some feedback, I read the story out loud to Jack and his sisters. After a startled meow, which I assumed meant she didn't like the trafficking angle, Josie stayed attentive through the end. Jilly slept through most of it, although she tried to be supportive by keeping one eye open from start to finish. Jack, always my toughest critic, had yawned widely through the last paragraph, then barked fiercely for several minutes. I'm sure that meant he liked it.

CHAPTER 15

JOE

Joe missed Diane fiercely. That morning's dream had been just one of many he continued to have about her. Or, for a surprising change, a woman who turned out not to be her. Nothing in his life was good without Diane, not night dreams or daydreams. After the initial shock of her disappearance and the frantic months-long search, time moved inexorably on, and he tried not to let his anguish show, burying himself in work and Belle's fur. He worried and waited, worked more overtime, and drank more bourbon, sometimes at home with Belle, often at the Daisy Lady with Terry. Finally, to fill his limited off hours and keep his thoughts from futilely spinning about Diane, he started flying a lot more, spending as much off-duty time as possible in the air. Belle liked to ride along as co-pilot. She was good company, despite needing a constant reminder that she couldn't stick her head out of the airplane's windows.

Joe had loved flying helicopters in the Marine Corps, had almost stayed in to keep doing so when his four-year commitment came to an end. But Diane had wanted stability while raising their as-yet unborn children, she didn't want to move every couple of years with kids in tow. A large part of Joe wanted to fly helicopters forever, but a larger part wanted to make Diane happy, so he resigned his commission when the time came. He didn't regret the decision exactly, but he did miss the camaraderie of the Corps. He also missed flying so much that after a few months back in St. Samuel, he had gone to the small local airport in Kingsland and inquired about flying lessons. They referred him to the flight training school operating out of the airport, Pryor Flight Training, where Joe earned his private pilot's license in two months. Unless the homicide unit was extremely busy, Joe managed to get a flight in weekly—twice a week if he was lucky—cruising above the Georgia coastline on moonlit nights, sometimes with Diane and sometimes solo. He took Terry up once, but Terry wasn't a fan of "mosquito jets," as he called the small aircraft, although Terry's three kids loved getting an aerial ride with their Uncle Joe.

Putting on his running shoes for real now that he was wide awake and starting his day, Joe recalled one hard day when he was trying to avoid thinking about Diane and the dire things that could have happened to her, so he decided to go fly. After a peaceful afternoon in the clouds, he and Belle were circling the airport before landing when Joe glanced down at the parking lot, looking for his truck. He spotted the vehicle without trouble because the dusty gray Ford was flanked by a bright red Mercedes sedan and a sparkling blue BMW.

Belle had barked as Joe deftly landed the little jet. He thought his dog might be suggesting they really needed a vehicle upgrade—an idea that had occurred to Joe too—but the truck still smelled slightly of Diane, so he had no plans to part with it. By the time Joe chocked and blocked the Cessna, turned in the key, and walked to the parking lot, the Mercedes was gone, but the BMW was still there. In terms of cool wheels, Joe told Belle, the Beamer was nice, but no match for his manly chariot. Belle peed next to the BMW's left rear tire to demonstrate her total agreement.

✱ ✱ ✱

Diane and Joe had met when he was stationed in North Carolina at Marine Corps Air Station New River. Diane was from Wilmington, working in Surf City as an executive assistant in a surveying company. She had accompanied a girlfriend to the New River Officers' Club one night and bumped into Joe on her way to the ladies' room, spilling his beer down both their sleeves. Joe took one look at that beautiful auburn hair and those sea-blue eyes and apologized, despite the fact she had caused the collision. She had been two-stepping to the country music instead of watching where she was going.

She had laughed up at him and said, "Come on, Marine, that was all my fault. Let me buy you a fresh beer when I get back to my seat."

Joe had readily agreed, then waited for her a discreet distance from the restrooms. Seeing him, she had flashed a wicked smile and said, "What, didn't trust me to hold up my end of the deal?"

He had grinned in return and said, "I didn't want to let a free beer get away."

After that evening, they spent most of their free time together. Diane was warm, attentive, had a terrific sense of humor, and didn't get upset when he deployed to the field for weeks at a time. She would run with him in his off-duty time, was always up for a hike in the woods, and loved days spent lakeside or at the ocean. As new lovers do, they talked about their hopes and dreams. Diane confessed to Joe that while she enjoyed her administrative job and found the work interesting, she'd always wanted to be a cop but hadn't summoned up the courage to take the leap. Her parents would have discouraged her going into law enforcement. She still lived at home with them but was ready to move out and start living her own life.

When Diane brought Joe home for the first time, her mom loved him instantly; dad took his time warming up to the crewcut Marine who was clearly over the moon for his oldest daughter. Diane's younger sisters thought Joe was to die for. Her little brother peppered the young pilot with questions about guns and helicopters.

After a year of dating, when Joe had six months left on his contract and he was debating whether to leave the Corps and return home to Georgia or sign up for another four years of flying helicopters, he popped the big question on the beach on a moonlit night. Diane cried, instantly said yes, and hugged him so hard he couldn't breathe for a moment.

Prior to Diane, Joe had dated a lot casually, but Diane hadn't dated much. She was friendly to people but a natural introvert. They married two weeks before Joe mustered out, in a small ceremony attended by a few of his fellow Marines, his parents and little brother, and Diane's family and friends. Once the couple moved to St. Samuel, Joe was immediately hired by the town's police department; they were recruiting veterans as often as they could. The young couple stayed with Joe's parents for a few months while the purchase of a property they found on Thomasboro Road went through. Once they moved in, Joe worked while Diane chose furniture and decorated, with Joe providing perfunctory opinions on just about everything. If Diane liked the blue couch, he liked the blue couch. If Diane wanted wooden floors, he wanted wooden floors. If Diane was happy, he was happy.

When the nesting was finished to Diane's satisfaction, Joe encouraged his new bride to follow her dream and apply for a deputy position at the Saddle County Sheriff's Office. Their new home was in Frances County, a much smaller, less rural jurisdiction. Saddle County was twice as big, a huge 571 square miles, and always had openings for deputies. Working up the courage to apply took Diane several weeks, but she finally filled out an application, an act rewarded two weeks later by the first interview in a three-step hiring process. When she got the call telling her to report for duty in five days, she started jumping wildly up and down before she even hung up the phone. Joe laughed with her, swinging her around and around in their newly decorated living room. Life for the newlyweds was great.

Despite being petite, Diane did well at the law enforcement academy. She could perform criminal takedowns better than many men, handled self-defense training like a pro, missed the sharpshooter award by only two points. Once out on the streets, she found she enjoyed helping the people she encountered every day, although like many officers, she hated domestic violence calls and those involving children, having high hopes for a houseful of her own. In those early years, the Morgans were focused on loving each other and keeping their respective town and counties safe from lawbreakers. Making babies was scheduled for later in their life plan.

Neither Joe nor Diane had ever dreamed anything could disrupt their future.

CHAPTER 16

DIANE (FIVE MONTHS EARLIER)

Eight hours, twelve minutes, and two gas stops after walking away from the dead child in the woods, Diane Morgan pulled a brown sedan into an almost empty motel lot. She had felt this day coming for months, the pull to escape her life as inexorable as the tide bearing down on the shore. Diane felt helpless, like the tiny grains of sand tossed against the never-ending waves. She had been tempted multiple times over the last several months to disappear with the help of her service revolver but could not bring herself to that act, despite her anguish over never being able to bear children. Joe, along with her family, would have been devastated. Better to leave without a trace so Joe could start fresh without her. Illogical thinking, Diane knew, but the best she could muster these days.

Besides the gas stations where she had filled up the tank and bought snacks, two t-shirts, and a pair of sweatpants, she had made one other stop. In a grimy area on the south side of Jacksonville,

Florida, she had walked into a local chop shop, which had posed for years as a legitimate auto repair business. She knew about the shop because Joe had worked an interstate auto theft case a few years earlier involving this place and fifteen others like it throughout the Southeast. The owner of this operation had received immunity for his testimony, so he was still in business, supposedly now legitimately. Diane doubted the legitimacy and wanted to make a deal with him.

Walking to the counter, she asked for Henrique, telling the clerk to let him know she had a special trade in mind. The bald-headed man looked at her curiously, then walked to the back. A few minutes later, Henrique came strolling out with a wary look on his face, followed by Baldy, who was ineffectively hiding a shotgun behind his right leg. Diane glanced at the weapon and turned her attention to the owner.

"I've got a two-year-old Dodge Charger outside I want to trade for the brown Honda sedan on your lot. Even steven."

Henrique went to the front window, looked out, and turned back to her, astonishment evident on his face.

"Are you crazy? You want to trade in a police car? The paint scheme is still on it, lady. What do you take me for? I ain't no fool."

Diane stepped close to Henrique, so close she could smell his sweat and the tobacco stench on his skin, and whispered in his ear. "You know full well you can turn that Charger into sardine cans in about two hours and make four times on the parts what the Honda is worth. I was never here, you and I never spoke, I don't know anything about your back room dealings, and you don't know anything about a marked patrol car from Georgia.

"As a bonus for you, I won't make an anonymous call to the cops to let them know you've restarted your greedy little chop-shop business. And that nicety on my part is on top of the extra money the Dodge's parts will bring in for you."

Henrique thought for a few moments. Business, both legitimate and illegitimate, had been slow since the trial; he could use the extra dough. And he believed this woman when she said she'd call the law on him. Ten minutes later, the Saddle County Sheriff's patrol car had disappeared from the repair shop parking lot and the brown Honda was on I-95 headed south.

✵ ✵ ✵

Turning off the engine in the inappropriately named Deluxe Rooms Inn parking lot, Diane sat motionless for a moment before she laid her head on the steering wheel, wanting only the oblivion of drug or alcohol-induced sleep. When the deafening sound of a faulty vehicle muffler reverberated through the car's interior a few minutes later, Diane raised her head. She knew she wasn't in the best part of Miami, the poorly kept motel exterior told her that in a way nothing else needed to. Spotting the dirty green panel van with the obnoxious muffler, she saw hurried activity several spaces down the lot. Two men had opened the back of the van and were urging four or five people out, herding them toward the last room on the ground floor. Too groggy from lack of sleep and hindered by complete disinterest, Diane couldn't tell if the people were male or female, adults or children. "I'm not responsible for citizens anymore and I'm too tired to care anyway," she murmured to herself.

Planning to hole up for a few days then head to Key West, Diane swung wearily out of the car into the early morning light and made her way to the motel office, trying not to think about the panel van or her retreat from Georgia. She had observed enough of the parking lot activity to recognize human trafficking when she saw it.

But she was no longer law enforcement and now a criminal herself after disposing of her patrol car, so she knew she couldn't interfere even if she wanted to, which she absolutely did not. The best she could do, if she could muster the energy, was call in an anonymous tip to the Miami Police hotline before she made tracks south.

Diane craved the solace of solitude and anonymity. She needed salt air or fresh pine-scented air, the restorative oxygen only the islands or the mountains could deliver. She needed to be somewhere that no one knew she was a woman broken by her inability to have children, somewhere Joe wasn't being so kind and conscientious and perfect. All Diane had ever wanted, besides being a cop, was to be a mom, specifically the mother of Joe Morgan's children. Once that dream was dead in the water, Diane turned completely inward, shutting out Joe, her family, her partners at work. She would never have believed she could become a woman this debilitated, yet here she was, running from a life she loved but couldn't now conceive how to live.

And Joe. Diane felt a physical stab of pain when she thought of her beloved Joe. He had tried his best to help, stoically undergoing every fertility test required by the specialists, supporting her as she underwent each and every treatment, by her side during and after each miscarriage and every failed regimen. He maintained an optimism she could not match and eventually could no longer endure.

From the moment they met, Joe supported her in everything she wanted to do, especially the things she was fearful of trying. Bungee jump? Done. Ten-mile hike in the mountains? Done. Tell her folks they were moving to Georgia? Done. After they settled in to their new place in St. Samuel, Joe encouraged her dream of working in law enforcement, scheduling her for ride-alongs with his fellow patrol officers, setting her up with administrative volunteer work at the station, telling her all about his long shifts, quizzing her on state and county law. He spent an entire afternoon digging up tons of inspirational quotes, writing them on sticky notes, posting them all over the house. He even quoted George Addair, some old motivational speaker she had never heard of, but who apparently was a genius at inspiring people. The morning Joe whispered Addair's words, "Everything you want is on the other side of fear," in her ear before he left for work, she took a long drink of coffee, jumped online, and pulled up a sheriff's office application. Joe was the best husband, friend, man, ever.

Shaking off thoughts of home, Diane entered the dimly lit motel lobby, taking in the worn interior and the empty space behind the check-in desk. A faded poster on a bulletin board proclaimed January as Human Trafficking Prevention Month. An equally faded sign sought a missing child. A third hoped for a missing dog. She rang the old-fashioned tabletop bell and waited. Three more bell rings and six minutes later, as Diane was resisting the temptation to go behind the counter and simply take a room key, a fat man with a poorly trimmed beard and wearing an ill-fitting polo shirt emerged from behind a curtain.

"Help ya?"

"I need a room for three nights. One person. Ground floor. Paying cash."

The man eyeballed her. "I don't put up with no trouble here. Cash customers are usually trouble."

Diane looked him in the eye and said, "You won't get any trouble out of me. I'm just not a credit card kind of gal."

Grunting, the clerk took three nights worth of money from her and handed over a key. "Ice machine is off limits after midnight. Wouldn't take no midnight walks in this neighborhood neither. Enjoy your stay."

DEATH WRITES ITSELF

※ ※ ※

Three days later, Diane watched the two men in the green panel van drive out of the parking lot. She had a full view of room ten through the gap in her own room's curtain. Except for a daily run out for supper and to buy packaged breakfast and lunch items, she had stayed in, numbing her senses on daytime television, long, restless naps, and a nightly bottle of red wine. The people in room ten, what Diane now thought of as the human trafficking room, had been equal homebodies. One of the men had left each day just after sunrise for about an hour but the other had constantly stayed in the room, as had the other occupants.

Diane called the one who stayed behind Nose Job because his schnoz looked as though it had been broken several times. She nicknamed the one who left each day James, reminiscent of "Home, James," for those folks lucky enough to have a chauffeur. Now, observing both men were gone together for the first time, she knew something was about to change. She also knew she should drive away, phone in a tip to the police, and head south, but her nature, her law enforcement training, her call to act were too strong.

Seeing the men leave, she knew she didn't have much time before they returned, potentially bringing reinforcements. Foolish or not, if she was going to act, she had to do so now. Diane took a deep breath, opened her door and walked quickly across the lot to the door of room ten. She rapped briskly on the door.

"Housekeeping." A rustling behind the door ensued, but no one answered.

Diane knocked again and called, "Housekeeping, I have clean towels."

As she waited, a mockingbird sang good morning from the palm tree at the edge of the lot. *That bird is mocking, alright,* Diane thought. *There's not much good about this morning or whatever's going on in this room.*

The door remained closed, impervious to Diane's knock and the bird's morning welcome. Wanting to walk away, Diane told herself to try once more. If no one responded she would drop the rescue attempt. Knocking harder, Diane said one last time, "Housekeeping. Open up." Two minutes passed. Diane sighed and turned away. As she did, the door opened a tiny crack, the chain still in place.

"Hello, hey, my name is Diane. I am not the police. I know you need help. Please let me in."

A dark brown eye watched her warily. Diane heard a whispered argument and saw movement through the thin spaces between the door's hinges. Three voices floated out, one speaking an Eastern European language she didn't recognize, one speaking English, and the third fluent Spanish.

"Look, I know you're in trouble. I can help you, but we need to move quickly before those men come back. Let me in or I'm leaving."

The yellowed, sun-beaten door closed briefly, then Diane heard the chain unlatch. She hastily pushed her way in. Eyes adjusting to the dim light, she saw five females in various states of undress, all staring at her in alarm. The Spanish speaker, a beautiful dark-haired, dark-eyed child of fifteen or so, started gesturing and speaking, pointing at Diane, then the door, clearly wanting her to leave.

Diane said, "Who speaks English?"

As she looked around, she realized that none of the females was an adult; all five were teenagers, except for two who appeared to be only ten or eleven. *I'm in it now*, Diane thought. *I can't leave these kids to God-knows-what, so the options are to get them out of here or die trying.*

A blonde girl who appeared to be about thirteen spoke up. "I speak English, and so do they." She pointed to the youngest girls in the room, curled up together on the far bed.

"That one by the wall speaks some kind of Russian, we think. And Maria mostly talks in Spanish, but she can say a lot of stuff in English."

"Okay, honey, thank you. What's your name?"

"I'm Elizabeth, but they said I had to go by Tulip now. And that's Rose and Petunia and Lily," she said, pointing in turn to the youngest girls and the presumed Russian speaker. "We're supposed to call Maria Violet, but she lets off an awful stream of upset Spanish when we do."

"Who are 'they'? Do you mean the two men who are with you? What are you doing here with them?" Diane asked.

Elizabeth, Rose, and Petunia looked at each other, clearly not willing to talk or unsure what to say. Maria angrily burst out in broken English intermixed with Spanish, explaining she had been hitchhiking from Texas to Florida when the two men had stopped on I-10 in the Florida Panhandle to give her a ride. From what Diane could piece together, Maria didn't like the driver's vibe, so she told them no thanks. He had tipped his ball cap to her, driven about twenty-five yards down the road, stopped the van, hopped out and chased her until he caught her by her long black ponytail. Several cars passed during the chase, but none stopped. As best Diane could tell from Maria's Spanish-infused narrative, the man had punched her in the head a couple of times and threw her, limp, into the back of the van. When Maria came to, she found herself with her hands tied, lying on the van's floor, being observed with frightened eyes by the other four girls, whose hands were also bound with zip ties. The men would not explain why the five had been taken or where they were going.

Tulip nee Elizabeth then asked if Diane could help them. They all just wanted to go back home, at least four of them did. None of them could figure out what Lily wanted. From overhearing their captors talk, they knew her age, that she wasn't an American citizen, and that the bad men had taken her passport, but that was all they knew about the pretty seventeen-year-old. While the youngsters looked at Diane anxiously, she thought about her need to get away, as well as the danger they would all be in if they couldn't get a big enough lead on the traffickers. But she couldn't just walk away from these girls. They were in danger with her or without her.

Resolutely, Diane replied, "Get dressed, grab whatever gear you have and each of you quickly go to the bathroom because we won't stop after we start. I'll get my car. When you see a brown sedan pull up in front of the door, move fast and jump in. Understand?"

The tall foreigner looked perplexed, but the other girls nodded somberly. Diane slipped out of the room and ran across the lot. In preparation for her own escape south, she had already put in her trunk what little she brought, so she just used the bathroom and picked up her purse and car keys before hurrying back to her car. She tried to formulate a reasonable getaway plan while cursing her own stupidity for getting involved.

✧ ✧ ✧

The barrel-chested desk clerk watched as the five girls streamed from room ten and jumped into the brown Honda. Picking up the office phone, he made a brief call.

CHAPTER 17

PHOEBE

The alarm woke me before I was ready Sunday morning. The DJ found me buried in the middle of an odd dream, groggy from being woken out of a deep sleep. In the dream, I had been jogging on the town trail (clearly a dream as I hate to run), my ponytail bouncing, when something hit me in the back, causing me to fall and roll down into the ditch. Just before I hit the muddy bottom, the alarm went off, saving me from certain ditch death. I burrowed in my warm nest for a few minutes, leftover dreamscape fogging my brain, wishing I didn't need to get up.

    I would have rolled over and gone back to dreamland, hopefully to a more pleasant dream, but I had promised to have brunch with my folks, who I hadn't seen in a couple of weeks. Mom had bribed me with her famous monkey bread, a delectable concoction much like cinnamon rolls only more delicious. That, along with freshly gathered eggs fried to perfection in her cast iron skillet, was more than I was willing to pass up, even for more time with Mr. Sandman. Plus Jack would never forgive me if we didn't go; I'd already told him Mom was making extra bacon for him like she always does. Being the only grand-dog within petting distance, Jack was a tad spoiled by Gram and Pop-Pop.

Prior to the weird dream, my beauty rest had been interrupted when my Lieutenant Joe started sending messages to my brain, an event quite similar to what happened the night I penned the human trafficking story. I woke up about two-thirty with the phrase, "the handsome detective and his partner pulled up in front of the abandoned building, while lightning flashed on the dark horizon," running through my head. The words wouldn't let go, stuck like a burr on a tennis shoe. So I got up, pulled a t-shirt over my head, and wrote for a couple of hours before falling back into bed, having no idea what I'd just composed. I was anxious to read my early morning scribbles, but my literary genius would have to wait, as I had a date with bacon, eggs, and a fat piece of monkey bread. Oh, and of course, my beloved parents.

Three hours later, Jack and I waddled back into the house, my jeans unbuttoned, his collar loosened. I put my purse and keys on the counter, opened the back door to let Jack out, and looked at the two felines giving me stink eye from the bar stools.

"Stop glaring at me. Yes, Gram sent you some bacon, just let me potty, then I'll give it to you."

A plaintive cry from Jilly informed me my need to pee was much less important than her need for bacon. I contemplated this piece of wisdom, communicated by a creature whose own potty business was cleaned up for her by the only mammal in the house with opposable thumbs and a high-functioning brain. Sometimes I do wonder whose brain really functions on a higher level, though.

The four-legged poopers or the two-legged pooper-scoopers? Possibly our furry friends are a lot smarter than we are.

Bathroom break complete, bacon delivered to high-IQ felines, and I was ready to review my pre-dawn work. Was it too early for a glass of wine? Yes, I should wait. After all that breakfast, wine would send me straight to the Land of Nod. And who can nod when there's writing to be done? Not me, the literary genius!

I settled for a cup of hot caffeinated coffee made with a grind called Carolina Morning from my favorite coffee shop on Main Street. The local owners import their beans from South America and roast them right in their shop. A delicious brew aptly named, the flavor did remind me of sitting on a porch in the Carolinas surrounded by jasmine and tea olives, watching the sun rise. I've visited friends in Charleston a few times, so I have some experience sitting on a porch in the southern Carolina which, not surprisingly, is much like sitting on a porch in southern Georgia.

Coffee mug in hand, I picked up the pad on which I'd scratched away during the wee hours and found about eight pages covered front and back. Wow, that's a lot! As I skimmed over the sheets, I discovered much to my relief that my Lieutenant Joe had returned once again, still searching for the killer who so rudely murders people while they bathe. Joe and his thus-far nameless partner (I can't quite decide what the partner looks like, so I haven't been able to give him a name yet) had narrowed down their list to a half-dozen suspects but were still interviewing people around town. Alright, not terrible.

Toward the end were some scribbles I couldn't decipher, then what seemed to be an unformed idea about a missing person. Not sure what that storyline would be. Who goes missing in a murder case? Well, I suppose the murderer is missing, although he—or she, I don't wish to stereotype just because most murderers are men—is technically hiding, and possibly some victims are missing, but do I really want to add a new story arc about someone disappearing? I'm having a hard enough time keeping up with the serial killer, my Lieutenant Joe, and my as-yet unnamed and unwritten-about heroine. I jotted down a note to think about it later: "Missing Person?"

All in all, not too bad, if you don't count the last page. The flying saucer showed up again, this time shooting paintballs from its turret. Sighing, I reached for my red pen.

CHAPTER 18

DIANE

Once in the car, the girls were quiet, understanding even better than Diane the gravity of their situation. Each of the youngsters was bruised or cut in at least one spot, a fact which infuriated the woman who wanted more than anything to be a mother. When Libby asked where they were going, Diane tersely replied, "South." In truth, Diane had no plan except to get off the main roads and away from this motel as soon as she could. If they did head south, they'd be in trouble when they reached the bridge that crossed the ocean to Key Largo. Highway One was the only road to the Keys from that point, with nowhere to hide on the two-lane road and water on either side. Diane would have to think of an alternate plan well before then. She supposed they should go north to Tampa Bay or to Charleston, but she was hoping not to keep the girls long, just long enough to get them away from the two men in the van and to a police station.

Diane was glad now she had replaced her phone with a prepaid one purchased the night before at the grocery store. When she left St. Samuel, her intent had been to stay completely off the grid—no phone, no bank, no credit cards, no electronics. Her first night in the motel, she had pulled the chip out of her phone, smashed it with her steel-toed boot, and pitched the pieces into the parking lot dumpster after nearly turning on the device and calling Joe in some desperate wanting she refused to examine. Back in Georgia, lying to herself about her true motivations, she had secretly stashed cash away for months, accumulating enough to live on for a long while. But since modern technology had replaced formerly common necessities like pay phones, yellow pages, and printed maps, traveling without a cell phone was proving to be more challenging than traveling without a credit card.

A quick internet search on the prepaid informed her the closest branch of the Miami Police Department was about twelve miles away. She thought about calling 911 to get the Florida Highway Patrol to meet them, but decided the safest course was to take the girls to the police station rather than waiting for an available trooper to find them on the road. Diane could usher the girls into the building, ensure they connected with the duty officer, then hurry back to the sedan and get on the road before anyone asked her name. Having set a plan in motion, she looked in the rearview mirror at the four girls in the back, checked out the roadway behind them, and looked in both side mirrors before glancing sideways at Elizabeth.

"So, what are your stories? I know how Maria came to be with you, but what about the rest of you?"

Elizabeth, who seemed to be the only extroverted member of the group besides the spirited Maria, said she was from Destin, Florida. At the beginning of the school year, she had made friends with a new girl named Chastity. Elizabeth's mom had recently remarried, and the stepdad didn't much care for Elizabeth and her siblings. With the extra freedom that comes with being a high school freshman with inattentive parents, Elizabeth started spending more and more time at Chastity's house. Both of Chastity's parents worked, but Chastity's big brother, Darin, was always around, even though he had graduated from high school three years earlier.

Darin always had money but no job, none that Elizabeth ever saw him go to, anyway. He was cute and funny and frequently took the two girls to the movies or to get ice cream or to the beach. Though she didn't say so, Diane could tell that Elizabeth had developed a huge crush on her friend's big brother. One day, Darin invited Elizabeth to come with him to meet some of his friends. Chastity encouraged her to go, but declined to come along herself, saying she had to stay home and watch her younger sister. Thrilled to be alone with Darin, Elizabeth put on her cutest top and some reserved-for-very-special-occasions mascara and hopped in Darin's truck when he pulled up in her driveway.

When they arrived at Darin's friends' apartment complex, a rundown building in a seedy part of town Elizabeth had not been in before, an instinct she'd never previously experienced kicked in. She told Darin she wanted to go home. He laughed and said, "Come on, babe, I really want you to meet my buddies." Hesitant but flattered by the attention, Elizabeth disregarded the primal voices warning her of danger and followed Darin up the stairs to find three young men in a dirty one-bedroom apartment. Two of them were smoking what she thought was marijuana, and the third looked at her with dead shark eyes, like she was bait for a trap. Elizabeth clung to Darin's arm.

"Hey guys, this is Elizabeth, my favorite girl. Lizzy, this is Pete, and the ugly guy is Bill. And that guy," pointing to shark eyes, "is my best friend since second grade, Bobby."

Elizabeth smiled nervously and gave a little wave, glued to Darin like a mollusk to its shell.

Bobby looked Elizabeth up and down while he told Pete to get the new arrivals a beer. Pete jumped up on command and went into what Elizabeth supposed was the kitchen. She'd never had beer and didn't want any now.

"Darin," she whispered, "I really need to get back home. Mom will be wondering where I am."

Darin looked down at her and said, "Don't be a buzz kill. It's party time! I'll get you home soon."

At this point in her narrative, a distant look formed on the young girl's face and the flow of words slowed. Elizabeth said all she could remember was reluctantly taking a few swallows of a nasty tasting beer while the boys encouraged her to drink it all. She recalled Darin pushing her down the hall and into the bedroom, his hand firmly on the small of her back, Bobby following close behind. The next memory she had was of waking up in the green van, the Russian-speaking girl tied beside her and the two younger girls on the bench across from them. Elizabeth didn't know how much time had passed or what had happened in the time between the bedroom and the van. Diane could guess what Elizabeth had endured but didn't share her thoughts with the traumatized teen. The young woman would let herself remember one day, that would be soon enough.

Diane eyeballed the rear and side views again for signs they were being followed. Seeing nothing of concern, she asked Lorelei and Libby to share their stories. The two girls were huddled together in the back seat, holding on to one another, clearly reluctant to speak. Gently, Diane asked where they were from. After some prodding and pinching from a silent Libby, Lorelei said they were from Fairhope, Alabama.

"And how did you get to that motel in Miami?" Diane asked softly.

"Our father, he brought us to the men in the green van."

"Your father? Why would he do that?"

"He owed a debt. We were the payment."

CHAPTER 19

JOE

Chief Paris knocked on Joe's door, then walked in and plopped heavily into an old armchair in front of his desk. Joe and Terry purposely kept uncomfortable chairs in their office so people wouldn't hang around too long shooting the breeze. Every time the facility manager offered to replace the chairs with new ones, both detectives said no.

The chief tossed two of the papers she was holding onto Joe's desk. "Looks like we have more trouble in the area than just our serial killer. When you're done reading that, tell me the latest about the case. Any luck with fingerprints?"

Joe looked at the dispatch from the Georgia Bureau of Investigation's monthly human trafficking report. The title blared, "MAJOR SEX TRAFFICKING RING SUSPECTED ACROSS FIVE STATES." He skimmed the article, which advised law enforcement agencies to send all their officers through refresher human trafficking training. The story also said when making arrests, particularly of prostitutes or during drug busts, to keep in mind the arrestees could be trafficked, and to report all suspected trafficking to the GBI immediately. The hot states for trafficking in the Southeast included Georgia, Florida, South Carolina, North Carolina, and Tennessee, although Joe knew this modern-day slave trade was endemic across the nation.

"You think trafficking in St. Samuel has started again since we cleared out that last bunch? Thought all of that had quieted down." Joe handed the report back to his chief.

"The vice unit says our city is clear, but I wanted you and your team to be aware and on the lookout. Your priority is these murders, but you never know how things connect."

Joe nodded his understanding, told her he'd brief his team, then updated her on the little information they'd gotten from the town cobbler.

CHAPTER 20

PHOEBE

Two days after my glorious early morning creative writing event, I was back at my kitchen table, desperate for a repeat. Nothing was coming to mind, so I decided to take the kids for a walk on the beach. Jack took point, as always, with me in the middle, and Josie following behind, none of us on the leash. Jilly hated the outdoors, but Josie was a funny feline with an unnatural affinity for deep water and swimming. She also loved chasing sand crabs and furiously tried to dig them up when she found one of their hidey-holes. Jack once rescued her from a crab's perilously close snapping claws, galloping up in the nick of time to push her away, enabling the crustacean's scuttle to freedom. Instead of giving Jack a thank you high five, Josie gave him an "I had it all under control" look and stalked off with her tail high. Siblings, so silly.

✯ ✯ ✯

I'm not originally from St. Samuel, but once my family arrived here, I fell in love with the Southeast Coast. What's that expression? "I wasn't born in the South, but I got here as fast as I could." That's me, all over.

My parents were itinerant farmers, so we moved around a lot, starting on the West Coast and moving east, stopping for a couple of agricultural stints in the Dakotas and one in Texas. I know, weird occupation for this century, right? My folks are friends-of-the-earth kind of people who used to go from one small farming community to another teaching farmers how to grow crops without using chemicals. After years of moving from town to town, they finally settled on a small plot of land on the outskirts of St. Samuel and opened a farmer's market with their own homegrown organic vegetables. We rarely had any money, and my parents still don't, but they love their life, which is more than most people can say. I've attempted to help them with my inheritance money, but they refuse all offers. And I still get free fresh vegetables any time I want, a definite win for me.

My sister, Sophie, and I were in grade school when our parents settled in South Georgia. One of the first kids I met was Paul, my future ex-husband. At recess on my first day of school, he offered to push the merry-go-round for me, an offer I—and ten other kids—immediately took him up on. Paul was a slight kid with no muscles, so the eleven of us didn't get much of a carousel ride. Sophie, who was one of the eleven kids, was thoroughly unimpressed with Paul's pushing abilities. She was in fourth grade, a year behind me, but that didn't keep her from trying to beat Paul up in our second week at school.

Paul insisted he was the fastest runner in fifth grade. Sophie insisted she could run ten times faster and soundly whup him. The two of them lined up against the fence on one side of the schoolyard, the plan being whoever reached the far-side fence first would be declared the winner. Three-quarters of the way in, Sophie tripped over a tree root, losing the race in a spectacular tumble. She rose from the dirt with fists cocked, declaring Paul had tripped her. Paul hit the finish line and was doing a victory dance when Sophie rammed into him, pummeling him left and right. Poor Paul didn't know what to do as he had been raised not to hit girls. I pulled Sophie off him, explaining she was clumsy and a poor loser to boot, a bad combination in a foot race. Sophie hated Paul from that moment on, even when she walked down the aisle as my maid of honor at our wedding.

By the time Sophie entered her freshman year of high school, she had fully transformed from tomboy to girly girl. No more fights in the schoolyard for her. Now she proved her mettle by acing every class and wearing more mascara than the entire cheerleading squad combined. With her intellect in full bloom, Sophie graduated class valedictorian and headed to medical school at the University of Kentucky on a full scholarship. The previous year I had followed Paul to Valdosta State University on no scholarship, unsure of what to major in except handsome, blue-eyed Paul.

Aunt Lucy was openly opposed to my going to the same college as Paul. Almost prophetically, she said I needed to flap my wings in a different direction and learn who I was without my constant shadow. Mom and Dad, as usual, thought Aunt Lucy was making too much of the matter. Aunt Lucy was my mom's much older and much more pragmatic sister. Mom and Aunt Lucy got along well enough, but Mom was a free spirit and Aunt Lucy, though fun-loving, was mostly practical and realistic. Mom thought her sister needed to lighten up. Aunt Lucy thought Mom and Dad needed to get jobs that would actually pay the bills.

I can hardly blame Aunt Lucy. She worked like a dog through her childhood years. I know only a few of the jobs she had as a kid: de-tasseling corn at ten, harvesting tobacco taller than she was, cooking in a diner, ironing for the wealthy people in her town, shining her parents' boarders' shoes. She saved all her money from those ventures to start a used clothing shop when she was in high school. Used items being a hot commodity in the aftermath of the stock market crash, the shop provided income for college. A dual degree in fashion design and business helped procure an internship with a well-known fashion designer, and Aunt Lucy's own amazing talent led to Lu's Labels, one of the top ten apparel lines in United States history.

Along the way, Aunt Lucy married four men, each of them richer than the previous one, although Aunt Lucy made plenty of her own money. Widowed by her first husband, she divorced the second, third, and fourth within a few years (months in one case) of the nuptials. I always thought Aunt Lucy's first husband, David, was her true love and her heart never fully recovered after his death. Aunt Lu never confirmed my theory in words, but she kept a photo of Uncle David beside her bed through all three subsequent marriages, which probably goes a long way toward explaining those divorces.

Back to my uneventful life. I ended up majoring in criminal justice, along with majoring in my beloved Paul, who was studying wildlife biology. I didn't plan to have a career in law enforcement, I just found the profession interesting. And of course I'd read my share of crime novels, Sherlock Holmes being my favorite sleuth, so clever at ciphering out clues and making awe-inspiring deductions. If I was more Sherlock-y, I would have already published a series of bestselling crime novels.

✶ ✶ ✶

As our little caravan traipsed along the ocean's edge, Josie darting off periodically to chase crabs, my mind wandered again, and I started to think about Uncle David's death and the random way events occur. What were the odds he would be on that particular street corner at that particular moment, putting him in place to get hit by a taxi whose driver drove up onto the sidewalk, a place a cab never should be? The driver was reaching into his glovebox for his cigarettes and, at forty miles per hour, crashed into my uncle, who was only on that street because the hotel concierge told him to turn right when the restaurant he was headed for was actually two blocks to the left of the hotel entrance. One tiny incorrect piece of information changed Aunt Lu's life forever, just like one inattentive landscaper back in Atlanta permanently changed the lives of Anna's family. And both of those random events changed my life completely as well. You know that song, "Isn't It Ironic" by Alanis Morissette? Listen to it the next time you need a reminder of the fickleness of the gods. You'll see my point.

CHAPTER 21

DIANE

Lorelei's revelation shocked Diane into momentary silence. Switching into cop mode, she asked several pointed questions, discovering the two girls were the daughters of a "bad man," who Diane learned, much later, was Sean Templeton, one of the largest drug kingpins in the United States. Apparently, Templeton's men had accidentally killed the son of a major East Coast rival drug czar, Frank Levy, whose criminal empire was so widespread even the rural Saddle County Sheriff's Office had once participated in a manhunt for the mob boss. Multiple law enforcement agencies were intimately familiar with his crimes, but Levy's organization was so compartmentalized no agency had been able to get close to the head man. The drug business wasn't the only criminal game Levy played. He had his share of the United States human trafficking trade from Florida to California, had his hand in money-laundering casino profits, and was suspected to be behind the murder of multiple informants and members of opposing criminal organizations. He was also known to execute his own people for the smallest of infractions.

As Diane was digesting what Lorelei had told her, the Eastern European teen started making hand motions, moving her hand repeatedly up and down to her mouth. Maria noticed and said, "Lily is hungry, and I'm starving, too. Can we stop for food? Those men hardly fed us in the motel."

Lorelei, Libby, and Elizabeth all nodded their heads in hopeful agreement, and though Diane did not want to take the time, she said they would stop at the first place they came to. Three blocks later, a local diner appeared on her right. After checking the mirrors for potential trouble and seeing none, she pulled into the drive-thru behind a red minivan. Half-listening to the girls reading the menu board, she kept her head on a swivel, checking the windows and mirrors for unwanted company. After several minutes, the minivan moved forward. As Diane inched the Honda up to the speaker to order, a white SUV whipped in front of her at an angle, blocking forward movement. Instantly Diane threw the transmission into reverse, then slammed on the brakes just in time to keep from ramming a black Hummer, which had trapped them from behind.

"Girls, get out. Get out and run, now now now!" With her door blocked by the restaurant's speaker, Diane couldn't go anywhere; Elizabeth, beside her in the passenger seat, was equally trapped by the large SUV. Diane wished deeply for her service revolver. On her hurried run to Miami, she had stopped briefly on a bridge and dumped the weapon, her uniform, badge, and holster into the river below.

Opening the back right door, Maria jumped out and ran about two yards before a large black man in a form-fitted suit snatched her by the hair and jerked her back to the Hummer. Lily had managed to scramble out of the sedan and was in a punching contest with a slight, tattooed white guy with a shaved head. The skinny man couldn't have been more than twenty. Lorelei and Libby simply clung together in the backseat, too frightened to open their door.

The black man tossed Maria into the Hummer and turned to help his tattooed colleague with his combative, foreign-language-spewing package. Lily was yelling what Diane assumed were damning curse words. Elizabeth clung to Diane, crying, while the former law enforcement officer watched helplessly as her simple escape plan imploded under the hot Florida sun. Scanning the parking lot for potential allies, Diane laid on the horn to get someone's, anyone's, attention, until a sharp rap on the window made her look over. A tall, handsome man with wavy black hair and an olive complexion, wearing a costly suit and pricey sunglasses, made a "roll down the window" motion with his hand. Hesitating, but unable to think of an alternate idea, Diane pushed the button.

"My name is Oscar Migliori. Listen to me. You will not lay on the horn again or attempt to do anything that will distract my men or interfere with this mission. You and these girls will come with us. These young women belong to my boss and now, so do you. If you prove useful, you will live. If you prove troublesome, you will die. Now, both of you get out and go to the SUV."

While the black-haired man made this speech, a fourth man pulled Libby and Lorelei from the backseat and pushed them toward the black SUV. Fair-haired and tall, he was wearing a t-shirt sporting a giant dill pickle in a straw hat and sunglasses. The caption below the artwork read "What's the dill?"

Watching each girl get tossed into a vehicle, Diane saw no other option. She disengaged Elizabeth from her arm and whispered,

"Come on, sweetie, we have to do what they say right now. We'll think of a way out later."

Elizabeth gasped for breath, wiped her eyes, and stepped slowly out of the vehicle, pulling Diane painfully across the console with her. In the SUV, the skinny tattooed man with the shaved head, who was now sporting a bloody split lip courtesy of Lily, put a blindfold on Diane and Elizabeth, then zip-tied their hands in front. Diane just had time to see the black man pull her purse from the front seat, meaning her phone was with them if she could figure out a way to get to it. In the vehicle, one of the kidnappers sat between Diane and Elizabeth. Diane thought it was Mr. Split Lip but couldn't see enough through the blindfold to tell. She asked why they were being taken and where they were headed but received no response. After several minutes of unbearable silence under the dark mask, Diane tried again.

"Who are you? Where are we going? Why have you taken us?"

"You will be quiet, or my colleague will quiet you forcibly." Diane recognized the clipped cadence as Oscar's, the well-dressed man from her car window.

"Look, if it's money you want, I'll get money for you. Just tell me what you want, and we can work something out."

As she spoke the last word, a ferocious blow snapped Diane's head back into the headrest. She could feel blood trickling from her nose but when she went to wipe the moisture away, a hand grabbed her wrists, squeezing the bones tightly.

"That is the only warning you will receive. Listen and act according to my instructions or sustain additional physical damage."

Silence fell in the vehicle, except for Elizabeth's muffled sobs. They drove for what seemed to Diane to be about an hour, but she had lost all sense of time the moment she had been hit. Eventually the vehicle slowed down, drove a few more yards, then stopped completely. Diane heard two doors open, then a breeze cooled her arms as her own door was opened. The person in the seat beside her, who did turn out to be Split Lip, took off her blindfold and told her to get out of the vehicle. He did the same for Elizabeth, groping the young girl's behind as she half-fell out of the car.

They were in a big warehouse stacked high with shipping containers. Diane could see markings in a foreign language on many of them. She looked rapidly around, trying to gather as much information about their whereabouts as she could. The four other girls tumbled out of the Hummer, their captors pulling off blindfolds one by one, but leaving their wrists bound. Oscar looked at the guy in the pickle shirt and said, "Take them to room five, Coffey. Don't let them speak to anyone you encounter."

"You got it, boss. Let's go, ladies." Herding Diane and the five girls up a set of metal stairs with Split Lip in the lead, Dill said, "Just do what the boss tells you and everything will be fine."

Diane thought that was the biggest lie she'd ever heard, but said nothing. The group turned left at the top of the stairs, walking along a catwalk that traversed the length of the warehouse. Diane watched from above as their two well-dressed captors, Oscar and the black man, strode toward the back of the building. Turning her attention to what she presumed would be their new home for a while, she found numbered rooms, all the doors with padlocks on the doorframes, some locked and some hanging unlatched. The warehouse was eerily quiet for such a large building. No one appeared to be about except those who had arrived with their unhappy group. The most noise came from several brown sparrows flitting from corner to corner, trapped just as equally as Diane and her new charges.

CHAPTER 22

JOE

As Joe told Chief Paris, Kurt Von Schuster hadn't had much to offer the investigation. He admitted to his penchant for stealing women's underwear, but claimed he was a reformed man and had kept his nose clean since he was last released from prison eighteen months ago. He had no desire to go back to jail. He swore he didn't know any of the dead women, claiming to have been in Alcoholics Anonymous meetings two of the four nights in question. Joe had a detective checking Kurt's story but felt as confident as a seasoned investigator could that the man was telling the truth.

Questioning Kurt about his skills, Terry had learned the repairman could make custom holes outlined with thread, but his work called for small eyeholes for laces, not one-inch buttonholes like the gashes found on the town's murder victims. He explained the sign in his shop window advertising custom garment buttonholes was for the alteration shop in town. That comment put the tailor next on the list to be interviewed and helped move Von Schuster further down the suspect list.

When the partners got back to the office, the Saddle County Sheriff's case file had been delivered. A quick review of the county reports confirmed the same pattern of brutal rape and strangulation used by St. Samuel's own killer, but didn't reveal anything new. Buttonholes on the corpse, a recently adopted kitten in the house, a lingerie drawer left open and rifled through, victim over five-foot-seven, thirty-three years old. The only item of possible interest was Saddle County's victim had played in St. Samuel's community softball league. Since two of the St. Samuel victims had also played in the league, checking with the softball organization to see if the three ladies played on the same team moved higher on the to-do list.

Having a little time before their lunch meeting with the Saddle County detectives, Joe and Terry held a short briefing with Agent Dalton and their two junior detectives to bring them up to speed. Terry then started making phone calls while Joe went to brief the Chief on their findings. Before he left, Joe tasked the young guys with comparing the sheriff's case file against the St. Samuel files detail by minute detail. Jeremy volunteered to help them.

Three hours later, Terry and Joe remained frustrated. So far, the file review of their own investigation hadn't revealed any new information or missed steps, and neither had the junior detectives' detailed comparison with the file from Saddle County. Lunch with the SCSO detectives had been useful for batting theories around but not for gaining any new data.

Joe stared out the window of his office, idly watching people walk down Main Street. He and Terry were waiting for the tailor's shop to re-open; apparently, the tailor and his assistant closed for Saturday siestas. Vehicle traffic was light, so when the county animal shelter truck rumbled by, Joe noticed it immediately. Cursing himself and Terry for fools, he stood and said brusquely, "Let's go."

Terry jumped up, grabbing his jacket. "Where we headed?"

"The animal shelter. When was the last time you thought about Henry DeSantos?"

"Oh, Lord," Terry said. "Not since he brought my sister that kitten a few years ago. I thought she was going to wallop him one. The cat turned out to be a handy mouser, though, so Sis got over it. But she avoids Henry whenever she sees him around town. She thinks he's weird. You're thinking maybe Henry's the connection between the kittens and the women?"

"Seems reasonable, at least reasonable enough to talk to the guy. He's always been a strange bird. Remember in high school when he offered everyone free tattoos of dog paws? But only if he could ink one on the top of your foot? And remember how mad he got if you said no?"

"Right, I have a vague memory of that, now that you mention it. Didn't he tattoo the head cheerleader on her foot? What was her name, Regina or Rosemary or something? And then the tattoo got infected, and she couldn't cheer for the rest of the season? I don't know who was angrier, her or her parents."

"It might have been me. Rosie was her name. The day she went to the emergency room for her foot, she and I were supposed to go on a date after the football game. Thanks to Henry, she had to cancel. I was sure I was going to get to at least third base that night." Joe laughed at the memory. Rosie had been a hot-to-trot walking mountain of trouble. He probably owed Henry a big thank you for taking the cheerleader out of the teen romance game that evening.

CHAPTER 23

PHOEBE

Hearing footsteps cross the old wooden porch, I looked out of the diamond-paned windows to see Henry DeSantos coming to the door. I was shocked. Henry had never been in the library, as far as I knew. I was curious to learn what he wanted.

My job is manning the information desk. I point people in the direction they need to go, help them find books, and assist with research. I also re-shelve returned books, the task I like best. Ours is a county library housed in a historic fire station, complete with an old-fashioned brass pole smack in the middle of the reference room. The pole runs from the second floor children's section to the first floor. Keeping the kids off that pole is a full-time job, luckily one I'm not responsible for. My idea of childcare involves a lot of duct tape, so the library director tends to keep me away from the children's area.

As Henry approached the desk, I welcomed him to the library and asked how I could help him. He said he was looking for information on serial killers. The voices in my head shouted at that bombshell.

"I'm sorry, you're looking for information on serial killers?" I tried to keep a perfect poker face.

"Yep, I want to learn how they find their victims and get them in a position to kill them. I want to understand how they think, you know?"

I wanted to say no, I most certainly did not know, but since I get paid (a miniscule amount, but I do get a paycheck) to help members research what they ask for, I smiled politely and said, "Well, let's see what we can find."

After thinking for a minute, I directed Henry to do an internet search while I delved into our database for books or journals about his gruesome subject. Turns out, a lot has been published about serial killers and we had multiple books on the topic. Even the FBI has published documents about serial murderers. You'd think they would want to keep those trade secrets to themselves, but evidently not. After doing this research, I'm certain I can now plan a murder or two and get away with them. The knowledge will come in quite handy for my novel-in-progress, so thank you, Henry DeSantos!

I'm not sure why Henry was researching serial killers, though the thought did cross my mind that he was thinking about becoming one. Or maybe he already was one and was researching to see if he's doing the job correctly. If my memory is accurate, Henry was a poor student in high school. In fact, seems like there was some question as to whether he would graduate on time, but I can't quite remember. I wouldn't think research would be his strong suit.

Since serial killers are reputed to be smart, St. Samuel is probably safe from Henry, especially if all of them are like Ted Bundy.

Bundy was reportedly charming, handsome, and intelligent, descriptors which would never be used in conjunction with Henry. And according to the research I just did for him, serial killers are usually anti-social (Ted must have been the exception to that rule), which Henry is, but they are also supposed to lack compassion and empathy. Our Henry has plenty of both . . . for animals, anyway. For humans, maybe not so much.

Possibly his dislike of humans does make him a candidate for a killer, who knows? Maybe I should have asked him why he was interested in the subject. But I'm glad I didn't, just in case that query may have marked me to be his first victim. The man appears pleasant when he's holding an adorable puppy or kitten, but without a furry friend in tow, he's kinda scary. Anyway, I gave him the call numbers for the books I found, then he stayed in the stacks researching for about two hours, making me glad I was on the early shift and could leave the building before dark. Silly, I know.

To keep up with the world and be able to make informed conversation with library members, I used to watch the evening news and read news stories online. But since people have gotten so ridiculous with everyone shouting at each other, fake news everywhere, and multiple talking heads who rarely have anything useful to say, I stopped watching the news completely and television in general, except for the occasional movie. I used to enjoy reading the paper, too, but last year our local paper closed up shop, like much of the print media across the country. So, except for the occasional glimpse of a headline online, I have no idea what's going on in the world. I rarely know what's happening in my own town. If a tornado was about to strike or someone was running amok killing people, I'd be the last one to know.

You might find my aversion to the news strange since I work in a library. If I was a good employee, I suppose I would continue to keep up with world and local events. But I figure if people are coming to the library to do research, ipso facto, they are typically looking up something that happened in the past, so I'm comfortable staying blissfully ignorant about the headlines. These days I read in the evenings with two cats and a dog fighting for my lap. Snuggles and a good novel always beat anything on television.

CHAPTER 24

DIANE

As Split Lip shut the door to room five, the girls clustered around Diane, eyes wide, tears streaming down every face except Lily's, who stalked stoically around the room, pacing in erratic rectangles. When Lily heard the padlock snap into place she walked quickly to the door and tried to open it, without success. Looking hopelessly at Diane, she resumed pacing. Diane felt hopeless herself. She could only imagine how much worse poor Lily felt, being unable to communicate with the rest of them. Diane wondered what the teenager's story was. Most likely Lily was from an impoverished home in a small Eastern European country and had been lured to the US with the promise of a good job, only to find herself in the hands of human traffickers upon arrival. Diane hoped one day they would be able to communicate with one another. Lily exuded an aura of impassive fortitude Diane found reassuring and calming.

"Alright girls, settle down. Obviously, we're in trouble." Diane saw no point in sugarcoating the situation. "I don't know any more than you do at the moment, so let's see what we have in the room that might help us, then we can talk about what to do."

The girls wiped their eyes and looked around, seeing nothing but cinder-block walls and a boarded-up window letting in thin rays of sunlight between the slats, the only light in the room. Luckily their hands were free. Their captors had cut off the zip ties while Dill pointedly told them misbehavior of any sort would lead to new restraints or worse.

Realizing Lily's pacing had led her through a doorway adjacent to the covered window, Diane pushed through the hovering girls to join her, where she found the teen examining a small bathroom. A makeshift shower was situated in the corner by a regular toilet and a small sink. Both toilet and sink were filthy, but Diane uttered a grateful prayer when she flushed the tank and the water flowed normally. The shower reminded Diane of the kind Joe had sometimes used in the field, when the Marine leadership was feeling gracious enough to let the troops have a shower. A black five-gallon bag hung from a hook in the corner, hose and shower head attached. A thin trench had been scraped into the concrete floor, but since there was no actual drain, Diane supposed the crevice only acted as a holding cell for the water. She reached up to open the water valve. Only a small trickle dripped out of the head. Neither soap nor shampoo were present anyway, so the odds of getting cleaned up seemed slim. Water did flow at a good rate from the faucet into the rust-stained sink, so all-in-all Diane thought the circumstances were about as good as they would get. A small amount of toilet paper on a roll, a few paper towels by the sink, and an empty soap dish were the only bathroom supplies in the small space.

Exiting the tiny water closet, Diane stopped to examine the window and found it was securely boarded from the outside with no evident way to push the boards out or pull them in. She sighed and moved to the only bed in the room, a standard twin with a variety of stains embedded in the thin mattress. No sheets or blankets. Diane dropped to her hands and knees to search under the black metal frame, finding nothing, not even mouse droppings. Rising from the floor to sit on the mattress, she mustered a weak smile as Maria and Elizabeth sank down beside her while Lily occupied the only other piece of furniture in the room, a decrepit plastic chair. Libby and Lorelei immediately scrambled into the corner of the bed against the wall, arms around each other, rocking slightly back and forth. Nothing else was in the room. Maybe they could take the bed or toilet apart to make a weapon, but Diane needed a moment to think.

While she could guess why the girls had been reclaimed, she had no idea why the men had taken her too, why they hadn't murdered her in the drive-thru lane and dumped her body in Florida's abundant alligator-filled marsh. She believed the girls would either be sold to a whorehouse stateside or in South America, or they would be kept here to be farmed out as sex workers by their captors. They could also be sold for domestic help, but given their young ages, Diane figured prostitution was their fate. She thought she was too old to fit the profile of a trafficked sex worker, but who knew what these men would do? Still in her thirties, Diane was aware she was an attractive woman and she had kept a trim, fit figure over the years. Until she could get some answers from one of the men, she wouldn't know her own fate.

"Diane, what's happening? Are those men going to hurt us? When will we eat? My stomach is grumbling bad." Elizabeth took

Diane's hand as she spoke while Maria let loose a tirade in Spanish, gesturing at the door.

Diane was saved from answering either girl by the sound of the padlock being lifted. The girls collectively held their breath as Split Lip appeared in the doorway, holding two white fast food bags. He walked slowly over to Maria, showing her the contents of one of the bags, a mouth-watering aroma filling the room. When she began to reach inside, he snatched the sacks away, grinning, then stroked the side of her face. "So what will you give me for a burger, baby? I need somethin' for my trouble."

Maria slapped his hand away, a diatribe of Spanish curse words pouring from her mouth. The bags went flying as Split Lip grabbed the teen by the neck, pulling her to him, pushing one hand between her legs as he growled, "You wanna eat? You need to be nice to me."

Diane jumped up and grabbed Split Lip's arm saying, "Look, this is a misunderstanding. Let her go. We'll cooperate."

Releasing Maria instantly, he backhanded Diane into the wall. Sliding to the floor, she could only look up at him as he stood over her and said, "Don't try to be a hero, lady. You're all gonna get what we give you, and you cain't do nothin' about it." Spitting on the floor beside her, he left, the sound of the lock clicking into place resounding through the door.

Diane got up slowly, gingerly feeling her jaw and cheekbone. Nothing seemed to be broken but her face hurt like hell after the two blows she'd received that day. Lily, who had picked up the food bags and retrieved the two hamburgers that had fallen out, solemnly handed the sacks to Diane. Diane looked at her, mustered a small smile and said, "Okay, let's see what we've got."

Their captors had provided six kids' hamburgers, three apple pies, and four small bottles of water. Not a lot, but better than nothing, and they could reuse the bottles to get water from the sink. Elizabeth and Maria gobbled their hamburgers like starving dogs while Lily and the two pre-teens chewed theirs slowly.

When Libby put half of her hamburger down and indicated to Maria she could have it, Diane stepped in. "No, sweetie, you need to eat the whole thing. We don't know what's to come and we all will need our strength."

Reluctantly Libby picked up the unwanted sandwich and slowly ate the rest, but Diane could not entice her to eat even a bite of her portion of the apple pies. As the sun set outside, the limited light coming through the thin slits in the boarded up window dimmed further, increasing the shadows in every corner of the room. Diane encouraged each of the girls to splash some water on their faces, thinking they might feel better if they could refresh themselves a little. Then she sat back on the bed and drew the girls up to her, all except Lily, who returned to the plastic chair.

"Okay, I don't know what's going to happen or what we're doing here, but I'll try to find out from these men tomorrow. Meanwhile, let's get some sleep tonight to be ready for whatever comes in the next few days."

At this, Lily made a small sound, as though she understood Diane's words. When Diane looked at her, Lily stared intently into her eyes. Diane figured this was Lily's way of saying she knew exactly what the men wanted from them. Diane nodded her head and shrugged slightly. Why whitewash the situation, even if she could say something reassuring in a language Lily would understand?

"I know Maria's and Elizabeth's stories, but it might be helpful if I knew how you and Libby came to be here, Lorelei. Could you girls share your history with me, please? You said your father brought you to the men in the van?"

After a slow start, telling the story in turns, eleven-year-old Libby and twelve-year-old Lorelei told Diane again their father was a bad man. They weren't sure what his business was, but they knew he was always looking out for the police. Their mother had stolen away with the girls about four years ago, slipping quietly into a moonless night and driving to Montana from their home in Alabama. They settled in a small town named Livingston where their mom, Ali, worked full-time as a barista in a coffee shop and full-time as a bartender in a hotel. She also worked part-time cleaning people's houses.

They barely had enough money to pay rent and eat, so when their mom cut their hair short and dyed it, she did the jobs herself; the results were less than glamorous. The girls weren't allowed to go to school. Their mom made sporadic attempts at homeschooling in between her three jobs; those results were also less than satisfying. Ali rarely let the girls leave the house, locking them in the tiny rental when she left to go to work with strict instructions to stay put. She made them learn new names, first and last, and told them never to talk to anyone in the town. She said the three of them were a family and didn't need anyone else. When asked about going back home to see Daddy, all Ali ever said was, "He is not a good man, and we will never go back there. Our life is here now. Just the three of us."

The girls, who were seven and eight at the time, knew their parents had argued a lot. They had often heard shouting and sounds of physical fighting as they huddled together in their room in Fairhope. The house they lived in was spacious with a pool in the backyard, and while they didn't have many friends, they had a lot of toys, went to Disney World every year, and loved to be read a story at night, especially when Daddy got home from work in time. But when the fighting started, the girls would scramble under the covers on Libby's bed, holding pillows over their ears to drown out the noise.

The day after a big mommy-daddy fight, Ali would have bruises or cuts all over and usually be walking slowly. She often had black eyes, too. She would always say she slipped and fell or bumped into a door, but the girls suspected their daddy had been mean to her. They whispered about it occasionally under the covers before they fell asleep, with Libby staunchly defending their dad and Lorelei vowing to pay him back for hurting their mom.

One evening in Montana while Ali was at her bartending job, someone knocked on the door. The girls looked at each other, wide-eyed. Their mom had told them never to answer the door, but the visitor kept banging on the wood. Finally, they heard a familiar voice say, "Libby? Lorelei? It's Daddy, open the door."

Libby gasped in delight and before Lorelei could stop her, she raced for the stepstool, climbed up to the top step, unlocked all four locks, and slung the door open wide. Their dad scooped her up in a big hug, then reached for Lorelei who shrank out of reach against the wall.

"I know it's been a long time, girls. Took me a while to find you. Where's Mommy? I need to talk to her." When Libby told her dad Ali was at work, a sly grin spread across his face. "In that case, let's go surprise her. She'll be happy to see us. But first, I need something to drink. You girls want something? I brought your favorite, chocolate milk." He waved a plastic grocery bag in their direction. "Come on, let's get glasses."

They went into the small kitchen, and he pulled out the chocolate milk, along with a big Mountain Dew. "Hey, you know what? Let's forget the glasses, just drink straight from the bottle. I know your mom won't like that, but this is a celebration, right? It'll be our secret. Now you both take big swigs."

The girls took turns drinking deeply from the bottle, enjoying this small act of rebellion. Mommy had so many rules, disobeying just this one was fun. Besides, chocolate milk was their favorite, and Daddy said they didn't have to use a glass. This bottle must have been close to going bad, though, because the taste was a little bitter.

"Alright now, get your coats on. It's chilly outside. You can stay in your pajamas." Daddy looked through the front window as he said this, as though he was looking for someone in the drive.

Lorelei walked slowly to the rack by the door and took down their coats. She didn't think going with Daddy was a good idea but didn't quite know why. Libby was so excited she kept jumping up and down. In the driveway they saw Daddy had gotten a new truck, a big one with a funny goat head on the front. He helped them into the backseat, then hopped in the front seat. Lorelei noticed a shotgun leaning against the console as Daddy backed out of the drive. When he got to the end of the street, he started to turn left.

Libby said, "No, Daddy, turn right to go to Mommy's work."

Daddy glanced at them in the rearview mirror but continued the left turn.

"No, Daddy, this isn't the right way. You need to turn around."

"We have to make one stop first, so just settle down. We'll be with Mommy soon."

Troubled, both girls sat back and looked out the windows, trying to find the moon dancing in between the clouds. Moon seeking was a game they played with Mommy in the back yard sometimes, hunting the moon on cloud-filled nights. As their father drove, they both soon fell asleep, waking only when daddy stopped for bathroom breaks. On these stops, he filled them up with more bitter-tasting chocolate milk and vanilla crème cookies. When they asked where Mommy was, he said she had gone to Memphis, Tennessee, and they were going to meet her there.

Eventually the girls woke to find bright sunshine but no Mommy. The truck was parked at a big gas station; lots of cars with Tennessee plates were coming and going. Daddy was standing at the front of the truck, talking with two mean-looking men. Daddy gestured toward the truck's cab, then back at the men, appearing unhappy with the way the conversation was going. Finally, Daddy nodded, the men shook hands, and Daddy came to open the back door.

"Okay, girls, get on out. Y'all need to go with these men."

"What? Why? Where's Mommy? We don't want to leave you, Daddy. And Mommy will be missing us."

"I know she will, baby, but I owe a man a big debt and the only payment he'll take from me is you two. Either that or he's going to kill me, and you wouldn't want that, would you? So y'all go on now and do what these men say."

As the girls screamed "No, Daddy, no!" over and over, their father scooped them up and handed their small wriggling bodies to the men, who stuck each little one in the arm with a needle. Thirty seconds later the girls were laid out in the green panel van, once again asleep.

CHAPTER 25

JOE

Monday afternoon, Joe exhaled with exhaustion as he stepped into Danny Taylor's shop to pick up a sports jacket he had dropped off four months ago. Diane had always done all their clothing repairs; she was a talented seamstress. These days he had to support the local economy when various articles of clothing needed mending. Joe was combining this personal errand with work; he hoped to hit the tailor up for a chat while retrieving his jacket.

Closing the door behind him, Joe was struck by the difference between the tailor's shop and the cobbler's store. Not one item seemed to be in its place here; the lighting was dim, the whole atmosphere unwelcoming. Joe supposed Danny stayed in business because he was the only tailor in town. As he waited at the counter for an employee to appear, he tried to tamp down his frustration with the case.

Saturday's interview with Henry DeSantos had been short and dissatisfying. Already upset that four kittens had each witnessed a horrific crime and been unexpectedly returned to the shelter, Henry had been unfocused and uncommunicative. The junior detectives were checking his alibis, but Joe didn't expect them to find that Henry had lied.

Although DeSantos admitted to taking a kitten to each of the victims, he denied killing the women or knowing anything about their deaths. The kittens alone weren't enough to make Henry a firm suspect, given the number of animals he had parceled out over the years. In the absence of DNA or anything putting him at the murder scenes, Henry would remain in the clear, assuming his alibis also checked out. He claimed to have been visiting his mother in My Mountain, Georgia, on one of the evenings in question. Joe expected Henry's mom to corroborate her son's story, even if untrue. Mothers rarely narc'd out their children. Video from the shelter's cameras proved Henry was working late at the shelter two of the evenings the murders had occurred, although there was a slim chance he could have snuck out, done the dirty deed, then slipped back in, given he knew the shelter entrances and exits well and not every door had a camera. Henry didn't have an alibi for the night Jillian Finn was killed, but Terry didn't believe Henry was their guy, and at this point, neither did Joe.

Canvassing the victims' neighbors had led to nothing. None of the women's neighborhoods had cameras and the few available ring doorbells didn't reveal anything suspicious on the streets the days or nights of the murders. DNA results from skin samples found under two of the victim's fingernails yielded nothing from CODIS, the national DNA database. Joe had hoped an interview with the tailor would help move the investigation forward, but his plan to talk with the businessman today was thwarted when Danny's niece informed him Danny had gone fishing at his secret fishing spot and wouldn't be around until the next morning.

Joe settled for interviewing Brenda since he was at the shop anyway. She was a chatty thing, but she didn't provide any useful information. Joe told her he'd return to talk with Danny the next day, paid for his newly repaired jacket, and headed back to the station.

Although anxious to find the killer and ready to get the tailor's answers to his questions, Joe knew from experience that the multiple parts of an investigation never came together in an orderly manner or at a time convenient for the investigators. In fact, most investigations stalled at some point before the acquired pieces began to fit together. If he had to wait until the next day for Danny's interview, he had plenty of other things to do until then. The press conference hadn't gone well, the Chief was breathing down his neck for a solve, and despite keeping a careful eye out, he'd had no further sightings of the auburn-haired woman or the blue BMW. He and Terry and the three other detectives in the unit were worn out from sixteen-hour days, minimum sleep, and maximum caffeine. Joe had requested two officers from other divisions to assist his team. They were supposed to report the next day. Chief Paris was still negotiating with the GBI for additional manpower; Joe hoped the agency would send them another experienced investigator soon.

✫ ✫ ✫

The two senior detectives took a short break from working the case Sunday afternoon and made a paternal stop at the county library. Terry's fourteen-year-old daughter had let slip that she was meeting her boyfriend at the library over the weekend. News of a male companion in his daughter's life was an unwelcome surprise to her father. In Terry's mind, his baby girl would live at home until she was forty and maybe then go on a date.

Despite the short, awkward conversation Terry had had with Ellen about boys, he insisted on going to check this boyfriend out. Joe felt like Maxwell Smart on one of his madcap missions as he and Terry surreptitiously entered the library. If Ellen saw her dad skulking around, she wouldn't speak to him for weeks, or maybe ever again. The pretty employee at the information desk was busy with several customers, so the stealthy sleuths were able to slink unnoticed around the shelves of books until they found Ellen sitting at a table talking to a pimple-faced boy with curly hair who appeared to be about twelve. As they watched the young pair, Ellen blushed prettily, laughing at something the boy was saying. Terry tensed, ready to pounce from behind the book stack, weapon drawn and handcuffs out. Joe put a hand on his best friend's shoulder.

"Relax," Joe whispered. "He looks harmless. They even have books on the table like they really are studying."

"Well, why does he have to sit so close to her?" Terry groused. "And how come she hasn't mentioned him to me before now? I never heard of this kid and all of a sudden he's her boyfriend? I'm finding out his name and running him through the system."

Joe smiled to himself, thought how futile reminding Terry of the illegality of a background check on his daughter's suitor would be, and suggested Terry talk to Ellen at supper that evening. He could get the scoop on the curly-headed kid, maybe even invite the boy to dinner later in the week.

Terry harrumphed as Joe added, "And maybe lock your weapon in your safe when you get home, Dad. Let's go, we've got work to do."

As they snuck quietly down the library stairs, Joe laughed openly at Terry's visceral response to the thought of his daughter dating. Terry scowled all the way to the car.

CHAPTER 26

PHOEBE

"Hey, Phoebe." I looked up to see Scooter, one of our more geriatric volunteers, leaning heavily against the counter.

"Did you see our celebrity? The guy who looks like Tommy Lee Jones?"

As I shook my head, Scooter pulled out his phone.

"Here, I snuck a video when he wasn't looking. Doesn't this guy look like Tommy Lee when he was younger?"

I had to agree with Scooter; the man in the video could have worked as the actor's body double in the first half of his career. In the clip, he was walking down the stairs with another man, seemingly unaware of his Hollywood looks, and moved with an assurance seldom seen outside of Tinseltown. Both men were dressed in nice suits. In fact, they looked a bit like undercover cops. But what would cops be doing in our library? The police had all kinds of electronic resources, right? No need for them to come slumming through our outdated computers. The county hadn't supplied funds to update our software in years. In fact, our systems were so unreliable, we still had the old card catalog file in the basement for backup.

Tommy Lee's lookalike was smiling, appearing to enjoy something his colleague was saying. I couldn't clearly see the man beside the handsome doppelganger, so I asked Scooter if the other guy also looked like a Hollywood actor. Scooter snorted and said, "Nah, that guy is as plain Jane as the rest of us."

Laughing, I told the old coot to speak for himself and waved him away from the desk. As soon as Scooter scooted, I stealthily pulled out the notebook I used to write down ideas for my stories. All my returned library books were shelved, and the desk was customer-free, so I had a few minutes to jot down potential plots and characters. Henry's visit had prompted some ideas I wanted to capture before a senior moment set in. And maybe our mysterious visitors would provide inspiration, too.

Although not bad at the game Clue, I'm terrible at puzzles and the kind of word games where you must guess an answer from a cluster of information. I don't know why I think I can write a crime novel. I should probably stick to romance, but I suck at that in real life. Maybe a kid's book? Please note aforementioned childcare theory. Science fiction? Ick. Historical novels? Hate to do research. Non-fiction? Don't like to read it, would die from boredom writing it. Maybe I should be like Henry DeSantos and completely change my desired career path. I wonder if the shelter has any openings. I suppose they will if he gets arrested for being a serial killer. Ha, what a thought!

As I struggled to capture the Henry-inspired ideas in my notebook, my thoughts roamed to some of my favorite authors. I'm always amazed at the way they can create stories. Writing experts say, "Write what you know." Really? Has Stephen King actually experienced his pets returning from the dead after they've been buried? Or seen perfectly sculpted bushes come to life in their animal form? Scary, if he has. And what about Diana Gabaldon and her popular Outlander series? Has she time-traveled back to eighteenth-century Scotland? I'd love to learn that nifty trick of space and time, especially if I could find my own Jamie Fraser. Although after a few days spent without electricity or indoor plumbing, I'd probably time-travel myself on warp speed right back to the present, sexy Scotsman or no sexy Scotsman.

Speaking of story creation, I heard an author being interviewed on National Public Radio recently. Richard Powers wrote a whole novel with trees as the core of the story. Trees, can you imagine? The man wrote a five-hundred-page book with only five or six human characters and entire forests of non-sentient beings as primary characters. And the book won a Pulitzer Prize! I can barely write ten pages with engaging characters, and this guy can make trees come to life in a novel? How does that happen? I gathered Powers hoped humans would reimagine their place in the world and realize just how connected we all are, especially to the ancient forests. He spent five years reading over a hundred books about trees while he wrote *The Overstory*. I couldn't last a full year trying to write one book; I'd be bored to death with the research.

Back to my own storytelling efforts (possibly I shouldn't digress so much), I did have another burst of inspiration over the weekend and was able to add five pages to my earlier ten. Keeping with the "killed in the shower" theme, now my Lieutenant Joe is befuddled about how the killer always knows the women are in the shower and how the bad guy gets into their homes undetected. My Joe is smart, so I'm sure he'll figure the mystery out within the next few chapters. One of us will have to figure it out soon or I'll be the one spending the next five years writing a book. Did I mention I don't have the patience for that?

While I added five pages of serial killer drama to my earlier efforts, after I put big red slashes through the flying-saucer-shooting-laser-light-beams idea and gave the high school sweethearts the same red-ink treatment, I was back down to seven pages total. Oh well. Surely inspiration will strike again. As Aunt Lucy would remind me, "In an operation this big, girl, there are going to be a few losses." Recalling that little witticism, I looked up to the heavens and whined, "Well, Aunt Lucy, if I have many more losses, I'll have a book full of blank pages!"

※ ※ ※

In other news, I had a date the other night. After much browbeating from my best friend Susie, I agreed to meet her first cousin once removed for drinks. Susie works as an adjustor at a local insurance firm in town and thinks I need a man even more than I think I do. We met a few years ago at the one book club meeting I've ever been to in my life. We both left the boring affair early, bumping into each other at the door in our hurry to skedaddle after an hour of listening to one woman drone on and on about her thoughts on Sue Monk Kidd's *The Book of Longings*. I loved *The Book of Longings*, think the novel is Kidd's best work. So I'm not much interested in hearing some close-minded blowhard talk non-stop about how Jesus could not possibly have had a wife, never, ever. Really? Come on, lady, the book is fiction. If Ms. Kidd wants Jesus to have a wife and ten kids, or a few beers with Judas before his friend throws him to the wolves, she can do that. May I say again? Fiction!

Whew, didn't realize I was still so worked up about that.

Anyway, that night Susie and I both turned to the right out of the library, heading straight for the Daisy Lady, one of my favorite bars in town. When we discovered we were both making a beeline to the same place for the same reason, we laughed and became instant friends. We sat in my preferred waitress's section, ordered drinks and nachos, and have been besties ever since. Our most excellent server was Eleanor, such a sweet girl. She told us that night she was taking classes to become a forensic scientist.

Susie is married to a nice guy named Gary who worships her but hates her spending habits. She is a master at spending money, both on things she needs and things she doesn't. The sneaky girl finally forestalled years of the same marital argument by getting a secret credit card Gary knows nothing about. How he thinks she acquires all the new clothes in her closet, I don't know, but the covert account has taken a lot of stress out of their marriage. I don't judge her. Honestly, sometimes the truth is overrated.

St. Samuel is home to a lot of bars, but I only patronize a few of them since the others require a six-shooter on the hip for personal safety. Well, I suppose that's usually only true during tourist season; the locals tend to stay calm. According to our mayor, St. Samuel is one of the top five safest places to live in Georgia. And while I do have a concealed carry permit, I don't usually carry a weapon, mostly because I haven't been able to find a holster that doesn't make my pants fall down. Also, shooting Scooter would be too tempting.

My other favorite spots in town are the Ducking Dog for delicious barbeque, and the Southern Biscuit, which sounds like a breakfast joint but isn't. The Biscuit serves amazing sushi and specializes in craft cocktails like the Funky Monkey and the Oyster Bomb. Personally, I prefer my oysters on the half shell accompanied by a cracker and a cold glass of white wine, but Susie loves a fancy drink. I usually stick to wine or the occasional beer. If I need a sipping drink in my hand to be sociable, Jack Daniels on the rocks is my preference. Susie always orders something brightly colored with an umbrella bobbing around the edge.

But I digress. Back to Susie's first cousin once removed. She had been bugging me for months to go out with him. My sister had chimed in from Boston, reminding me I wasn't getting any younger (thanks, Sis), I hadn't been on a date in months (thanks again, Sis), and no matter how much I loved him, Jack could not be the only man in my life forever. After that long-distance barrage, I conceded to meet Cousin Chauncey at the Ducking Dog for happy hour, emphasizing when I spoke with him on the phone that I could only stay for one drink, as I would have to get home and wash my hair.

No, I didn't really tell him that, but I did invent supper with my parents so I had an excuse to leave when I was ready. I figured with a name like Chauncey he couldn't amount to much and I was right. He was tall, with pretty blue eyes, but thin and pasty-looking, weird for a man who lives close to the ocean. He was a clinical psychologist and seemed to spend the whole evening analyzing me. He watched me so closely all my nervous tics revealed themselves, wriggling in my seat, tapping my foot, drumming the tabletop with my fingers. I finally gulped down the last of my wine and beat feet. I don't know why Susie thought Chauncey was a good fit for me—he was nothing like my Lieutenant Joe.

One good thing did come from the date though, all because The Ducking Dog carries the most interesting appetizers in town. That night a new one appeared on the menu called Dollhouse Ducks, which turned out to be flaky, miniature biscuits shaped like ducks and drizzled with warm honey butter. Delicious! While Chauncey had droned on about his job, the little shapes started me thinking about dollhouses and the tiny families living inside them, which led me to imagine one tiny doll murdering another tiny doll, and now all the other tiny dolls are going crazy trying to ferret out the murderer, but the little dolls in the little rooms keep getting knocked off one by one in some bloody and horrific manner, and of course they can't escape because they are trapped inside the dollhouse.

Ah. Now I see why Chauncey was observing me so carefully. I was clearly plotting my little dollhouse murder mystery in my head while he picked the cashews out of the complimentary nut bowl. I'm certain he won't be calling for a second date, but at least I got a free glass of wine and a potential story idea out of the evening.

CHAPTER 27

DIANE

Libby and Lorelei fell asleep shortly after they finished the tale of their journey into this nightmare. Diane had seen the worst of humanity during her law enforcement career, but this ranked easily as one of the top heinous crimes she'd seen committed. To sell your precious little children into a life of prostitution. Diane couldn't understand and fervently hoped she'd come across the girls' father one day so she could assist him into an early grave. Joe would have been furious. He hated human traffickers above all other criminals, even mass murderers.

She sighed and closed her eyes. The room wasn't freezing, but cool enough for a sweater and blankets, none of which they had. Diane had asked Dill for blankets, sheets, and towels before their captors left the room. The man had looked at her and shrugged.

Split Lip had leered at her, saying, "You get what you pay for, bitch. Whatcha goin' to pony up?"

Just as Split Lip was about to underscore his comments by groping Diane's breasts, Dill had grabbed his colleague's arm. "Keep your hands off the merchandise until you get permission, homeboy. You know how Oscar feels about that. He may let you take a shot at one of them, but not if he finds out you've been sampling without his say-so. He'll slit your throat if you aren't careful, and I won't cover for you if he asks how things are going."

Split Lip had made a face but dropped his hands and turned away. Diane had shot Dill a grateful look and said, "One more thing. Water for the shower. Please."

Neither man had replied to that, they had simply walked out of the room without acknowledging her plea.

Except for Lily, the younger girls had all fallen into a troubled sleep on the bed, surrounding Diane like exhausted puppies. The European teen sat resolutely on the chair, back straight as a ramrod and eyes forward. Diane could barely see her in the dark room but spoke in Lily's general direction.

"You may as well get some sleep, sweetie, who knows what will happen tomorrow. We'll make room on the bed if you want to come over."

Whether Lily understood her or not, Diane had no idea.

✯ ✯ ✯

Diane woke the next morning to find Lily had made her way to the bed in the dark and was now sleeping curled up between Maria and Elizabeth. Lorelei and Libby were still propped up against the wall in the corner, snoring with their mouths open. Diane's arm was hanging off the bed. Another inch and she would have rolled off onto the concrete floor. She shivered and sat up, moving as slowly as possible so she wouldn't disturb the girls. No reason for them to wake back into this hellhole any sooner than necessary.

Weak light leaked in through the miniscule openings in the window slats, but Diane had no idea what time it was. She was reluctant to use the nasty toilet, but with a screaming bladder and no other choice, she slipped off the mattress and made her way into the makeshift bathroom. After a lengthy drip-dry on the seat, she threw some water on her face, combed wet fingers through her hair, and managed a quick finger brush of her teeth and tongue. Didn't help much, but she supposed the minimal ablutions were better than nothing. She longed for a cup of Joe's homebrewed coffee, and for an embrace in his strong arms.

Standing in the doorway of the bathroom, watching the girls twitch in restless sleep, she contemplated their situation. Though he was clearly the boss and therefore the most dangerous, she thought her best bet was to talk with Oscar. He was the one with the power. If she could figure out how to connect with him, maybe they could strike a deal. Not that she had any leverage or anything to offer; he and his goons held all the cards. But surely she could think of something.

Just as she decided to tuck herself back into the warm nest of bodies on the bed, the outside lock clicked and Split Lip walked in. Diane tensed when she saw him; he was hot-tempered and unpredictable. She would rather deal with Dill. Split Lip slouched over to Diane and threw two blankets and two towels at her feet, grinning wickedly. Diane looked at the pile on the floor, looked back up at him, and started to say thank you. Before the words left her mouth, he grabbed a handful of her hair, pulled her head back and kissed her viciously, forcing her lips open with his tongue and teeth. She gagged on his sour breath, slapping at his face until he released her.

Laughing, he said, "The boss wants to see you. Put on your nice dress and we'll go down. But first, I'm supposed to give you electricity. Personally, I'd keep you bitches in the dark all the time, but the boss figures one night without light is enough. Gives him something to take away if you don't behave."

At the conclusion of his little speech, Split Lip pulled pliers and a screwdriver out of his back pocket and turned to the light switch beside the door. Unscrewing the switch plate, he used the pliers to work some magic inside the box, then flipped the switch. The overhead bulb spread light into most of the room, leaving only the corners in shadow. Diane watched covetously as their captor shoved the tools securely back into his pocket.

The girls, who had woken up when Split Lip entered, gasped at the new lighting in grateful surprise. Split Lip surveyed the sleepy-eyed group for a moment, then sauntered over to the bed and sat down, causing Lorelei and Libby to attempt the impossible and shrink even further against the wall. He laid a hand on each girl's thin thigh, rubbing slowly up and down. Seeing that Maria was about to launch herself at him to protect the little ones, Diane stepped in and said, "Hey, jackass. Thought you said the boss wanted to see me?"

He stopped rubbing the sisters but left his hands on their skin, turning his head to look at Diane. He stood up slowly and moved to stand inches from her.

"The only reason I don't smack you for that is because you're goin' to see Mr. Migliori. But call me names again, an' I'll bust you to hell and back. Or maybe I'll just do somethin' the boss cain't see." With that, he shoved his hand down her pants, pinning her against the wall as he rubbed spitefully between her legs.

Diane pushed him with a fury, but he held tight, sneering in her face and groping her crotch, until Lily came up from behind and punched him hard in his left ear. Split Lip howled and grabbed his ear with both hands, turning on his attacker like a feral dog.

Diane, realizing she needed to get the situation under control before the bastard did real damage, grabbed his arm, saying, "Okay, okay. You said I had to go see the boss. You don't want to keep him waiting, right?"

Split Lip looked at her, shook her hand off his arm, then turned to look at all the girls. "You keep sticking together, you're all going to get it. Right from me. Every day. Think about that. Plenty of places on you sweet young things bruises don't show. You be nice to me, you hear?"

Turning back to Diane, he said, "Let's go, bitch. And don't say nothin' to Oscar about anythin' that goes on in this room when I'm here. I'll be up here a lot. He won't."

CHAPTER 28

PHOEBE

Back at my kitchen table, laptop open, pen in hand, legal pad beside the mouse, I'm ready to write more of my Lieutenant Joe's story. Maybe I should concentrate on my thus far non-existent heroine. Or maybe focus on the serial killer my Joe is trying to track down before the guy commits another shower murder. But my favorite character is my handsome detective, so I start thinking about him. Should my Joe have two brothers or one sister, rich parents or poor, a fancy college education or a community college background? Or did he join the military after high school? Maybe his siblings should be adopted. What are his leads and who is he investigating? Oh wait, I know this one. He and his partner must be investigating several people in their town, the butcher, the baker, the candlestick maker . . .

No, wait, that's a dang nursery rhyme. So, let's see. Oh, I've got it. Maybe Joe is investigating the cobbler, the tailor, and the manager of the local animal shelter. Ha, what an idea, I think I'm projecting. Much as I'd like to, I could never get away with crafting a story about those three St. Samuel citizens. The old-timers in town would know instantly who the characters were. Besides, the crazy water conservationist is my working plotline, so wouldn't Joe start with interviewing the members of my mystery town's vocal environmental group?

As I sit with fingers poised over the keyboard, waiting for a Ouija-board effect to begin, my insubordinate brain goes to Joe's personal life. Should I give him a wife? Maybe he has one I don't know about yet. Shouldn't a handsome professional law enforcement officer in his thirties have a wife? But if my Joe has a spouse, where will that leave my heroine whenever the two finally meet? They will meet, right? If I give him a wife, then what do I do with her? My Joe must be free to fall in love with the heroine. No unrequited love is allowed in this story.

Do you see now why I have trouble getting words down on paper? My brain just goes round and round, never landing on one spot, like a carousel horse that can never catch his brightly painted girlfriend just two rows up.

Besides a wife, Joe needs a work partner, too. Every homicide detective has a partner, right? So, should the partner be tall and handsome like my Joe? Or short and tubby, like a Mutt and Jeff match up? No, that storyline has been overused, especially in the movies. I think the partner will be tall, but not as tall as Joe, and nice-looking, but not as nice-looking as Joe, naturally. Oh, and here's an idea. I can name the partner Terry, after the real-life detective I met in Atlanta. When I become a rich and famous novelist, being cast in my first book will be a nice thank you to him for being so kind to me after the Anna episode. Okay fingers, here we go, I'm typing, I'm typing, I'm typing . . .

I'm not typing. Where are the spirits of the great dead authors when you need them?

I give. I'm going for an airplane ride.

In case I haven't mentioned it, I'm a qualified pilot. Yep, saved up my baby-sitting money and joined the Civil Air Patrol when I was in high school. Learned to fly gliders, which was scary but so fun, as well as single-engine aircraft. Taking off and flying were fun, landing not so much. I did contemplate joining the Air Force after high school, but Paul's big brown eyes and delicious lips talked me out of it. I kept up with flying through college though, maintaining my qualifications each year, making short runs up and down the coast, free as a bird. I even took a three-day aerobatics course one summer—such a thrill! Paul never came along on my flights, he hated to fly. Possibly that was a clue to our future failed marriage.

I usually take a plane up a couple of times a month. Susie comes along occasionally, but typically I go alone. I like being solitary in the clouds, makes me feel like Nut, the Egyptian goddess of the sky. In the interest of family togetherness, though, I brought Jack out to the airport once and encouraged him to hop in the passenger side of the small plane I had rented for the afternoon. He peered in the cockpit door, then walked around the plane, stopping to pee on each tire. Then he sat down with his back to the Cessna and refused to look at me. I took that to mean he had no interest in soaring with the eagles.

After that display, I left Jack at home on flying days and never asked Josie or Jilly for their opinion, thinking their responses would be even more negative than Jack's. I fly out of the Kingsland Airport, not too far down the road towards Jacksonville. The airport is tiny, but Pryor Flight Training operates out of one of the hangars, so small planes come and go constantly.

One Saturday after a glorious afternoon flight, beautiful weather, perfect wind currents, a pair of eagles slipping the surly bonds beside me so close I could have reached out to touch them, I finally had to land or risk coming in on fumes, something frowned on by the Pryor Flight Training people and the Federal Aviation Administration. As I taxied in, reluctant to come down to earth, a Beechcraft Bonanza taxied out, closer to my aircraft than was usual, so I checked out the cockpit to see if I knew the pilot. Who to my wondering eyes should appear but a man lucky enough to look a lot like a young Tommy Lee Jones.

If I'd had enough gas, I would have taken off again and chased him down. Or would the correct verb be flown him down? Whichever, I'd give a lot even to meet Tommy Lee Jones's lookalike. I did ask at the operations desk if the actor had rented a plane for the afternoon, but the clerk looked at me like I was a nut and shook her head. Then she suggested the sun had been too bright on the tarmac and my eyes deceived me. She was probably right. The pilot was most likely a firm-jawed Marine from the training base up in Beaufort with no relation to the hot TLJ at all.

CHAPTER 29

DIANE

Oscar was as well-dressed as he had been the day before, in a perfectly pressed dark brown suit with a pale yellow shirt. The open collar revealed a touch of dark brown chest hair. He motioned Diane to a chair, telling Split Lip to leave and close the door behind him. Diane studied her surroundings as she perched on the edge of a beautifully upholstered chair. For an office in a warehouse, the room was comfortable and well appointed, hosting a large oak desk, two wing chairs in a lovely brocade pattern, a buffet holding serving ware, and a glass coffee table.

The space also housed a small conference table surrounded by six chairs. *As though these criminals would hold daily staff meetings,* Diane thought, tamping down fierce anger at the normalcy of the space and the impassive demeanor of her captor. She was determined to find some way to escape this ordeal, even if she had to jump through the room's plate glass window. When Oscar interrupted her thoughts to ask if she'd like something to drink, she looked at him, debating.

Cozy up to him? Be aggressive with him? Flirt? Be recalcitrant? She wasn't sure, so she settled for an even toned, "Water would be good."

Oscar opened a small refrigerator and pulled out a twelve ounce bottle of water. He eyed several lead crystal glasses on the small buffet, then handed her the bottled drink saying, "I would prefer to serve you in a nice glass but given your position here, you may feel you have no choice but to use the crystal as a weapon. I would hate for our association to end too quickly."

Diane took the bottle without comment while Oscar settled into the chair across from her.

"So. Who are you, Diane Morgan? What are you doing with these young women? Your phone is empty of activity and personal information. Tell me. Why is that? And before you waste my time by lying to me, I already know you are a deputy sheriff in Georgia.

When Diane couldn't contain a look of surprise, Oscar said, "The internet is a beautiful thing. You live in a nice town. You have a handsome husband, a good job, and a beautiful home in the woods. Now, explain to me…what are you doing with these girls?"

Thinking furiously, Diane cursed modern technology. What website could have possibly pulled up any information connecting her and Joe? Or given the address of their home? After a few moments, while Oscar watched her with probing eyes, she figured telling as much of the truth as possible wouldn't matter one way or the other, so she told him about arriving at the hotel, observing the activity around room ten, and her subsequent efforts to help the girls escape.

He nodded. "For what reason did you leave Georgia?"

Diane squirmed and drank some water. "Personal reasons, nothing to do with this," she said, waving her hand around the room. Her "this" hung in the air, an unspoken accusation.

Oscar nodded again, contemplating her, hands folded under his chin, thumbs forming a resting tripod.

"Why do I think you are part of a law enforcement sting against my organization? You are, after all, a sworn officer of the law. Although one traveling without a badge or gun or uniform."

Diane sighed, understanding how this looked, knowing she had no means to convince him her presence was just a horrible twist of fate. Despite those five vulnerable girls upstairs, she dearly wished she'd never knocked on that motel room door. "Look. I left my life in Georgia behind for reasons I will not share with you. I was headed to Key West to bum for a while. I got caught up with these girls out of pure coincidence. I saw they were in trouble and wanted to help. That's all."

Oscar studied her, a shrewd glint in his eye. "Very well. I will believe you for the moment. Now the question is, what do you want to do? As you have likely surmised, these girls will be paid escorts. They have no option. You do. You are an attractive woman, a little older than what our clients usually request, but still, a market exists for your age and your looks. Because I prefer to keep an eye on you, I will give you a choice. You may stay here, where I will allow you to remain with the young ladies, and you may work as an escort. Or, if you prefer, I will sell you to one of my clients who eagerly buys items I no longer need."

Diane closed her eyes and exhaled heavily. Merchandise, that's what she and the girls were to this man. Worthless resources to be used up and disposed of. Little did he know just how much feeling worthless had played in landing her in this predicament.

"They are just girls, sir. Young girls. You have a mother. Do you have sisters? Or daughters? How can you trap these children in a life like this?"

"The logic is quite simple, Deputy Morgan. These young females are runaways, cast-offs. No one wants them or is even aware they are gone from the ratholes in which they originated. And given that you appear to be a runaway yourself, I am guessing no one is looking for you, either. Or if someone is, you have erased your tracks well enough that you will not be found. And those two girls with you who are sisters? They are here to pay for the death of my boss's son, a loving boy who was also my godson. And pay they will, until they are dead in their graves."

Oscar took a sip from his coffee cup. "Now, what is your answer?"

CHAPTER 30

PHOEBE

Susie and I had dinner the other night, just the two of us, for the first time in a while. She's been extra busy at work, and I've been trying to be more disciplined with my writing schedule. My author efforts are not going as well as her work efforts. Apparently, all the drivers in Georgia have recently decided to crash into each other at an exponential rate, so she's been hopping across the state, investigating claims for her company's clients as quickly as possible. The woman has worked so much overtime she hasn't had a chance to use that secret credit card, but she'll have a nice bundle built up to pay off the bill when she finally does.

We went to Southern Biscuit since Susie needed rum therapy. After her stressful weeks of work, she was craving a Funky Monkey. I was sipping a lovely white wine blend. Deciding to skip the raw seafood this time since we were both starving and Susie wanted comfort food, we dove straight into a four-person platter of nachos with extra jalapenos. Having both been raised to be ladies, at first we attempted to politely eat one cheese-covered piece of deliciousness at a time, but hunger won out and, while I would never say we gobbled the next several handfuls like piglets, I will say the Beatles song "Piggies" was playing in the background.

Second Funky Monkey drained, half the platter devoured, chewing slowed to a more lady-like pace, Susie and I settled back into the booth with satiated sighs. I was confident we would finish the nachos, but we needed to get our second wind first. Signaling the waiter for another round, Susie, who in between bites had been ranting about the stupidity of Southern drivers, suddenly stopped herself mid-sentence. "I'm tired of talking about work. Did I tell you what happened after you left me and Gary at the Daisy Lady the other night?"

My mouth once again full of chips and jalapenos, I shook my head.

"Well, we moved up to the bar to listen to Sally while we finished our drinks, and you'll never guess who we saw sitting at the far end. It was a guy who looked like Tommy Lee Jones! Well, Tommy Lee when he was younger, anyway. Does he have a son? Gary wanted to go ask for his autograph, but I told him the guy wasn't Tommy Lee and even if he was, not to embarrass me by asking for an autograph like a backwoods Georgia hick. I wanted to get a better look when we left, but he and the guy he was drinking with took off before we did."

I thought back to the day I taxied by a pilot who resembled the actor and to the two well-dressed men leaving the library a few days ago. So odd. That's the third sighting of someone resembling my Hollywood crush. Did the famous actor's son buy a home on the Georgia coast? Can't imagine that happening; there's not much to attract famous folks to St. Samuel. Or am I just so engrossed in my fantasy detective my subconscious envisions his double everywhere? But Gary and Susie wouldn't conjure up the actor from my subconscious, and neither would Scooter, so that can't be it. Who knows? Maybe there was a Tommy Lee Jones doppelganger contest somewhere and I hadn't heard about it since I never watch the news or read the paper. I said as much to Susie, then plunged back into the nacho platter.

CHAPTER 31

DIANE

Back in room five, Oscar's question ringing in her ears, Diane sat on the bed while the girls crowded around her, all talking at once, wanting to know what happened and what was going to happen. Diane looked at them, not knowing if she should tell them outright they were going to be prostitutes or make up some platitudes until she could decide what to say. She knew she would have to explain what a prostitute was to the youngest ones. Right now, she simply didn't have the heart.

"Okay girls, give me a minute and I'll tell you all about it. Did they bring up some breakfast?"

"Yes, we saved you a biscuit," said Maria, handing over a round, paper-wrapped package. "And a milk."

Thanking Maria with a one-armed hug, Diane slowly unwrapped the biscuit and opened the small milk carton, stalling for time. When she finished eating the frugal meal, she sighed and looked at each girl. She had always believed ripping off a bandage in one swift, painful motion was better than peeling it back slowly, so she forced herself to begin.

"These men, they are part of a human trafficking ring. They are going to force all of you to become prostitutes. In other words, those men out there will find other men who will pay to have sex with you. If you don't cooperate, they will beat you or drug you, or both."

Five pairs of eyes looked at her, three in confusion, two in frightened disbelief. Libby and Lorelei looked at each other and asked simultaneously, "What's sex?" Maria and Elizabeth both exclaimed in horror, Maria spewing torrents of rapid Spanish. Lily may or may not have understood Diane's words, but there was no mistaking the rest of the group's reaction—the news was bad. She sat silently on the folding chair, watching Diane without expression. Diane had the feeling Lily knew exactly what was in store for their little posse.

Feeling a tug on her arm, she looked down to find Libby trying to get her attention.

"We don't know what sex is. Would Mommy let us have some sex?"

The young girl's innocent question brought tears to Diane's eyes. She reached for Libby and Lorelei's small hands and explained, as best she could, what sex was. The more Diane talked, the wider their eyes got, tears spilling down their faces.

"We can't do that, we can't do that. We can't. Mommy would not let us do that."

"Shh, shh, calm down now. We will find a way out of here before anybody has to have sex. We will."

"What about you, Diane? Will you be a puta with us?" This came from Maria, who had stopped cursing and was looking at Diane with flat eyes.

"Yes," Diane replied. "If I cooperate, we will all get to stay together. I will try my best to get us out of here as soon as possible. Hopefully before any of us have to be an escort to anybody."

As things turned out, as soon as possible wasn't soon enough for any of them.

CHAPTER 32

JOE

Except for Joe and Terry, the rest of Joe's unit leaned toward Kurt Von Schuster as the killer, his criminal history and underwear fetish being primary influencers. A new lead had cropped up, which posed additional questions for Henry DeSantos, but the senior detectives weren't confident the right suspect was even in their sights. For one thing, they still had to interview the tailor. Joe was more than mildly curious about his handmade buttonhole skills and his whereabouts on the days of the murders.

Also, two other potential suspects had popped up, former convicts who lived not in St. Samuel proper, but Frances County, both out on parole despite being convicted of aggravated assault. One of the parolees was charged with attempted murder in addition to assault, having thrown his wife headfirst into a concrete wall. The woman was now breathing on a ventilator with little hope of ever drawing a breath of her own again. The other convict had started a fight in a bar, punching his opponent so many times in the midsection six ribs broke, one of which punctured the unfortunate man's right lung. Dalton and Hoffman were headed out to find both men and bring them in for questioning.

The new questions for the animal shelter manager revolved around the years Henry had lived away from St. Samuel. DeSantos had left town for a time after high school. None of his old classmates or acquaintances knew where he went, nor had he mentioned living anywhere else when the detectives interviewed him the first time. A routine background check had brought up an old address for him in Franklin, Tennessee. Apparently, he had lived in the Volunteer State during his hiatus from St. Samuel.

One of Joe's detectives had grown up in Franklin, and he recalled several murders occurring in that area around the same time Henry lived there. According to the NIBRS database, the Tennessee killings had never been solved. Although the Franklin victims were male as well as female, and without disfiguring buttonholes, they had all been strangled. Joe thought the timing was enough to warrant a second interview with DeSantos.

Jeremy was waiting for a callback from the Franklin Police Department detective who worked the cases. If Henry had ever been questioned or suspected in those murders, their own interest in him would rise exponentially. The fact Henry had lived in two towns where a series of homicides occurred was unusual. Most people go through life without coming close to one murder, much less two sets of them. A patrol unit had been dispatched to bring Henry into the station for a second, more formal interview. This conversation would be less friendly than the first and include detailed queries about the animal lover's life in Tennessee.

✳ ✳ ✳

When he had stopped at the alteration shop to pick up his repaired jacket, Brenda had convinced Joe she had no idea where her uncle's secret fishing hole was. Joe guarded like a military secret his own favorite hunting and fishing spots, so he could appreciate the tailor's reticence. Joe had had little inclination to track the man down while he was fishing, but during their conversation, a few of the niece's comments had made Joe's intuition quiver, especially when she said, "Well, you know Uncle Dan. He'll be happy to talk with you as soon as he gets back. He'll be anxious to do whatever he can to help."

Every person Joe knew described the reclusive tailor as unfriendly, shy, and distant. So much so, few people could recount ever meeting the man or what he looked like if they did. But Brenda had talked at length about her uncle being a gregarious, likeable fellow who had the best interest of the community at heart. According to Brenda, Danny treated her like a daughter and would do anything for her. He supposedly loved having a beer with the boys after work, frequently won at monthly poker nights, and usually hunted with a group during deer season. Brenda's recount of her uncle's personality was completely opposite of Joe's impression of Taylor.

Joe's intuition told him something was off. He hadn't had a chance to parse through all the niece's words yet, but a line from Shakespeare's *Hamlet* had popped into Joe's brain during their conversation: "The lady doth protest too much, methinks." Joe needed to talk with Terry about his interview with Brenda but hadn't had the opportunity. His partner had been busy tracking down different manufacturers of sewing thread and the team rosters for the women's softball league, in addition to making calls about the Franklin murders.

To stitch his signature buttonholes, the killer used a heavy-duty, dark red thread, the kind found in multiple areas of the sewing industry: leather jacket repair, upholstery, shoemaking, even artisan tapestry. Terry was grumbling his way through that research, wishing they had an extra rookie detective on whom to pawn the tasks off. All Terry had discovered so far was the sewing thread was so common it would likely be impossible to track. The softball rosters had only shown the three victims had played on different teams in the league with no evidence indicating they knew each other from the ballfields.

The Joint Task Force Joe thought would materialize after the Richardson murder had still not come to fruition. Saddle County, knowing eventually they wouldn't have a choice, still weren't interested in joining forces just yet. They were operating with barely enough manpower to keep their homicide unit open, never mind trying to man a task force.

Chief Paris had reached out several times to the Georgia Bureau of Investigation and the Federal Bureau of Investigation, requesting a federal and state joint task force, but the GBI had their hands full with two other statewide task forces, one investigating complex financial crimes worth millions and one trying to bring down a complex human trafficking ring. Apparently, Georgians were misbehaving all around the state. The GBI had promised to juggle manpower to free up more personnel to assist St. Samuel soon, but the Feds were "looking into the matter" before deciding if they wanted to engage. Between the bureaucracy of multiple agencies and a shortage of manpower in every law enforcement agency in the state, Joe wasn't sure if a task force for his murders would ever get off the ground.

Joe wasn't surprised by the bureaucracy, that being a condition afflicting most organizations, especially government and military.

He remembered flight orders changing multiple times before takeoff when he was a Marine aviator because someone up the chain couldn't make a decision. Or the Army, Air Force, or Navy had come up with a different idea that required hashing out first. In Joe's experience, the more organizations involved in an operation, the more likely the undertaking would turn into a goat rope.

Besides Henry DeSantos' missing Tennessee years, the only promising lead the two detectives had was an interesting tidbit unearthed while reviewing the case. They had been surprised to discover Danny Taylor was dishonorably discharged from the Royal Australian Navy, something they only found out because fate inserted her fickle fingers, for once in a helpful way.

Terry had been multi-tasking, researching a hoped-for family trip to Australia online while he and Joe brainstormed ideas about the killer. One of the junior detectives popped in to ask a question about Danny Taylor at the same time Joe brought up the niece's perspective of her uncle's personality. Listening to Joe, answering his other colleague's question, and thinking about snorkeling at the Great Barrier Reef caused Terry to combine "Danny Taylor" with "Australia" in the search engine line. Shockingly, Taylor's name popped up on a Royal Australian Navy personnel roster. A few international phone calls revealed Taylor had been dishonorably discharged for assault on two female sailors in his unit. Prior to his discharge, Danny had spent eight months in the brig for the attacks.

Although not necessarily suspicious, the fact Taylor was a native Australian was news to both Joe and Terry. The few times they'd heard him speak, neither man had detected an Australian accent. The assault charges were definitely suspicious, though, and notched the detectives' interest in the tailor up several pegs. Joe phoned an old buddy who worked for Immigration and Customs

Enforcement and asked for Taylor's immigration history. While they were waiting to hear back from his ICE contact, Joe picked up the phone and called the tailor shop. When no one answered after a dozen rings, Joe glanced at the clock. Four-thirty, a little early for quitting time. Hanging up the receiver, he said, "Let's go for a ride."

Terry gladly closed the folder on the paperwork he was reviewing, pulled on his jacket, and asked, "What's up?"

"We're going to find the tailor, even if we have to disturb his fishing spot. He should be sewing away at this time of day, but no one's answering the phone."

CHAPTER 33

DIANE

As a result of Diane's amended arrangement with Oscar, she woke, exhausted and bruised, to find the sun streaming through the bedroom window of her little group's new living quarters. She remained unsure if Oscar had taken a liking to her or if he was practicing one of Sun Tzu's *Art of War* techniques: "Keep your friends close and your enemies closer." She suspected the latter since the man was emotionally barren, and she was, without question, his enemy.

Through their six-week confinement in the warehouse, he had continued to question her extensively about how she got mixed up with the girls and why she left Georgia. Her answers never varied. She thought he would tire of the same queries at some point, but he called her to his office two to three times a week, asking the same questions in a different way. He even ordered takeout, which they shared over the coffee table in front of the couch. At first

Diane was reluctant to eat with the man, but finally decided the more time she could spend out of room five and in Oscar's company the more details she could discover about his organization and the location of the warehouse where they were jailed. The more data she could gather, the more likely she was to devise a successful escape plan.

Although he retained his formal and formidable presence with her, she found the grit to ask about his personal life, as well as the organization he worked for. He never answered her questions directly, but in their conversations about other things—his preferred topics being politics and United States government policy—he had dropped enough information that she had pieced together a few facts about his life.

He was divorced, with a young daughter and an older son. His ex-wife disappeared after their split. From his comments, Diane intuited that the wife disappeared with some help from Oscar's henchmen. She suspected the woman was decomposing in the concrete foundation of an Oscar-owned building. Her captor also once remarked he lived locally, though she had yet to cipher out where local was. She was fairly confident they were still in the Miami area but unsure as to their exact location.

The only information about Oscar's criminal enterprise Diane had been able to glean was the network was international and involved multiple trades, some legal and some not. She tried to coax the name of the organization out of Oscar in the hope she would have a better idea of who she was dealing with, but he deftly avoided any detailed questions about the criminal group or his boss, except to let slip that the head man was Frank Levy. When Diane learned that detail, she knew immediately she and the girls were in more trouble than she originally thought.

Levy's tentacles stretched across the nation, firmly hooked in multiple illegal enterprises. The level of violence he committed to accomplish his goals far exceeded that of his rivals. He killed and mutilated within his own organization to obtain and maintain loyalty. He unhesitatingly murdered outside his organization to acquire and grow his dynasty. Now that she knew who the head crime boss was, Diane realized if her gang ever escaped, they would need to run far, run fast, and not trust a soul. Levy would have eyes and ears everywhere—in law enforcement, the judicial system, even the corner grocery stores. Libby and Lorelei were in more danger than the rest of the group since they were reparations for Levy's son. He would never give up looking for the sisters.

Though discouraging because of his reach and ruthlessness, knowing Levy was the top dog was also helpful, if only for understanding the depth of danger they would face upon escaping. Diane had every confidence they would find a way out, the only question was when. Even more useful than learning about Levy, though, was the amended deal she made with Oscar. The new bargain she struck resulted in the captives' upgraded living arrangements, and was why she found herself waking that morning in a comfortable bed with sunbeams streaming through the curtains instead of in a dark room in a warehouse.

✯ ✯ ✯

After four days of dire living in the warehouse, Diane was desperate to find a way out. Recognizing she had nothing to trade with, except the obvious, she told Oscar if he wanted their continued docile acquiescence, they needed decent rooms with a fully functioning bathroom and all the items a woman required. This bargaining session took place in Oscar's warehouse office during their second meeting, three days after he had given her the choice to stay with the girls or be sold to one of his subordinates. In those three days, Lily and Elizabeth had developed runny noses, none of the group had showered because of the lack of water and supplies, and none could get a solid night's sleep because there was only the one twin bed. Maria's period had started, with only a few paper towels available to stem the flow.

When Oscar heard the words "…wanted their continued docile acquiescence…," he had smiled and said, "You realize you will cooperate, willingly or not? We prefer not to drug our escorts, but we will. We prefer not to abuse our escorts, but we will do that, too. So, you will acquiesce, or you will suffer."

Diane had looked Oscar coolly in the eyes as he said this, but her insides shriveled at his words. She was tempted to tattle about Split Lip's constant groping if company policy was not to abuse the escorts, but right now she had a more important mission. They needed a tolerable place to live and one more likely to provide an opportunity for escape. The warehouse room was not only barely inhabitable, there was also no way to get out. None of them had been called for escort duty yet, and she hoped to forestall that for as long as possible. The only stall technique she had been able to think of was to beg for improved living quarters.

Plastering an earnest expression on her face, Diane pled her case. Oscar pursed his lips as she talked, sipping whiskey, watching his captive carefully.

"I see the problems, though your comfort is not something I care about. We care only about the money your bodies will bring to the organization. But your points about the inevitable menstrual periods and body cleanliness are well made." Smiling slightly, he continued. "And I like you, Deputy Morgan. You have mettle and courage, so I am willing to make some allowances."

Oscar had paused, watching Diane over the rim of his glass, the crystal reflecting the sun's rays in a beautiful rainbow. "Allow me to offer you a different deal."

✳ ✳ ✳

Those eight words were the catalyst for Diane waking to sunlight streaming across a flowered bedspread on what she thought might be a Sunday morning. They had no access to watches or calendars, so she was rarely sure of the day or time anymore. Though the sun's rays brightened the room and was a major improvement over the dimness in warehouse room five, the light did nothing to lighten Diane's mood.

She had woken up gasping from a disturbing dream. Her slumbering brain had transported her to the running trail in St. Samuel. In the dream, she had been running for several miles, her ponytail bouncing with each footfall. Joe was running behind her calling her name when he suddenly hit her roughly in the back and knocked her down. As her dream self rolled off the trail towards the ditch, she gasped and woke up, looking wildly around the room, calling out for Joe. Only then did she realize the woman in the dream wasn't her but someone else with an auburn ponytail. Diane wiped the sleep from her eyes and sat up slowly, swinging her legs over the edge of the bed, missing her husband desperately, trying to compose herself. She didn't want Lily to hear and realize how close she was to breaking down. Diane knew she had to stay strong or all of them would succumb to paralyzing fear.

The new deal with Oscar was straightforward. Oscar desired female companionship, but he didn't want the complications of a standard relationship. He wanted a consistent consort for meals, conversation, and sex, not necessarily in that order. If Diane agreed to be his paramour until he tired of her, she would not only be relieved of escort duties, but he would also provide her and the girls with decent housing. Diane had tried to think through all the implications of this proposition but in the end, uncertain of the best decision, agreed to his conditions. She felt guilty about the children working as prostitutes while she would serve only one man, but she reminded herself different quarters and time with Oscar might eventually reveal a route to freedom.

Acknowledging their contract with a nod, he had risen, indicating their meeting was over. Diane had stood also saying, "I do have one condition before I accept this deal. I want to approve the new rooms."

He had laughed out loud when she said that, shook his head in regret and said, "You expect much, Deputy. Do not confuse this offer as a gesture of kindness or some type of affection for you. I am not kind and I do not get emotionally involved. You have no approval authority here. I take when I wish, and I give when I wish. Since you do not seem to understand that, allow me to prove my point."

With those words, he flipped Diane over the front of his desk, pinned her by the neck, pulled down her pants, unzipped his, and took her from behind in five long, brutal thrusts. She was so tightly restrained and shocked, she couldn't muster the wherewithal to fight him. When he was finished, he dropped her to the floor, zipped his fly, and walked out of the room.

CHAPTER 34

JOE

Shortly after discovering the local tailor was a criminal who had been evicted from the Australian Navy, Joe and Terry pulled up in front of Danny Taylor's shop. The standalone building shared one wall with a liquor store. The front parking lot was empty on the tailor's side, but the package store seemed to be doing brisk business for a Thursday afternoon.

Slamming his door as he got out of the passenger side, Terry was the first to notice the closed sign. He walked up to the door and peered through the glass, but the lights were off, and no one seemed to be about. Terry jiggled the doorknob. Finding it locked, he turned to Joe and said, "Around back?"

They moved together around the side of the building, noting the absence of vehicles, surveillance cameras, and any activity, other than a stray dog rummaging through an overturned aluminum garbage can. The dog observed them warily but didn't move from the half-eaten hamburger trapped under its front paws.

Joe pounded on the back door. No answer. He looked at Terry. "Didn't that sign up front say they were open until five-thirty weekdays?"

"Yep, sure did. Guess we need to get his address and go to his house."

Joe dialed dispatch and asked for a residential address for Daniel Taylor. The dispatch officer returned to the line after a minute and gave him an address on the outskirts of town. Joe's spirit eye was awake and pinging, causing him to reach back and touch his service revolver, ensuring the weapon was in place. Then he bent down and pulled up his pant leg to double-check the presence of his back-up piece.

Observing his partner's movements, Terry said, "Expecting some trouble?"

"I don't know, but I don't like the smell that's starting to form around our favorite tailor. Just don't want to get blindsided."

"Yeah, me neither. Let's see if we can find him at home."

Twenty minutes later they parked in front of a small, yellow, ranch house built in the early sixties. The yard was mown but covered in clover. The flowerbeds had not seen a weed pulled or the prong of a rake in months. No cars in the drive, no lights visible, no activity around the home. The two detectives sat in silence for a moment, watching the house. Then Terry said he would go around back, Joe could take the front. Joe nodded and exited the Crown Vic. Joe gave Terry two minutes to make it to the back door, then knocked loudly on the front. Thirty seconds passed with no answer, so Joe pounded the door with his fist, simultaneously pushing the doorbell.

"St. Samuel PD, open up."

Still no answer. Joe frowned and looked through the six-pane window. Closed blinds blocked his view. Testing the knob, he found the tailor practiced good security, keeping his doors locked when absent from home. He went around back to find Terry standing on a lawn chair, peering through a window.

"See anything?"

"Nah, blinds are drawn tight. Door's locked, too."

"Alright, I put my card in the door with a note to call me, so we'll give him a few hours to see if he does. If not, I'm putting out a BOLO on him. Do we know anyone else he, or maybe the niece, might hang around with?"

"Nope, far as I know, the guy's a loner. Where does the niece live? Maybe he's at her place."

Joe shook his head. "No, she lives with him. Maybe they're eating dinner somewhere or grocery shopping. Or fishing."

Getting back in the car, they decided to wait for a while to see if the missing tailor or his niece returned home. Terry called his oldest son for the third time this week to ask him to start cooking supper. Joe reached for his phone to call Diane before he remembered she hadn't answered her phone in five months. Belle didn't have her own phone yet. Or opposable thumbs to answer one.

CHAPTER 35

DIANE

A few weeks after Oscar raped Diane the first time, Split Lip and Dill entered room five and ordered the group out. Surprisingly, the girls still had not been called to escort duty, but Diane had been forced to see Oscar several times a week. The order to leave frightened the youngsters, as none of them had been allowed out of the room in the time they'd been held. Now they submitted to zip ties around their wrists without complaint, except for a few Spanish invectives Maria muttered under her breath. Diane asked Dill where they were going. He told her she'd find out soon enough.

The small squad moved silently down the stairs, the sparrows chittering overhead as they flew in endless structure-bound circles. Arriving at the same vehicles in which they had been kidnapped, the whole group cringed when Split Lip pulled blindfolds from his pocket.

"Come on now, be sweet to old Jakey-Jake. Don't fight me here."

"Shut up, Jake. Get your skinny white ass in gear and tie up the masks. You're such a dumb shit."

This insight came from a man Diane had never seen before, a short, middle-aged white guy who looked like he could have been a professional mixed martial arts fighter. Jake shot the new guy a hateful look but kept his mouth shut as he and Dill blindfolded their captives.

Determined to discover their location, Diane unobtrusively pushed her blindfold up a smidgen as she climbed into the SUV. She couldn't see much but if she tilted her head at the exact right angle, she could view bits of buildings and the road as they drove. Neither man was seated next to her, so she had some freedom to move her head around. She began counting the moment they drove through the warehouse doors, hoping to calculate how far they were being driven. Even though she didn't know where the warehouse was, she thought knowing how far they were being taken away from where they spent the last few weeks may come in handy. *Grasping for straws,* she thought, *but it's something tangible I can do.*

She hoped they were being taken to new living arrangements and not to a whorehouse. The girls weren't aware of the deal she had made with Oscar; they only knew she had come back troubled and trembling after her second meeting with him. In the weeks since, she hadn't wanted to get their hopes up. She wasn't sure he would hold up his end of the bargain after he had so violently demonstrated he wasn't going to play "let's make a deal."

Approximately twelve-hundred seconds after getting in the vehicle, the SUV turned left and slowed. Angling her head up as best she could, Diane saw a large gate with a security talk box beside it. The new guy, who Diane had dubbed Mr. MMA, rolled down his window, punched in a code, then drove through as the gate slowly rolled back. Trees were all Diane could see now. They drove for another couple of minutes, stopped, moved forward several yards, then halted, the big engine dying immediately. When her door opened, Split Lip—whose real name apparently was Jake—reached in and cut her zip ties with a short-bladed knife.

"Whooo-eee, you girls is lucky ducky. Guess it pays to screw the big man."

Diane couldn't see him, but she heard in his voice the lecherous grin he wore most of the time. Thankful to have her hands free, she wished more than anything she could knock ol' Jakey-Jake to the ground and stomp his face.

Once he untied the blindfold, she found herself in a two-car garage, glad to see the rest of the girls exiting the Humvee which had pulled into the second vehicle slot. She constantly worried Oscar was going to separate them from her.

The garage was drywalled and painted but otherwise didn't look like any garage Diane had ever seen. Except for the two cars, the building was empty. Not a tool or a sprinkler or a rake, not even an oil stain on the spotless concrete. The space was as sterile as an operating room.

Their three captors motioned the group into the house through the interior door. Split Lip sneered "Welcome home, ladies" as they filed in through a small utility room, which held a washer and a dryer. From there, they stepped into a clean, modern kitchen with quartz countertops. The house's open floor plan revealed a small dining area and a living room with a grateless fireplace in which no fire had ever blazed. Bars covered windows which looked out at a forest of oak trees.

"Check the place out and get situated," Mr. MMA said. "We need to bring in some stuff."

Diane led the way down the hall, the girls padding silently behind her. The first door revealed a medium-sized bedroom with two twin beds and a bathroom connecting to a second similar-sized bedroom, also with two twin beds. The master bedroom was at the end of the hall. Though much larger than the other bedrooms, the master also had two twin beds, along with a large bathroom.

The furnishings weren't fancy, but the beds were covered with matching floral spreads, towels hung on the towel racks, and carpet ran through the house, a giant step up from their previous prison. Bars had been installed on each window in the bedrooms, just like the rest of the house. Diane recalled vaguely these security bars were required to have emergency release latches and hoped their captors hadn't thought of that. She would look for the quick release fastenings at the first opportunity.

Since none of them had any extra clothing or other personal items, the only task to get themselves situated was to determine who would be in which room. Diane pointed at Lily, then to herself, then to the master bedroom. "Lily and I will bunk together in here. Maria, you and Elizabeth take the first room. Lorelei and Libby, take the other one."

The girls chittered excitedly about the new quarters, momentarily forgetting they were prisoners in this space, just as they had been in the dreary warehouse. Diane was uneasy, knowing what the new living arrangements meant. And knowing she would have to inform the girls their reprieve was over.

✵ ✵ ✵

A few days before their move, while she had been waiting in Oscar's outer office at the warehouse, Dill and the black man who had been wearing a suit the day she was kidnapped walked in. She hadn't seen the black man since that day but believed he was the Spencer she had overheard Split Lip talking about. Before they realized she was sitting in the corner of the couch, she overheard the presumptive Spencer tell Dill the boss's local whorehouses were overstocked from a recent raid down in Mexico. Until some of the whores got shipped up north or down south, there was no room for new bodies, but it was past time for the group in room five to begin working. Word had come down that Diane's crew needed to start earning their keep. Since the escort service didn't operate out of the warehouse, Oscar had chosen the ranch to stash them until space in a brothel opened up.

Dill had looked at Spencer with a smirk on his face and said, "You think they're going to the ranch because of a lack of space or because the boss has something going on with the redhead?"

"Doesn't matter why," Spencer replied. "It's the ranch for the time being. They'll start work the day after they get there. And if I were you, I'd keep my mouth shut about the boss's personal life."

Now Diane assumed "the ranch" must be some type of compound given the tall fence, but she was no closer to figuring out their exact location than she had been in the warehouse. She hoped the deal she'd struck with Oscar was the reason why her little band was here, rather than a lack of space at the brothels. The fact that none of her group had been forced to perform escort duty yet was puzzling, but she'd been too afraid of the answer to ask Oscar about it during their meetings. Besides, she was more than grateful for the delay.

Prior to being relocated to the ranch, the girls had fallen into a routine in room five, sleeping for twelve to fourteen hours a day, reading out loud from a ragged Harry Potter paperback Dill had given them, and performing a once daily wash with cold water from the sink. Diane made them run a finger over their teeth to rub as much gunk off as possible at least once a day. All their breaths stank, but Diane's appeal for toothbrushes and toothpaste had gone unanswered. She also made the girls run in place for five minutes each day, do ten pushups, and knock out twenty-five sit ups. Not only did they need things to do to pass the time, they also needed to stay in physical shape. If they ever found a way to escape, the group would probably need to move fast.

On good days in the warehouse, the girls would make up word games, and Lily, who had an operatic voice, would sing songs in her native tongue. Each night when they climbed into bed, Lily would softly sing a haunting tune so mesmerizing Diane wished she could understand the words. They all took turns trying to teach Lily English, with a little success. On bad warehouse days, all five girls had tended to stay curled up in the little bed, dozing off and on. Bad days were the days when Split Lip would come into the room, pawing and groping, until Diane could find a way to maneuver him out of their space.

As the days progressed, Diane realized the younger girls had been lulled into believing this routine would continue until rescue arrived. She perceived Lily was aware that a life of horrific abuse hovered at the edge of each sunrise. The teen would often give Diane a knowing look after Diane returned from a meeting with Oscar. Diane had the impression Lily guessed the nature of her deal with the devil.

✵ ✵ ✵

In the new quarters with the room arrangements settled, Diane and her small crew walked back into the living room. The men had put multiple brown grocery bags on the kitchen counter. Looking from the men to the bags, Diane asked what was in them.

"Food. Women stuff. The toothpaste you've been whining for. Don't waste anything. We're not going to be resupplying you very often. You probably won't be here too long anyway." This piece of info came from Mr. MMA.

"Now listen up. We'll be close by, so don't get any funny ideas about escaping. If you haven't noticed, there are cameras everywhere in here. We monitor the video feed twenty-four seven. Oh, and when one of you gets a date, we'll bring you some clothes to wear. Until then, you wear what you've got on."

Split Lip, who had laughed when his colleague mentioned the video cameras, walked over to Elizabeth and put his arm around her, drawing her in close to whisper in her ear, "I monitor the cameras, baby. Can't wait to see you in the shower." He licked her ear as she cowered, then pushed her abruptly away. "Let's go, chumps. We got better things to do."

As the men left, Diane looked up into the corners of the living room and spotted a camera in each corner. Walking through the house, she found several cameras in each room. The overlapping angles of each lens covered every bit of space in the rooms as far as Diane could tell, even in the bathrooms. Both the back and front doors locked from the outside, as did the door connecting the utility room to the garage. Between the locked doors, the cameras, and the barred windows, Diane was beginning to believe they had been better off in the warehouse. As of this moment, she saw no avenue of escape. Maybe with time she could figure out a way to circumvent the barriers to the outside.

Hearing commotion coming from the direction of the kitchen, Diane walked in to find Maria organizing food into the cabinets and the refrigerator. From the look of things, they would be dining on inexpensive brands of frozen dinners, cereal, and canned fruit. There appeared to be only a few days' worth of groceries.

Pulling toilet paper and menstrual products from the bags, Maria dispatched Elizabeth to the bathrooms with them, then shrieked with glee as she pulled a small bottle of laundry detergent from a bag. The girls' clothes had not been washed since they were taken. Although they would have to walk around naked or wrapped in a blanket while the washing machine and dryer did their work, Diane knew having clean clothes would be a morale booster—something the crew would need as soon as she told them they would be starting work the next day.

Diane instructed the girls to check every nook and cranny in the house to see if they could find anything to use as a weapon. She started in the kitchen, finding nothing more deadly than a plastic fork. Even the six glasses were cheap plastic. Looking at the twelve-ounce cups, Diane was reminded of drinking beer with Joe after a community league softball game Diane's team had won. From the keg to the red cup to a celebratory toast to a laughing kiss, the moment was just one of a thousand good times the two had shared.

Quickly shaking off that memory, Diane wondered if she could make a shiv from a toothbrush. Or maybe she could break off a tine of one of the forks, tape it to a toothbrush and make a miniature bayonet. A further search revealed no tape or string of any kind, so even that far-fetched idea was out. The girls' hunt didn't turn up anything suitable, either.

Except for the thrill of their first shower since capture and the blessed relief of minty paste against tooth and tongue, their little posse spent an uneventful first night in their new prison. The next morning, after Diane awoke from the dream about Joe on the St. Samuel running trail, she discovered Libby, Lorelei, and Elizabeth curled up together on Maria's bed, sleeping as soundly as newborn puppies. She supposed even in sleep they needed the comfort of each other, the knowledge they weren't alone. Lily, like Diane, had stayed in her own bed. Diane had heard the teenager talking restlessly in her sleep but had no idea what the foreign words had meant.

After a hot shower, during which she tried to forget about the monitored cameras, she wrapped the bedspread around herself, gathered all their clothes, and put the filthy pile into the washing machine. Lily had hopped into the shower after her, but the younger ones hadn't stirred. Diane went into the kitchen to fix a bowl of cereal for breakfast and figure out how best to tell the girls they would be starting work today. As she pulled the store brand version of Cheerios from the cabinet, she heard a car pull up out front. Going to the barred window, she was dismayed to see Split Lip and Spencer getting out of the SUV, two clothes bags and a makeup case in hand.

The front door lock popped open with an audible click. The men stepped into the living room. Diane looked at them, her expression unwelcoming. Split Lip gawked at her shoulders, naked above the bedspread, running a greedy tongue over his lips.

Without preamble, Spencer said, "Violet and Rose have jobs tonight. Take these. Clothes, shoes, jewelry, makeup. We'll be back by five to watch you dress them. Before we get here, put their makeup on but not their clothes. Violet's needs to be heavy. Just a little mascara and lip gloss for Rose." Thrusting a black garment bag at Diane, he continued. "This is for Rose. The blue is Violet's. Do the makeup right or one of you will suffer the consequences."

Before Diane could ask a question or utter a word, the men walked out, Split Lip giving her one last leering look before slamming the door and clamping the padlock into place. Diane looked at the case on the floor and the bags in her hands, then turned to find Lily watching her with a question in her eyes.

CHAPTER 36

JOE

While Joe and Terry were staking out the tailor's home, Detective Bradley Hoffman, the Tennessee native, began Henry DeSantos's second round of questioning. Bradley and his cohort, Archie Maxwell, interrogated Henry until he was sweating when their bosses returned. The senior partners observed the end of the interview through the two-way glass and patted each other on the back for training the young guys so well.

Joe stuck his head in the room and motioned the pair out. "What's the back brief? Did Henry cop to knowing anything about the Franklin murders?" He unwrapped a piece of gum while he waited for the answer.

"No sir, not so far. He doesn't remember most of the dates in question since it's been so long. He has no idea where he was on any of the days the murders were committed. He also says he didn't know any of the victims. Seems like he's telling the truth. He hasn't asked for a lawyer, and except for being nervous, he's cooperating." Hoffman spoke with a pronounced Tennessee twang, distinguishable from a South Georgia drawl, but not by much.

Maxwell piped up. "The detective in charge of the Franklin murders called back. Said DeSantos never came up in their investigation and wanted to know if they should take a look at him now. I explained what was happening down here and why we were asking. He said if we got a bad vibe from Henry to let him know. Also said to call if we had any other questions for him. They're going to overnight their files to us. Oh, and he said they have some fingerprints from two of their crime scenes which never matched in the national database."

At this Hoffman chimed back in. "We thought we'd ask Henry if we could take his prints. He's not charged with anything, so we have to get them voluntarily. Maybe he'll agree and we can run them through the system. If he says no, we haven't lost anything. But if he gives consent, we can match him or clear him from the Franklin scenes. If he's not the Franklin killer, he probably isn't ours, either."

Joe acknowledged the fingerprint request was a good next step, told the two to finish up the interview and let him know about the prints or if Henry said anything useful. Then he and Terry went to their office to go through the mound of case file information and reset priorities.

CHAPTER 37

PHOEBE

In an attempt to improve my writing skills last year, I started to read a book unimaginatively titled *Writing Tips for Beginners*. The title alone should have been a major clue that the four-hundred-page tome wasn't worth reading, but a best-selling famous author wrote it, so I thought her advice may be useful. Why this author is famous or why I thought reading her how-to book was a good idea, I don't know. I've always thought she was an awful writer, ergo the reason I'm not naming her. A few years ago, I tried to read one of her best-sellers, but my goodness…so wordy, and not in a good way. I remember wanting to holler at the pages "Get on with it, already, will you? Too many useless words! This is boring!"

For the record, while I may carry on conversations with my four-footed family members, I am not so kooky that I would talk to a book. Unless, of course, I'm speaking to my own written pages, which is a completely different situation.

The wordy novelist would do better if she would subscribe, as I wholeheartedly do, to E. B. White's dictum, "Omit needless words." E. B. White, as I'm sure you know, is the amazing American author who wrote *Charlotte's Web* and several other famous children's books. One of the reasons he's a great writer is because he is capable of perfectly describing something in limited words. In fact, despite Stephen King's novels tending to run several hundred pages long, the sci-fi master also subscribes to the theory of using only necessary words. He particularly hates adverbs, so I try not to use too many in my own writing, just in case Mr. King ever picks up one of my future bestsellers.

Shortly after returning that boring author's self-help book to my workplace unfinished, I heard her speak in person at a writer's conference. The woman proved to be a pompous stuffed shirt who, no surprise, spoke beyond her allotted time. She was full of advice for anyone wanting to become a bestselling novelist. The tip she emphasized most was the importance of imagery and how the writer must get the technical aspects of whatever is being described exactly right, a view which explains why her books are so wordy. Well, I do agree one shouldn't try to describe a gorilla using words that depict a mouse, but some amount of creative license on the author's part must be allowed. Metaphors and similes exist for a reason.

An example of perfectly written imagery using a small amount of latitude is that song, "Wind Beneath My Wings." The ballad is a lovely tribute to someone who always stands in the background while their lover, parent, sibling, or friend becomes famous or ascends to living their absolute dream. You know, the person who always encourages you but never tries to undermine your success? My person used to be Aunt Lucy, but now is Sophie. As I may have mentioned earlier, my little sister consistently boosts my self-confidence when the topic is my writing and reassures me when I'm ready to forget the whole endeavor, just like Aunt Lucy did when she still walked among us.

Aunt Lucy's favorite words of encouragement? "I have all the confidence in the world in you, Pheebs."

I sure miss that woman.

Now, regarding Bette Midler's phenomenal hit. When you listen to "Wind Beneath My Wings," what does your mind see? A lifting up from underneath, right? Maybe you visualize your own personal hero hoisting you to his or her shoulders while you grab the stars. Well, I hate to be a bubble burster, but anyone who knows anything about aeronautics (have I mentioned I'm a qualified pilot whose number of successful takeoffs still equals successful landings?), understands for the plane to take off and fly, the wind flow over the wings is much more necessary than the wind flow under the wings.

A little complicated to explain, but the bottom line is wind over the wings equals airplane taking off and staying aloft more than wind under the wings. The wind factor is a contest between Newton's Third Law of Motion (under the wings wind) and Bernoulli's Principle (over the wings wind). Newton plays second fiddle to Bernoulli here, by a smidgen, anyway. For a more definitive explanation—remember, I majored in criminal justice, not physics—check the internet.

Back to our song and the challenge of creating an accurate visual image when writing. Were the songwriters aware of that important nugget of aeronautical physics? Who knows? Who cares? If they had written "you are the wind over my wings," the song would have crashed and burned in the recording studio, not flown up to iconic status. Wouldn't have won record and song of the year Grammys, either. So, Ms. Wordy Woman author, I'm thinking constructing an image in one's creative work is important, getting each detail *perfectly accurate* maybe not so much. Unless, of course, you're writing a manual on how to launch a nuclear missile. Then too much creativity may be a bad thing.

CHAPTER 38

DIANE

Diane waited until after the girls ate breakfast to tell them the day had come to begin escort duties. They looked at her in shocked disbelief before bursting into questions all at once. Diane's heart broke when little Lorelei asked if they could somehow escape before five o'clock.

They spent much of the day in cowed silence, not talking or looking at the kids' books or the puzzle on the end table by the couch. Three books and one five-hundred-piece puzzle were the only entertainment in the house. The rooms held no televisions or radios. After Diane's post-breakfast announcement, Libby crawled back into bed, followed shortly after by Lorelei. Maria, Lily, and Elizabeth, full of defiance, again helped Diane search for ways to make weapons or to break out of the house without success on either front. At one point, Maria turned to a camera and shook her fist angrily. Diane could imagine their jailers laughing at their frustration.

Early that afternoon, Diane was summoned. A man they had not seen before came into the house shortly after they finished a peanut butter sandwich lunch. Without introduction or greeting, he handed her a pair of white linen pants and a powder-blue sleeveless tank, along with a pair of flat leather sandals, and told her to put them on. Judging his demeanor, she determined querying him about where she was going would be of no use, so she walked to her room and changed. She assumed she was going to see Oscar. No jewelry or makeup had been provided, a small blessing, as Diane had no desire to make herself attractive for him. No bra had been provided, either; the men had taken their bras away back in the warehouse.

The new jailer was a small, well-muscled man, shorter than Diane by a few inches. She noticed his surfer blonde hair, but if he also had a typical surfer's bright white smile, Diane didn't find out as he kept his mouth in a tight line and spoke minimally. Returning to the living room in her new clothes, Diane took a chance and asked him what was up. He simply said Oscar wanted her, motioning her towards the door.

Expecting to go back to the warehouse, Diane was surprised to find no vehicle in the driveway. Instead, she followed Surfer Dude across the lawn to the front of the large house she had sneaked a peek of yesterday under her mask. Her suspicion that Oscar might live there was apparently correct. As she walked over the green grass, Diane inhaled the fresh air like an addict snorting cocaine. The day was warm, with clouds flitting between the sun's rays, heavenly after being cooped up inside for so long.

She took the opportunity to look around as much as she could, gathering data. She noted a large, gated complex, the tall, maybe eight-foot-high, fence, two other cottages like their own, and multiple poles around the carefully manicured lawn. At first, she couldn't figure out what the poles were for, but then realized each of them had security cameras mounted at various heights and angles. Discouraging but not surprising.

As they walked around to the front of the house, Diane saw a large outdoor area with a firepit, and a lanai connecting to the back porch. Just to be aggravating, she asked Surfer Dude if Oscar lived in the house. He declined to answer and rang the bell, stepping back after so she stood in front of him. A loud click indicated their acceptance. Surfer Dude reached around her to turn the knob, motioning to her to enter. She stepped into a beautifully appointed foyer, large gray flagstones covering the floor. As they moved farther into the house, she glimpsed richly furnished rooms, elegant carpeting, full wall coverings. The house reminded her of a Spanish hacienda from the 1800s.

Oscar appeared to be signing papers. He was seated at an antique desk with a cut crystal glass full of caramel-colored liquid sitting beside an old-fashioned inkwell. He looked up when the duo entered, pen paused in mid-air. At Oscar's nod, Surfer Dude backed out of the room, closing the thick wooden doors behind him. Without speaking, Oscar looked Diane up and down, took a sip of what she presumed was expensive whiskey, and motioned her to the couch, a fine piece of craftmanship covered in dark leather. Returning to his task, he completed his signature, neatly tucked the stack of papers into a folder, and put the folder in the bottom left drawer, locking the drawer with a small key. Diane wondered what was so important it needed securing in Oscar's own house.

"I trust you approve of your new accommodations?"

She chose to ignore the sarcasm in his question and simply nodded her head.

Oscar walked to the buffet serving double duty as a wet bar and poured red wine from a decanter into a sparkling crystal wineglass. Apparently, his concern that she would use a glass as a weapon had abated. Handing the goblet to Diane, he sat across from her in a wing chair, regarding her openly. Diane looked back, wondering how such a handsome face could grace such a black-hearted, callous man.

"I believe Spencer and Jake have already informed you the girls will begin work tonight. They will explain the rules to you. I expect them to be followed without question. You and I will continue our relationship as before. Any questions?"

Diane had a million questions, but few he would answer. She simply said, "Thanks for the cottage and food. I know it doesn't matter to you, but we are much more comfortable."

"No, your comfort does not matter at all. I suggest none of you get too used to being here. As soon as we resolve some logistical problems, you'll be moved to different accommodations with the rest of the escorts. Rather, the girls will be. You will stay here with me until I decide differently. Now, lunch is ready. Bring your wine and we will go into the dining room."

Startled at the notion of being separated from the girls given their previous agreement, Diane said, "I thought the six of us would be staying together as long as I cooperated with you?"

Oscar shrugged, a graceful move enhanced by the well-cut black suit covering his torso. "We will see what the future brings. Do not worry about these matters now, Deputy. We have a delicious meal to consume, then we will enjoy private time in my guest room. Many afternoons and nights are before us."

Seeing Diane's raised eyebrows at the mention of his guest room, Oscar smiled slightly and said, "No one enters my bedchamber except for me. We will be comfortable in the guest room conducting our business."

Diane tried to keep a look of disgust off her face.

✳ ✳ ✳

As five o'clock approached, eleven-year-old Libby, renamed Rose by their captors, cried silent tears while Diane tried to force the afternoon with Oscar from her thoughts and swiped mascara onto the little girl's wet blonde lashes. After several minutes of futile effort, Lorelei had finally stepped in and told her sister she had to pretend like Mommy had told them to when they left Alabama for Montana. Mommy had suggested they imagine they were in a fairytale on the way to a new castle. Play-acting was the only thing that had made the trip and leaving their daddy bearable.

After this stern sisterly chat and several nose blows into multiple tissues, Libby's tears subsided into soft hiccups. Diane had rebelled against their captors' demeaning instructions and dressed Libby in the supplied garments: a plaid knee-length skirt and white blouse with a Peter Pan collar—clearly a girls' elementary school uniform, complete with white knee socks and black Mary Janes. Diane tried not to think about the kind of man who fantasized about having sex with young girls dressed in a school uniform.

Maria, already adept at putting on makeup, also dressed in her working wardrobe: a dark pink shrink dress which barely covered her rear end, leaving a small amount of space for a supplied pink lacy push-up bra, but no room for panties. Her kit also contained dangling fake diamond earrings and a fake diamond necklace, but no shoes. Maria wondered why she would be going barefoot but couldn't come up with a reasonable explanation. She didn't care enough to consider the question for long.

When Split Lip and Spencer arrived right at five, Libby shrank against Diane, gripping her hand as tightly as a tick latching onto a hound dog.

Spencer looked at Libby, then Maria, and sighed. "You know how Oscar feels about his instructions being followed."

"I'm not going to allow two underaged children to be dressed in front of grown men. That is not happening," Diane retorted.

"I fail to see why you think you have a choice. And just what do you think they'll be doing later?" Turning to his colleague, he motioned at the group with his hand.

"Pick one. Make the point. But just once."

As rapid as a rattlesnake, Split Lip backhanded Elizabeth, who had the misfortune of being closest to him. The blow landed so hard, she fell backwards to the floor, crying out in pain. He advanced on her, preparing to kick her in the ribs with his heavy work boot when Spencer stopped him.

"Jake. I said just once."

Split Lip looked up with a vicious glint in his eye, clearly wanting to inflict more punishment. Diane had cried out when he struck Elizabeth, and now, in a steely voice said, "You should have hit me. This was my decision."

Spencer looked at her and said, "The point, Deputy, is to prove what we say goes. If you fail to comply, one or more of you will be hurt. Keep that in mind the next time you want to be disobedient." He pointed at Libby and Maria. "Now, you two get undressed."

With Split Lip still hovering over Elizabeth, all Diane could do was turn to the trembling Libby and help her with the buttons. When the little girl was stripped down to her underwear, Spencer said, "Everything comes off."

Shaking with rage, Diane helped the little girl step out of the panties. Spencer motioned to Split Lip again. With a lascivious smile, he moved between Diane and Libby, and shoved two fingers into the girl's vagina, wriggling them around until Spencer told him to stop. Libby gasped in shock and pain, then began to cry, while Diane and the others watched helplessly. Maria, who had slowly undressed, stood stoically as Split Lip came to her and probed her roughly. She gritted her teeth but didn't make a sound.

"I'm glad to see you didn't plant a note inside them, Deputy. That would have been a grievous mistake. Jake will handle the contraband check before each escort task. And after, as well."

Spencer said this as though he were explaining the inner workings of the organization to a new employee. Diane exploded in pent up fury, shaking her fists at the two men.

"How the hell would I write a note? There are no pens or pencils or crayons in this place, you stupid, degenerate SOBs!"

At these words, Split Lip lunged for Diane, ready to teach her a harsh lesson. Spencer restrained him with a hand on his shoulder and a hard look. Ignoring her outburst, he calmly reached into a brown bag Split Lip had dropped on the couch and pulled out a slinky pair of four-inch black stilettos. Handing them to Maria, he said, "Put these on; it's time to go."

Looking at the shoes, Diane could see why they hadn't been included in the garment bag. They were the perfect weapon to jab into one of their captors' eyes. As the door closed behind the men and the two girls, the rest of them looked at each other in dismay. A long night of waiting began.

※ ※ ※

Three hours later a motion light on the front porch switched on, the lock clanked, and the door opened, revealing a defeated, head-bowed Maria and a sobbing Libby. Before Maria could run to her bedroom or Libby could wrap herself around Diane's waist, Spencer barked, "Get undressed. Now. Unless you want Jake to make another point."

Maria pulled the pink dress over her head and unhooked the bra, standing with shoulders stooped and head down in front of the men. The stilettos weren't in sight. Diane assumed they had been confiscated the moment Maria got back into the car after her escort duties were over. She helped the shaking Libby undress, saw blood and bruising on the young girl's inner thighs, and waited angrily while Split Lip performed his inspection of both girls. Gathering up the clothing, Diane stuffed the outfits into one bag and thrust it at the men.

"You've had your fun. Now get out and leave us alone."

The next night all five girls were required to work. The schoolgirl plaid returned, this time for Lorelei. Diane was forced to braid the child's hair in pigtails with ribbons at the ends to complete the effect. The rest of the outfits were cheap, tight dresses accompanied by costume jewelry pieces and the late arrival of dressy, high-heeled sandals. Apart from Lorelei and Libby, the girls stood stoically through Split Lip's degrading finger probe. Lily looked as if she would strangle the pedophile with her own hands; Diane half-wished she would. But tonight, Spencer and Jake were accompanied by Dill, and Diane didn't like the odds. She and Lily, with Maria and Elizabeth's help, may be able to overpower two of the men, but without some type of weapon, three were too many. The three of them had talked through strategies earlier that day, with Lily listening intently, but hadn't come up with a workable plan.

After the men had left the night before, Diane had gathered the girls around, telling them all to hold hands. When they were locked in a tight circle, she had looked each one in the eye and said, "We will only survive this is if we keep mentally strong. Maria, never again bow your head to these men, and none of the rest of you do either. They are scum. Try your best not to cry. No matter what they make us do, we will not let them cow us, do you hear me? We will take care of each other until we're free and then we'll find these men and punish them."

Looking at each of the girls in turn, she held their gaze until each one nodded. Surprising them all, Lily spoke, arms swirling in angry gestures. No one could understand her words, but the teenager's long, beautiful hands articulated a clear message of defiance and determination…and hope for future freedom.

✯ ✯ ✯

Having regained some of her spunk after Diane's speech, Maria muttered Spanish curse words under her breath the next night while Split Lip performed his invasive inspection, but stood tall with shoulders straight. Libby and Lorelei cried silent tears through their ordeal while Elizabeth bit her lip to keep from crying out. The three girls looked pleadingly at Diane as the men ushered them out the door. All Diane could do was hold up a formed fist to remind them to stay strong. Lily and Maria kept their eyes forward as they marched defiantly to the vehicles.

Another long evening of waiting, but this time Diane was alone, without any of the girls to comfort. The thought struck her this was the first time she had been completely alone since she knocked on the door of room ten at the motel. She used the time to go through the house yet again, searching for an exit, a weapon, anything that might enable an escape. She had already checked for emergency release latches on the window bars and found them all disabled, so sneaking out through the windows was not an option.

The doors appeared to be the only potential escape points, but disabling the locks, which were on the outside of the doors, seemed like an impossibility. No matter the avenue, Diane knew the first order of business would be to take the cameras out of the equation. Looking closely at the ones in the living room, she saw that hanging clothing over the lens wasn't feasible because the cameras were mounted too close to the walls. But could they be adjusted? She stood on the couch, pushing a lens carefully with her finger. To her surprise, the mechanism moved easily. Well, that was interesting. If they could adjust each camera a smidgen, perhaps they could open a corridor out of their captors' line of sight.

Since Diane didn't know much about the property, she was unsure whether a run to freedom was even feasible. The fence appeared too tall for the little ones to climb, but maybe not. Was the fence electric? Did attack dogs guard the property? Were their quarters and the outside areas alarmed? Were the cameras really monitored around the clock? She didn't know any of the answers, but she did know their choice was simple: escape this prison or live a nightmare until they all died early deaths.

※ ※ ※

Over the next several weeks, a debilitating, cruel routine set in. The men would come about mid-morning to drop off clothes and makeup, then return about five in the afternoon to take the girls to their jobs. The outfits their captors brought varied, apparently determined by the fantasies of the client. The schoolgirl plaid was popular, a fact that didn't surprise Diane but made her ill to her core. Most of the other garments were short, tight-fitting, low-cut dresses with high heels too unstable to comfortably walk in. Diane's heart ached to see the girls, especially Libby and Lorelei, made up and dressed like streetwalkers. She knew the men on the receiving end paid a premium price for such young flesh, and she wished she could chop off each one's penis and shove it, along with their balls, down their sick throats.

While all the girls didn't work every night, each one usually worked five or six nights a week. A light night included one or two jobs; a heavy one was more than two. Often the girls were forced to service as many as six men in one evening. Diane learned to tell what type of evening they had endured by the look on each girl's face when they returned to the house. After a particularly bad night, Lily's features would be hard as granite, and she would refuse to sing their goodnight lullaby, no matter how much the girls begged. Maria adopted an air of nonchalance, as though she'd been out picking daisies in the park, but her eyes were as hard as flint. The three youngest girls simply came in looking exhausted and shell-shocked. More often than not, the girls were marked in some way, bruised from a punch or scored with red welts from vicious pinches. With each passing night, Elizabeth, Libby, and Lorelei faded slowly away, each of them becoming wraithlike and brittle.

Diane worked almost as many days a week as the girls did, Oscar calling for her four or five times, sometimes in the afternoon and sometimes in the evening. Their meetings were always the same. They ate an exquisite meal cooked by Oscar's private chef, then copulated like the two strangers they were, Oscar always seemingly satisfied, Diane always unwilling. When Oscar felt Diane wasn't being cooperative enough, the sex would be rough and painful, so Diane did the best she could to act accommodating, meanwhile plotting all the ways she could steal a knife from the kitchen and plunge it directly into her captor's black heart. While outwardly cordial, an air of tension always sheathed their meetings, Diane sensing danger in the air no matter how politely Oscar spoke and behaved.

Early in their stay at the new quarters, Diane had asked Oscar about the lack of writing utensils in their house, requesting at least one pencil. Amused, he had looked at her and said, "I do not trust you or any of your group enough to provide something which may be used as a weapon. Most of our women have grown used to their new life and are no longer threats to my people. I do not believe you have."

Diane had interpreted this comment to mean most of the kidnapped women they had turned into unwilling prostitutes had been deliberately hooked on drugs to guarantee their compliance. She made no response when he continued, "I cannot trust you will come to, if not enjoy, then at least accept your current situation. If I have not been clear on this point before, allow me to say this now. Please listen carefully.

"Your girls will work for us until they can no longer satisfy the customers. As for you, I do not believe your story that you just happened to get tangled up with these girls. Since you may be a mole for the Federal Bureau of Investigation, a question I am working with my federal colleagues to get an answer to, I will continue to take extra precautions with you. So no. No pencil."

* * *

One evening as Diane stepped out of a long shower spent scrubbing off her time with Oscar, she looked up at the cameras and realized all of them were fogged over by steam. In all this time, she'd never noticed the cameras fogging up. Several weeks earlier, Diane had tried an experiment with the surveillance equipment. She had moved one of the foyer cameras to the right about three inches. Two minutes later the front door lock had clicked, followed by Surfer Dude carrying a small tool bag. He looked at the cameras in the foyer for a minute, grabbed a chair, realigned the lens she had moved, and said, "Don't mess with the cameras. It only pisses us off."

A week later, Diane readjusted one of the cameras in her bedroom. This time no one came until late the next day, but when he finished readjusting the camera, Surfer Dude viciously grabbed her by the arm, pinching the soft skin above her elbow.

"Just stop it. Do it again and they'll hurt one of you. Or I'll hurt you. You don't need all of your fingers or toes to be a whore."

Rubbing her bruised arm, Diane thought. *So, a fifty-fifty chance of them not realizing immediately a camera has been moved. Which response is more consistent? And what if I didn't move them three inches? What if I only moved them an inch? Maybe they wouldn't notice at all. And maybe they don't monitor the feed every minute of every day. Maybe.*

Now as Diane contemplated the fog-covered lenses, an idea began to form. Their jailers believed they'd thought of everything. But they hadn't thought to put a fog-proof solution on the camera lenses. Diane smiled just a little.

CHAPTER 39

JOE

Belle woofed softly as Joe throttled back the engines and taxied slowly to the small Cessna's marked parking space. He rubbed her ears, reluctant to leave the cockpit and return to their Diane-less home. Joe had gotten home from work that evening dispirited and discouraged, having made almost no progress on the case that day. Diane was intensely on his mind in a way she hadn't been for a while. Despite not having eaten since lunch, he wasn't hungry and couldn't settle, so he had consulted Belle. Both had agreed they needed to get out of the house.

Now, after a two-hour flight through the late-night sky, Joe looked through the windshield at the midnight stars, extremely bright here in rural Kingsland, and wondered if Diane was looking at those same stars. Or if she was looking up at the three-quarter moon while she made her way home to her husband and her dog. He still couldn't fathom what had caused her to disappear, her own hand or foul play, but knew only something truly bad could keep her away this long. Endless possibilities ran through his mind, a slideshow made more vivid by the horrific crimes he had witnessed over his years in law enforcement.

Hand buried in Belle's ruff, rubbing his sweet beast softly, Joe leaned the seat back and closed his eyes, forcing Diane out of his thoughts, only for his mind to drift to his murder cases. Something had to break soon, or another woman would be killed and he'd be out of a job, and rightfully so. In the quiet of the cockpit, he thought he could feel the spirits of the murdered women waiting for him to find their killer and bring him to justice.

I may not be able to find my wife, Joe thought to himself, *but I am damn sure going to find this killer and find him soon.* Maybe that bit of luck would bring Diane home.

CHAPTER 40

DIANE

Still musing on the potential benefits of a fogged up camera lens, Diane found all the girls had returned while she was in the bathroom. She looked at Lily and Elizabeth as they trudged past her to the shower. A thorough scrubbing was each girl's priority when they returned in the evenings. Elizabeth looked even more dispirited than usual, eyes bleak and shoulders hunched. The girl was scarecrow thin. She barely ate more than a bowl of cereal each day, no matter how much Diane and the girls encouraged her. Diane reached out to stroke her gaunt arm.

"Honey, do you want to talk about it?"

Elizabeth shook her head and slipped into her room before Diane could persuade her to talk.

Diane had learned from the girls that their escort duties followed a basic pattern. They typically went to one of three motels, all rundown and dirty, in a seedy part of town with no street signs and busted-out streetlights. They were given condoms, which the men did not always use, then taken into separate rooms with instructions to answer the door at each knock, admit the customer, do whatever the customer wanted, and repeat the sequence until a knock revealed one of their captors.

When queried about their handlers' behavior, Elizabeth said one of them stayed outside each door until all the jobs were done for the night, but Lorelei said, "No, I came out before you one night, no one was at your door. I think they only keep one person at the motel for all of us. Until we get into the car to drive back here, then the others come back."

Diane asked how the customers paid but the girls didn't know. They had never seen money exchange hands. Occasionally, a customer would throw some cash on the bed or floor as he left, but not too often. As proof of this, Maria turned her back to the cameras and surreptitiously pulled two crumpled twenty-dollar bills from her pocket. The girls had made a pact not to tell their jailers about the cash, even though Dill had told them they weren't allowed to keep any money given to them. He'd threatened to slice off their thumbs if they did.

***

One morning when Split Lip opened the door to drop off that evening's costumes, he had a new jailer with him, a woman of indeterminate age and large stature, about six feet tall and two hundred pounds. Diane stared at her, dismayed but not surprised. She knew from her time in law enforcement that human traffickers were both genders and all races. As was the case with Elizabeth's friend, Chastity, women were often used to lure other females into the net. Diane looked at the woman with disgust while addressing her request to Split Lip.

"Hey, we'd really like some hot tea. Could you bring us a teapot?"

Split Lip looked at her and laughed. "You want somethin' new? Go suck Oscar's dick for it. By the way, he wants to see you. So maybe if you're extra sweet to him, you can get your teapot today." As he threw down the girls' garment bags, he stuck his thumb out towards the woman. "This here's Wanda. She's new. Don't mess with her just 'cause she's a girl."

Wanda gave Split Lip a look that told Diane the skinny bird-brain would pay for his comment later. Then she turned to Diane. "I see you eyeballing me, wondering if you can take me. You can't. Others have tried. So stop thinking about it."

Diane couldn't stop herself, even though she knew her words were pointless. "Why do you do this? Why would you help them turn me and these young girls into prostitutes? Why?"

The Amazon shrugged her shoulders. "Money, why else? I got two kids at home. Need to send them to college. This is easy work and good dough. Now come on, Oscar don't like to be kept waitin'."

***

A few days later, Maria and Libby had a rare night off. They were watching television with Diane, who was savoring a cup of tea, when Dill and Wanda returned with Lorelei and Lily, but not Elizabeth. During Diane's most recent meeting with Oscar, she had petitioned him for both the teapot and a television. To her surprise, both luxuries had been delivered to the cottage two days later, complete with teabags and a cable hookup. Split Lip had herded all of them into the master bedroom before letting the cable tech in the house. When he freed them from the bedroom, he had sneered at Diane and said, "You must be something special in the sack, lady."

As soon as Dill and Wanda left the house, Maria turned off the TV and asked where Elizabeth was. Lorelei started to cry, putting her arms around Lily's waist. Lily encircled the girl's narrow shoulders, then started talking and gesturing with her hands.

Watching without comprehending, Diane finally said, "Lorelei, honey, what happened? Where is Elizabeth?"

After a moment, Lorelei unhooked herself from Lily and mumbled, "Lizzie went crazy. She went crazy, Diane. And now she's goooonnnne..."

Diane exchanged glances with Maria and gathered Lorelei into her lap, saying "Tell me what happened, sweetie."

In fits and starts, accompanied by uninterpretable exclamations from Lily, Lorelei told them at the end of the night Elizabeth had gotten into the car holding her jaw as though it hurt, two black eyes swelling her face. About halfway to the ranch, she had started to rock back and forth, then began to cry, and finally started screaming. No matter what their captors said or did, Lizzie would not stop screaming, rocking, crying. When they got back to the ranch, the men took the still shrieking Elizabeth to a different cottage before bringing herself and Lily here.

Diane went numb all over. If Elizabeth's spirit had broken, they would drug her or kill her. No in-between existed for the sweet thirteen-year-old. She would try to get Elizabeth back through Oscar but didn't hold much hope for success. Oscar was only interested in them to the degree they brought in business. If they couldn't work, they were useless to him. Aside from Elizabeth's mental state, her absence brought up an additional difficulty. Diane and the girls had been devising potential escape plans for weeks. If Elizabeth wasn't with them, how could they leave? She could only hope the girl would be returned to their cottage in the coming days.

※ ※ ※

A week had passed since Elizabeth's disappearance. Diane had been minutely adjusting the cameras in the house each night, hoping the dark would cover her actions. Either their jailers didn't monitor the cameras closely or the picture was too dim for them to see her because no one had barged in yet to stop her. She was adjusting them just enough to form a corridor she hoped was invisible to anyone monitoring the video feed. Her original thought, and the reason she had requested the teapot to begin with, had been to fog the cameras with steam, but too many lenses made that idea unworkable. With Elizabeth's meltdown, Diane felt their situation was becoming more and more precarious. They urgently needed to break out of the compound.

When asked, Oscar had simply told her Elizabeth was no longer her concern. He shut down all discussion of returning Elizabeth to Diane's care. None of their jailers offered any clues to the girl's whereabouts or well-being. Unsure at first whether to proceed with an escape plan, the final straw came on the fifth day of Elizabeth's absence.

Lorelei had returned from her evening jobs, coughing, and holding her side. When Diane finally got her alone in the bathroom, a hot tub filling for the little girl to step into, she saw massive bruising on the child's torso. The coughing stopped, but Diane's request for Lorelei to draw a deep breath elicited a shriek of pain from the tiny girl. Clearly, she had at least one broken rib, given to her by one of the johns she had serviced that night. For the past three nights, all the girls had returned with various amounts of bruising on their breasts, arms, and legs. Diane knew the time had come to leave before any more of them went crazy. Or died at the hands of men to whom they were objects to be used, abused, and tossed away.

Diane washed Lorelei gently, then wrapped the girl in a dry towel and tucked her into bed. Shaking her head at Libby who wanted to cuddle with her sister, she gently told the younger girl to sit on the floor and hold her big sister's hand, but not jostle or squeeze her. Libby nodded, staring at Diane, gray eyes huge and filled with tears.

Walking wearily into the kitchen to boil some water for a much needed sugar-laden tea, Diane was surprised to see Lily standing by the counter holding a napkin in one hand and a lipstick tube in the other. Sometime in the last few days, their captors had begun leaving the makeup kit at the house, a development Diane hadn't realized provided the prisoners a writing tool until just now. Lily looked at her, then wrote down five numbers, shielding the napkin from the cameras' view.

Diane looked at the numbers, then looked at Lily. "I don't understand."

Lily wrote the numbers again. Diane repeated, "I don't understand," this time shaking her head back and forth for emphasis.

Lily raised her eyes to the ceiling in frustration, then wrote the numbers on the napkin a third time. Diane took the lipstick from her and drew a question mark. Lily paced the floor, forward and back, forward and back, forward and back, then with a yelp, snatched the tube from Diane's hand and began a clumsy sketch, the waxy lipstick making a poor drawing tool. At first, Diane couldn't figure out what the square with smaller squares inside represented. Then she suddenly got it.

Unlike most security gates which opened automatically when a car pulled up to depart, the one here at the ranch required a code to get both in and out. Because of the double security measure, Diane had dismissed the idea of escaping via that portal. They wouldn't have been able to get out of the gate without the code. Trying to evade capture while hanging around in the bushes by the gate until a car entered or left seemed irrational. But if they had the code, and they could break out of the house, they could simply open the gate and run like hell.

Diane looked at Lily. "Are these the numbers to the gate box code?"

Lily steadily returned her gaze, then began writing a number beside each square on her drawing.

"Oh my God, Lily, you've done it. We can get out of here!" Diane hugged the teenager close in astonished excitement.

✫ ✫ ✫

Even without Elizabeth, Diane knew they had to leave. She hated to abandon the young teen but felt they had no choice. Split Lip refused a doctor for Lorelei and refused Diane's demands to see Oscar. The young girl was deteriorating quickly. They had forced her to work the night after her rib injury, and she had come back to the cottage barely breathing, doubled over in pain. At that moment, Diane decided they would escape the next night or die trying. She talked the decision over with the remaining girls while Lily sketched the landscape outside their cottage on a napkin and listened closely. Although none of them wanted to leave Elizabeth behind, they knew the time was now or never for Lorelei, and on some level, they had each accepted Elizabeth would never rejoin them. With luck, they would be able to notify the police in time to save Elizabeth from wherever she was being held, assuming she was still alive. Diane doubted it but didn't say so.

While Diane, Maria, and Libby discussed a potential plan, Lily walked out of the room. Returning with an object in each hand and carefully standing in the slim corridor Diane had created by adjusting the cameras, Lily opened her hands. Diane stopped in mid-sentence and stared. The teenager was holding two homemade knives carved from toothbrushes—one end whittled to a sharp point, the brush serving as a handle at the opposite end. The weapons looked exactly like shanks a prisoner would make.

Diane gawked at the girl, not knowing what to say. Then she jumped up, went into the kitchen, returned with the teapot, and handed it to Lily. Taking the pot, Lily grinned.

Maria looked at the two women and said, "What, what? Que es?"

Lily handed her the stainless steel pot. Maria almost dropped the jug before realizing its surprisingly heavy weight. Pulling off the lid, she found the pot full of sugar, three pounds from the new groceries delivered yesterday. Maria beamed.

✻ ✻ ✻

When Split Lip and Wanda delivered work clothes the following morning, Diane was relieved Lorelei was not on that evening's schedule. If she had been, they would have had to implement their plan during the day, before they were fully prepared to execute and without the cover of darkness.

Diane and Lorelei spent a quiet evening while the other girls went to work, Lorelei in bed fully dressed, with Diane sitting quietly on the floor beside her, holding her hand. When the remaining three girls returned about midnight, Diane moved quietly into the living room to stand close to Wanda. Wanda looked at her suspiciously for a second, then turned back to watch her partner. As Split Lip began to perform the nightly contraband inspection on Maria, the teenager reached over with a forced smile and cupped his genitals, massaging gently. Leaving his fingers in place between her legs, the pedophile stopped probing and looked at her in surprise, a grin spreading across his face.

"Really baby? It's about time. I been waitin' for ya' to warm up to me."

He was leaning forward to kiss Maria when Lily attacked, fiercely driving one of the carved toothbrushes into his neck, twisting and pushing until only the bristles were visible. Split Lip fell, convulsed once, twice, then lay still, eyes staring blankly, blood gushing from his carotid artery. The instant Lily made her move, Diane grabbed the weighted teapot she had hidden in the chair cushion and walloped Wanda on the back of the head. Wanda went down with a grunt, then rose from her knees, swinging blindly. Powered by months of stored rage, Diane swung the teapot again, smashing the woman's face with the makeshift weapon. Then, before Diane could stop her, Lily pulled the second shiv from her back pocket and drove it deep into Wanda's right eye.

In the following stillness, they all looked at each other, shocked with what had just occurred, even though they had orchestrated the attack. Finally, Diane shook herself and said, "Let's move. I'll get Lorelei."

Their fifty-fifty gamble on whether the feed was continuously monitored had paid off as no one was in sight when they scooted quickly out the front door. A perfect lie, Diane thought. A good way to keep them in line, making them believe the cameras were constantly monitored. The brave group's willingness to gamble on that lie, combined with a monumental misstep on their captors' part, had formed the foundation of their plan.

A few weeks earlier Diane had noticed a huge security breach their jailers had overlooked. No matter who came to get the girls for work or to drop off clothing, the traffickers never locked the front door while they were in the house. Those occasions being the only time a door was left unsecured, their escape plan had to revolve around pick-up and drop-off for the evening jobs or the mid-morning clothing delivery.

Now the fivesome moved quietly around the side of the cottage towards the gate, Maria holding up a gasping Lorelei, Libby supporting her sister's other side. Having never left the compound, Diane wasn't familiar with the route to the gate, so Lily led the frightened group, keeping as close to the tree line as possible. When Diane had the gate in her sights, she let herself hope just a little that this implausible scheme would work, and they would all get out alive.

As they got closer to the code box, Diane reached out and touched Lily on the shoulder, motioning her to stay near the bushes while she moved up to put in the code. Lily nodded and turned to help Libby and Maria with Lorelei. Just as Diane entered the last digit, a spotlight came on, followed by shouting from the direction of the cottages. As the gate rolled slowly back, Diane pushed Lorelei and Libby through the small opening, Lorelei coughing and holding her side in pain. Diane turned to let Lily and Maria go next when gunshots started booming.

Maria gasped, clutched her chest, and started to fall. Diane caught her, pushing her through the exit. Without fully opening, the gate began to reverse course and close. As bullets flew around them, Diane stepped halfway through the opening, keeping one arm around Maria's waist, then turned to grab Lily and pull the young woman through. As the gate bore down on them, Lily shoved Diane to the opposite side, then backed away, holding eye contact with Diane before touching her hand to her heart and holding her palm out. Then she turned and ran, yelling in her native tongue, drawing the men away from the escaping hostages. Diane screamed for Lily to come back as the gate locked in place.

Irrationally, Diane wanted to climb the fence to go after Lily but a muffled sound from Maria made her look down. The teenager's chest was covered in blood, and she was gasping for breath as she began to slide to the ground. Libby and Lorelei looked on in horror. Diane cursed and stooped to help Maria up. "Come on, honey, we made it out, we have to move."

Maria protested but managed to stand with Diane's support. Diane looked at the sisters and told them to run down the road as far as they could and not stop, she and Maria would be right behind them. Though barely able to stay upright, Maria was attempting to reach into her shirt pocket. Grasping the teen's flailing hand with her own, Diane got Maria moving slowly. The wounded girl hobbled a few steps, then collapsed heavily to the road. Diane knelt over her as she drew a final shuddering breath, dying just a few steps into her hard-won freedom.

Hating to leave her but knowing she couldn't wait any longer, Diane stood. She walked two steps then, agitated, turned back to Maria. Kneeling, she reached into the pocket the young girl had been scrabbling at, pulling out a wad of bills soaked in Maria's blood. Silently blessing this brave young woman, Diane kissed Maria softly on the forehead, gathered her wits, and ran to catch up with the two remaining members of their diminished posse.

CHAPTER 41

PHOEBE

I woke from a dream in which I'd been walking between the hedges at the University of Georgia's huge football stadium, heading to a stage set in the middle of the field to receive the Pulitzer Prize for Literature, Jack walking proudly beside me with a bow tie attached to his best collar, Josie and Jilly prancing several feet ahead, each carrying a piece of bacon in her mouth. As I approached the steps to the stage, Kurt Von Schuster came down to greet me, holding a bright orange flip-flop in one hand and a large sewing needle laced with red thread in the other. Henry DeSantos was on the right side of the stage, using a miniature sewing machine to sew a giant plaid shirt, and Danny Taylor was on the left of the stage, cornered by a dozen rowdy puppies. When I reached up to take Kurt's hand, I found myself already at the top of the stairs, dancing a tango with Tommy Lee Jones.

Blinking myself fully awake, I laid in bed for a moment, replaying the scene and wondering what I'd eaten the night before that caused such a crazy dream. Must have been the jalapenos and beer. Or maybe the hot fudge sundae at midnight. Or maybe the creative side of my brain had clashed with the logical side while trying to spark new ideas for my water-conservationist-as-murderer storyline.

Who knows? I thought to myself. *But I should probably go out and buy Jack a bow tie, just in case I do win the Pulitzer.*

CHAPTER 42

DIANE

Shaking with shock and terror, Diane, Libby, and Lorelei wound their way as quickly as they could through the edge of the tree line. Diane didn't dare walk on the road or venture too deep into the woods. The road was too visible, the woods too thick with brush, live oaks and other large trees Diane didn't recognize. She assumed the compound's driveway would lead them to a road where they could potentially flag down some help. Of course, they needed to evade capture first. As poorly as Lorelei was breathing and as slowly as they were moving, Diane didn't hold much hope for the longevity of their freedom. But she was determined to make the most of Lily's sacrifice, so she pushed the little girls as fast as she dared.

As the moon moved across the night sky, Diane and the girls trudged forward. Twice they ran into the bushes and hid, once when the familiar white SUV drove slowly by, searching the edge of the woods with a spotlight. Fear kept the three as still as deer avoiding a hunter's gun. Twenty or so minutes after the spotlight disappeared, the threesome heard men's voices a short distance from them. They stopped again to bury themselves in a bush until only the sounds of crickets and frogs filled the night.

What seemed like a lifetime later, the trio came to an intersection with the road going straight, left, and right. Diane debated. *Turn or keep going straight?* She rotated in a three-quarter circle searching the sky for lights and the roads for signs. Nothing. Just as she had decided to turn left, using the logic that most people stay the course or turn right when given a choice, Libby tugged at her arm. The little girl pointed straight ahead, but to what Diane couldn't tell. No matter which way they went, they were going to lose the tree line and most of their cover, so Diane propelled the girls forward to follow Libby's finger. The little girl must have possessed the eyesight of an eagle because about thirty feet down the road, a sign proclaimed "Oswald, pop 4500, 2 miles."

Since the foliage wasn't as thick along this route, Diane moved them into the brush, keeping her charges moving as steadily as possible against small branches reluctant to yield. Again, the SUV came drifting slowly by, seeming to beam the spotlight right at them. Again, they crouched and froze until the danger passed. When Diane finally saw bright lights in the distance, she feared she was hallucinating, but soon her exhausted brain registered a huge gas station in the streaming light. A giant travel center, of all things, in Oswald, population 4500. Diane breathed a sigh of relief. Several minutes later they arrived directly across the road from the brightly lit plaza, and she stopped the girls so she could think through their next move.

Since the gas station was so large, Diane doubted their traffickers could maintain spies at every pump, but she had to assume

Oscar's men would at least periodically cruise the parking lot and the store. She hated to make the girls sleep in the dirt overnight, particularly because she didn't like the way Lorelei was breathing, but she thought their best choice was to lay low until morning, then see about hitching a ride north with a trucker. She contemplated running over to the station to borrow a phone and call 911 but felt sure Oscar would have local law enforcement infiltrated with his own people.

✻ ✻ ✻

The sun will come up tomorrow, Diane thought, as the sun did, indeed, rise in the east the next morning. She had been awake all night, watching the girls toss and turn on the hard ground, murmuring soft words to them when they were on the verge of waking, humming as much as she could remember of the bedtime tune Lily had sung and resorting to "Jesus Loves Me This I Know" towards dawn. Lorelei felt feverish and coughed often, wincing in pain with each convulsion.

With the sunrise came decisions. Diane had passed the dark hours concocting a story she hoped would sweet-talk a trucker into giving them a lift. She could see the parking lot slowly coming to life. Waking the girls, she helped them pee in the bushes, showing them a trick she had learned as a young camper to keep the urine from running down their legs. Then she moved them as close to the road as they could get without being seen. She told the girls to wait, she would be back. They both grabbed her, begging her not to leave them alone. Diane briefly explained her plan. Reluctantly they let go of her waist and sat, despondent and exhausted, in the dirt.

Diane combed her fingers through her hair, attempted to wipe off the grime she presumed covered her face, and prayed for a Good Samaritan. Crossing the road, she looked closely at the big rigs gassing up. At this hour of the morning, there weren't as many long-haul drivers as she had hoped for, but she would choose from what was available. Positioning herself at a gas pump, she observed the truckers coming from the store, ready to begin their long day driving. Not sure what criteria she was using, she dismissed some at first glance, considered others, and finally settled on one she thought might be receptive to the tale she had conjured up during the long night. Looking in every direction for anyone who might be on Oscar's payroll, she walked toward her chosen mark, an affable looking red-headed, bearded man, gassing up a rig with "Got freight? Go Grate" stenciled on the side of the trailer. The cab door indicated the truck belonged to Grate Trucking out of Sedalia, Missouri.

"Excuse me," she called softly. "Can you help me? I'm in a bit of trouble."

The barrel chested man eyed her warily, looked behind her, then to each side of her. "What is it? I need to get on the road. I've got a deadline."

"I just need a ride. Well, me and my two daughters, we need a ride. Where are you going? I could pay a little for gas."

"I'm headed to Jacksonville. Gotta pick up I-10 there." He looked around the parking lot.

"Where are your daughters? I don't usually give rides to hitch-hikers." He was eyeing her suspiciously, taking in her dirty clothes and face and general dishevelment.

Diane broke down then, none of the hot tears fake, and explained how her boyfriend had threatened to kill her and her daughters, she had run away from him last night, spent the night in the woods, that's why she looked so terrible, they just needed to get away from him, she didn't have much money, she couldn't think what to do except come here and ask for a ride. Couldn't he help them? The lies flew easily, driven by desperation for herself and the two girls she had left to save.

"Why don't you call the cops?

"My boyfriend is a cop. A local cop. And he knows all the other cops around here. If I call them, they'll call him. Look, my name's Diane. I promise, if we can just get away from here, there won't be any trouble. Please, sir. I beg you. I have friends who live a little north of Jacksonville if we can just ride with you there."

The truck driver rubbed a hand down his beard, returned the gas handle to the pump, looked at his watch, and said, "Alright. But any funny business and I'll kick you out on the side of the road, kids or no kids. I'll get the rig going. Get your girls. Three minutes or I'm gone without you."

Diane had instructed the girls to watch for her. If she waved her arms, they were to run across the road to her as quickly as they could. She walked rapidly to the edge of the lot and signaled them, experiencing a moment's panic when two blonde heads didn't pop up immediately. Red Beard's truck was belching smoke as he drove the big machine slowly toward her. Finally, Diane saw the girls burst out of the bushes and sprint without first checking for oncoming traffic. Luckily the roads were empty, especially since Lorelei stopped running halfway through, only managing a slow, hitching gait the rest of the way. Libby turned back to help her sister move across the road. Finally, they reached Diane and the waiting vehicle. Diane boosted the girls into the back seats, then scrambled up and buckled herself into the front.

As they pulled onto the road, their savior said, "My name's Fred, but folks call me Rusty. Is your daughter alright? She's breathing kinda funny."

"Yes, I know, thank you. I'll get her tended to when we get to Jacksonville. Or St. Samuel, that's where my friends are."

"Sure you don't want to go to a hospital now? There's one about four miles from here. She doesn't look too good."

"No, no hospital. My boyfriend's the one who hurt her. He'd find out if we go for help around here. He has contacts everywhere. His sister works in the hospital ER. Just get us to Jacksonville, please. I'll get her taken care of there."

Rusty shrugged and turned on the radio.

About eight hours later, the big rig pulled into another large gas station where I-10 intersected I-95. The red-headed driver had proved an interesting companion after the first hour, entertaining them with stories from his years driving America's highways. The girls had slept much of the way, Lorelei's breathing calmer but still hitched and out of rhythm. As Rusty maneuvered the truck into position at one of the pumps at the busy station, Diane pulled a twenty from Maria's stash.

"I know it's not much with the price of gas, but here, please take this. I am so grateful to you."

Turning off the engine, Rusty glanced at the bloodied bill, gave her a steady look and said, "No, ma'am, I won't take your money. Helping you was my pleasure. Wish I could take you on further and I hope things work out for you and the little ones."

They said goodbye at the back of the huge semi, Diane giving Rusty a firm handshake and a warm peck on the cheek. He squatted down to give the girls each a hug, then turned to the gas pump. Diane took a small hand in each of hers. They all needed the restroom and hot food, and Diane needed to figure out how to get them the final stretch to St. Samuel. She had decided to take the girls home and turn herself in. Anything else seemed undoable and too complicated with little money, no identification, no credit cards, and no phone, not to mention the angry cartel boss searching for them. Joe may be furious with her, but he would focus on keeping the girls safe. She just wasn't sure how to traverse the sixty or so remaining miles. She knew Oscar and Levy's operation ran the length of the coast and couldn't bear the thought their little trio could be recaptured.

Contemplating the problem while scarfing down a burger and fries, Diane pulled Maria's money from her pocket to see how much cash the young girl had secreted away. She counted out one hundred and twenty dollars. Not enough to rent a car or call a taxi so she guessed she'd have to throw herself on the mercy of a new trucker and hope they found another angel like Rusty. Diane murmured a prayer for Maria, blessing the girl for her brave heart and foresight. Then she whispered another one for Lily, who had saved them by drawing the men away from the gate.

As she tucked the bills deep into her back pocket Lorelei whispered, "Wait, put this with it." Diane looked over to see the sick girl holding two twenty-dollar bills.

"I've got some, too," Libby piped up. Two more twenties sat in Libby's outstretched hand. "Mr. Rusty gave it to us."

Diane's eyes filled with tears, thinking about the kindness given by this man after the cruelty they'd suffered at the hands of others. Then, resigned to trying to find and persuade an honest trucker to take them to St. Samuel, Diane parked the girls at a picnic table partially hidden from the road and looked over the rigs in the lot. Settling on another red-haired trucker who was filling up a pink cab with "AnnaLine's Logistics" and a breast cancer emblem embossed on the doors, she rehearsed her story in her head as she walked toward him. Halfway to the pump she heard someone call her name. Turning, she was surprised to find Rusty hurrying to catch up with her.

"Hey, are you going to talk to William?"

"Who's William? I'm going to see if the guy driving the pink truck will give us a ride north."

Rusty grinned. "Good choice. He's my buddy, William. We cross paths on the road all the time. I talked to him in the store. Says he's willing to give you a ride to St. Samuel. You'll be safe with him."

Amazed by the goodness of this man who had been a complete stranger just hours earlier, Diane didn't know what to say. Rusty made the introductions, Diane took the girls into the store for a final bathroom stop, and ten minutes later they were barreling up I-95. About twenty minutes later, Diane, who was finally getting used to the lengthy sightline offered by the cab of these big rigs, saw vehicles slowing a mile or so in the distance, and blue lights flashing beyond the stop-and-go traffic. Until she saw two ambulances, she panicked that Levy's men had persuaded the state patrol to establish a checkpoint to look for them.

As they inched along in the slow-moving column, Lorelei and Libby, who had been playing a back-and-forth singing game, went suddenly quiet. Diane turned around instantly to find both youngsters staring in horror out the window. She looked down and out of her own window, freezing in her seat when she saw Dill, Surfer Dude, and a man she didn't recognize in the white SUV one lane over.

"Oh, my God. Girls, get down and don't sit up until I tell you it's safe. William, may I borrow your ball cap, please?"

William pulled the gold Jacksonville Jaguars hat from his head and handed it to her bill first.

"What's up?"

Diane hurriedly stuffed her now-short hair up into the cap. She had borrowed scissors from Rusty and chopped off her distinctive auburn waves in the women's bathroom. She should have cut the girls' hair as well but hadn't been able to bring herself to do it.

"Remember I told you about my ex we're trying to get away from? Looks like he's figured out where we're going. He's in that white Suburban over there. He must have remembered I have family in St. Samuel."

Diane recalled Oscar had found plenty of personal information about her online, plus he'd had her wallet and purse. She should have realized he would send his goons to her hometown, assuming that would be the place she would run to. How stupid of her. She should have taken the girls west with Rusty. In the heat of their escape, the thought that Oscar would pursue her outside of the immediate Miami area hadn't been foremost in her mind. But now she remembered the girls were payment for his dead godson and realized that while this brutal man and his boss might have let her go, they would never rest until the little girls were back in their control or dead.

She had planned to go straight to the St. Samuel police station without calling Joe first, mostly because she couldn't fathom what that conversation would sound like. Now she would have to come up with a different plan. Since her former captors obviously had St. Samuel in their sights, Diane had to assume they would be monitoring her home, the police station, and the SCSO headquarters. She also had to assume they could trace calls to Joe's phone as well as the stations' landlines. *Could they?* She didn't really know. She only knew Oscar's reach was long.

She was rapidly thinking through different scenarios when William said, "Why don't I take you to a hotel at exit three? It's not far from St. Samuel and that scumbag looking for you won't be able to search every random hotel, even if he figures out you didn't go all the way home. You have people you can call once you get close, right?"

Diane nodded, recognizing William's plan as a good one. She probably had enough money to pay for two, maybe three nights at a cheap motel. Meanwhile, she could figure out how to contact Joe or Terry or her sheriff in some way that didn't include telephone lines or visiting St. Samuel in person. Diane sighed and rubbed her neck to relieve the tension. *Would this nightmare never end?*

A few minutes later, the traffic cleared and normal speeds resumed. The white SUV disappeared down the far left lane. Diane took a deep breath before telling the girls they could sit up. No sing-along now, the girls were wrapped around each other, petrified.

✵ ✵ ✵

William deftly pulled the semi into the parking lot of a cheap-looking motel at exit three, the Red Wheel Inn. Lorelei was sound asleep so William said he would stay in the cab with her while Diane checked in. Libby climbed out, needing to stretch her legs and wanting to stay close to Diane.

With the key to room 202 in hand, Diane and Libby returned to the truck to retrieve Lorelei. William was in the back with the little girl. He had woken her to explain where they were and what was happening. Handing her down to Diane, he hopped down himself. She thanked him for his kindness and held out the Jaguars cap to him. Smiling, he wrapped her in a big hug, then pulled a fifty-dollar bill from his wallet.

"No," Diane protested. "You've done enough just getting us here. I can't take more from you."

"Listen. I've got three kids at home. You need help. I can help. I figure you've helped your share of folks in the past and you will again down the road. Don't argue with me about it 'cause you won't win. Now, I'll watch 'til you get safely into your room. Take care of yourself and keep those young'uns safe."

Diane hugged him again, so grateful she couldn't find words. Libby and Lorelei managed small smiles of exhaustion, waving at him from behind Diane's legs. The threesome walked as quickly as they could to their room, turning to wave at William for the last time before they closed the door.

Running a hot bath for the girls, Diane put them in the water together with a cheap bar of motel soap, then she sat in the lone chair, musing about the best way to reach out to Joe. She had no credit card and not much cash. No buses ran from here to St. Samuel. She couldn't get a ride share without a credit card. Maybe a taxi? The room didn't have a phone so even if she had felt safe calling a cab, she couldn't do that, either. Diane got up to pace, periodically looking through the curtains of the depressing motel room to scope out the parking lot, paranoid that Oscar's men had somehow discovered their whereabouts.

On her third lap, she saw activity by the pool, causing her to pause and watch, half hidden by the dingy curtains. The pool, empty of water but full of leaves and trash, sported a broken wooden wheel in place of a diving board, splotches of red indicating a once-fresh paint job. An idea formed as she observed a short young white male standing by the broken wheel surreptitiously exchange cash with a teenaged Hispanic kid for a tiny package. Transaction complete, the teenager moved rapidly to a waiting Lexus while the short guy beat feet to a rusty four-door black sedan. The sedan looked like its best days were way behind it. The white guy sat in the car for a few minutes. Diane couldn't see what he was doing, but she guessed he was enjoying the fruits of a just consummated drug deal.

Making an instant decision, she ran out the door and down the stairs, arriving at the sedan breathless. She rapped sharply on the window of the driver's side door. The young man startled and looked at her in fear, eyes dilated. She made a roll-down-the-window motion. When he shook his head no, she said, "I'm not a cop. I want to make a deal with you. Do you want to make fifty bucks? Open the window."

Wiping white powder from under his nose, he rolled the window down two inches.

"I need you to take a message to someone for me. And let me borrow your car tonight for an hour. I'll pay you fifty bucks." Diane tried not to sound desperate.

The young man looked at her like she was an alien who had inexplicably popped up from the pavement.

"Nah, I don', I don't think so. I need my car, man."

A minute passed while he tapped the steering wheel erratically, head twitching. Diane waited, fairly certain of the young man's next words.

"But, well, if I do it, could I get the money now?"

"I'll give you ten now, ten after you deliver the message, and the rest when I bring back the car. The message is going to someone in St. Samuel. Can you take it now?"

"Uh, sure, yeah, I guess." The young man looked bewildered, his fingers continuing an irregular drum beat on the steering wheel.

"Okay, wait here. Let me get some paper."

Diane ran into the motel's office, borrowed what she needed from the clerk, and wrote a few words on a sheet of notepaper. On a separate piece, she wrote Joe's name and the St. Samuel Police

Department address, not trusting her messenger to remember who he was looking for or where to find him. She wasn't sure this guy would follow through, and she felt bad about him driving under the influence, but as Joe's granny would have said, "Needs must."

Her need was great and time was short, so she headed back to the car, gave him the folded-together notes, a ten-dollar bill, and detailed instructions on how to find Joe, then crossed her fingers and went back to room 202. The sedan pulled out of the parking lot a few minutes later.

CHAPTER 43

JOE

The morning following Joe's flight, Terry picked up the ringing phone on Joe's desk while his partner stared out the window, squeezing a flex ball in one hand, holding a coffee mug with the other, and distractedly watching a white Chevy Suburban pass slowly by the station. Without apparent reason, Joe's spirit eye flared. Having had no success finding the tailor yesterday at his shop or his house, the detectives were going back to his business this morning as soon as Joe met with Chief Paris. She had summoned him earlier and he was waiting now for her to get out of a meeting.

Terry's professional "Saint Samuel Police Department, Homicide, Hampton" greeting was followed by a full minute of silence as Terry listened to the voice on the other end. Joe's spirit eye blazed higher. That plus the silence caused him to turn towards his partner. Observing the stunned look on Terry's face, Joe stopped squeezing the ball and put down his coffee as Terry ended the conversation.

Dropping the phone into the cradle, Terry exploded in a big grin. "Uniforms have Taylor. Let's go get him!"

As they hustled out of the building, Chief Paris forgotten, Terry explained the phone call was from the 911 call center supervisor, a veteran dispatcher of twenty years. She knew they had been looking for Danny Taylor and had called to let the detectives know a patrol unit had been dispatched to a call where a woman had been badly beaten. Upon arrival, the responding officers had found the woman unconscious and Danny Taylor being detained somehow, the supervisor didn't know by whom. That was all the info dispatch had at the moment, but she thought the detectives would want to know soonest.

Joe was thanking the police gods that they wouldn't have to continue to track Taylor down when his cell phone rang. Caller ID showed his ICE contact's number. Joe answered with a brief, "Morgan" and Jerry Wang immediately started talking.

"Joe. Haven't been able to track down Taylor's exact arrival and subsequent movements in-country yet, but did discover he's wanted in Australia for questioning in the disappearance and suspected murder of several women. I'm still working on the rest of his background but wanted you to know this piece immediately."

Now it was Joe's turn to look stunned. Terry watched as his partner pumped his fist in the air and replied, "We're on our way to pick him up now, Jerry. Sounds like he's probably our guy. Thanks for the help and the call. We'll be back in touch." Joe looked at Terry. "Well, partner, I think this case may have just broken wide open."

Focused on Wang's call and the possible scenarios they might encounter when they reached Taylor, Joe was still ignoring his fevered intuition and barely registered the white SUV cruising past again as he and Terry jogged down the department steps. When the pair stepped down to the sidewalk, a short man in his twenties with a tiny fuzzy moustache popped out from behind a fully grown crape myrtle tree.

"Mr. Morgan?"

Startled, Joe looked over to find the guy twitching and rubbing a hand under his runny nose. Joe didn't recognize him, but he looked like a tweaker from the back alleys of St. Samuel.

"Here, some lady told me to give you this," the young man said, pushing a piece of small white paper into Joe's hand. Joe stared after the stranger as he hustled down the sidewalk. When the messenger disappeared from sight, Joe opened the paper to find a handwritten note from Diane.

Joe
In trouble. Need help. Our woods. Tonight, 1900.
D

CHAPTER 44

PHOEBE

I was tuned in to a previously played college football game, blank writing pad on my lap, watching my Valdosta State Blazers get pummeled by one of those annoying Southeastern Conference teams, when the announcers started talking about how the coach of the Valdosta team had a lot of faith in his young and inexperienced players. The coach's big challenge was getting those players to have equal faith in themselves. The announcers' comments got me thinking about my own self-confidence, unusual for me, introspection being something I usually avoid at all costs.

    I have a modest amount of faith in my writing skills, but Aunt Lucy was always my biggest fan, telling me multiple times, "All you need in this life is ignorance and confidence, then success is sure." I'm fairly certain she stole that line from Mark Twain, but the phrase fit Aunt Lucy's outlook on life perfectly. That philosophy is what made her a successful businesswoman.

My sister, Sophie, also says she loves my attempts at writing—short stories, poems, limericks, whatever. But she loves me, so would she really tell me if my writing was terrible? Sophie keeps bugging me to write a long novel with my own original characters. Of course, her ulterior motive is to be the star in my first book. I actually should try to build a character around her, because I'd have a ready source for all things medical, as well as a protagonist with the perfect personality.

The graceless but phenomenally intelligent Sophie ended up becoming a renowned neurosurgeon (apparently clumsy feet belied extraordinarily steady hands) and she now heads her own neurology practice in a prestigious Boston office. Yep, my baby sister, the brilliant neurosurgeon. If I didn't love her so much, I'd hate her. At our holiday dinner tables, she tells funny stories about the things people say when they are undergoing brain surgery, so I could easily tap her neural pathways for ideas and make her my heroine. Not only is she an amazing doctor with runway model looks, she has a handsome husband and two adorable, well-behaved children. You know that birth order personality theory? The one that says the first born child is always the overachieving Type A personality? Totally backwards in my family.

Sighing at the repeat of the Blazers' third loss of last season (we got stomped in this rerun, too, no surprise), I switched off the television, stared at my legal pad, and took the cap off my Bones Oral Surgery pen. I swiped it the last time I got a crown, not that the fifty-cent pen made up for the eighteen-hundred-dollar surgeon's bill. Made me feel better, though.

So, let's see, time for some creative writing. *Joe, Joe, where are you, my Joe?* I closed my eyes, meditating for a few minutes to see if my Lieutenant wanted to come out and play. His backstory needed a lot of work, I still needed a heroine, and my water conservationist serial killer plotline was trying to dry up on me. I clearly needed inspiration. Hmm…before becoming a cop, should Joe have been a college football player? Maybe dating a beautiful cheerleader majoring in pre-med…whose name just happens to be Sophie? Touchdown! I started scribbling rapidly.

CHAPTER 45

DIANE

Relief flooded her veins as Diane finally saw Hank pull into the motel lot and park, leaving the engine running. Diane had asked his name before he left on her errand so she could call him something besides "the druggie" in her head. She had watched the parking lot from the window all afternoon, waiting as patiently as she could for the run-down sedan to return. The girls snuggled in the bed with the TV on, watching some cartoon Diane wasn't familiar with, falling asleep and waking off and on. Though her cough was almost gone, Lorelei's breathing still wasn't normal. Diane knew she needed to get her to a hospital. *As soon as I find Joe. We'll take the girls to the emergency room, and they'll be protected by him and by people I trust.*

When she saw Hank drive up, she told the girls to stay put, she would be right back. They didn't protest but she could tell by the looks on their faces they didn't want her out of their sight. She kissed them both on the forehead, told them they could watch her from the window, promised pizza for supper, and ran down to see if Hank had accomplished his mission. He had been gone longer than she thought he would be, forcing her to spend long minutes hoping he hadn't made another drug deal and gone rogue on her.

Hank rolled down his window and demanded his money as she approached the car. "I found him and give him the note. Now gimme my money."

"Did he say he would meet me?"

"I didn't stick around for him to say nothin'. I ain't gonna hang around no police station any longer than I got to. Had to wait a long time for him to come out as it was. My money?"

Diane held the ten-dollar bill just past his grasp while she quickly reached in the window and snatched the keys from the ignition. Hank shouted in protest until she said, "The deal was I could also borrow your car. Here's the next ten. You'll get the last thirty when I get back tonight."

"Well, what am I 'posed to do 'til tonight? I don' live near here."

"I don't care what you do, maybe go get something to eat at the Waffle House across the street. When was the last time you had a good meal?"

Hank didn't answer her question but exited the car without further complaint, a sheep accustomed to complying. He wandered over to the pool, contemplated the accumulated debris in the bottom, then laid down in a broken lounge chair and appeared to go to sleep.

✲✲✲

As the sun went down, Diane cleaned up the detritus from their cheese pizza dinner, then sat on the bed with the girls. She explained she was going to meet a friend who would help them, but they couldn't come along. She told them to stay quiet in the room, she would be back in a couple of hours, then they would be safe. They would take Lorelei to the doctor and her friends would find their mom and bring her to Georgia.

Both sets of gray eyes lit up at the mention of their mom, but Libby's mouth trembled as she begged to go with Diane, Lorelei nodding in agreement beside her. The ailing child was feverish and limp with pain. Diane knew she needed a doctor, but the priority right now was keeping them out of Oscar's grasp, which was why she refused to take them with her tonight. If she got caught, at least the girls wouldn't. She needed a posse of law enforcement professionals to ensure their continued freedom. Both children had displayed an incredible amount of fortitude over the last months. They just needed to stay tough a bit longer.

Libby continued to plead. "We don't want to be left alone. Please, Diane, please take us with you. We'll be good, and we'll be quiet, and we won't be any trouble."

Diane sighed as she took Libby's tiny hand in hers, massaging the little palm with her thumb. "Sweetie, I don't want to leave you, but it's too dangerous for you girls to go with me. You'll be safe here as long as you stay in the room and don't answer the door."

Giving Lorelei a worried glance, Diane continued, "Besides, I don't think Lorelei feels much like moving. You stay here and be a good nurse. I'll be back soon with ice cream and people to help us. Deal?"

In response, Libby slid back down under the covers, snuggling as close to Lorelei as she could. The little ones were frightened and unhappy with the idea of being alone, but Diane couldn't do anything to alleviate their fear. *A few more hours and we'll all be safe,* she thought as she placed the "Do Not Disturb" sign on the handle and closed the door behind her.

CHAPTER 46

JOE

Our woods. "Our woods," Diane had written, the woods where they had spent countless hours discussing and planning their life. The three children they would have, a boy, a girl, then another boy. Chief of police eventually for Joe, chief of detectives for Diane. Hours of lovemaking in the treehouse Joe had built, talking over all the major life events. Rehashing the multitude of holiday dinners spent with his family and hers where they had stuffed themselves with food and love. Problems at work with supervisors and fellow officers, arrests gone bad, victims helped, bad guys convicted. Hours of desperate anguish with each repeated pregnancy failure. At some point the tree's magic no longer worked and they went to the treehouse less and less, until finally staying out of the woods for good.

Joe had built the circular treehouse six feet off the ground, with a trap door for the opening. He would pull himself up onto the wooden platform, then give Diane a hand up, closing and locking the door under them. The couple had moved a mattress and blankets into their foliage-wrapped world, Joe cursing a blue streak while hauling the mattress up with a rope and pulley. They kept snacks in a squirrel proof metal box, brought wine or beer as the mood suited, and in the first few years of their marriage, relaxed in camp chairs under the shining galaxy several times a month. Their woods were on the south side of town, between the five-mile running loop and the edge of their twelve-acre property.

Reading Diane's note, Joe blanched and swayed slightly. Terry, after watching the twitchy young man retreat rapidly down the sidewalk, looked at his partner with concern and pulled the note out of his hands. In the two seconds it took Terry to read the words, he started to shake his head.

"Nope, no way, no, Joe, you are not going into those woods on the basis of this note. You don't even know if Diane sent it."

"That's her handwriting."

"And how do you know she wasn't forced to write it for some nefarious reason? Like maybe by someone with a grudge against you who would just love to get you alone in the woods at night, with your mind all clouded because you think you're going to find your missing wife?"

"All the more reason to go, Terry. No matter how you slice it, Diane's in trouble, whether she wrote the note voluntarily or under coercion. My job, as both husband and law enforcement, is to help her. You won't talk me out of it. And no, before you say it, you can't go with me, either. I'll go alone. I'll be careful and I'll walk away if the slightest thing seems out of place."

Terry started to protest again but Joe, putting a hand in the air, stopped his friend. Looking Terry straight in the eyes, he said, "She's my wife. This is mine to do. We are too swamped with this serial killer to bring in the rest of the department for something that should just be between me and Diane. Let's go get the guy we think is our murderer. We'll collar him this afternoon, question him until we get the truth, and I'll go meet Diane tonight. No arguments, Terry."

Terry knew when a battle was lost, so he gritted his teeth and didn't say anything more. But he was determined to back up his partner, no matter what.

CHAPTER 47

PHOEBE

I had just let Jack out into the back yard for some squirrel chasing when the doorbell rang. After a morning of sweaty yardwork, I had the shower warming up, so I hoped the visitor was UPS with the books I'd ordered and not company. I also hoped the doorbell didn't presage Henry DeSantos at my door. He had brought me a kitten last week, and I wasted an entire hour convincing him Jilly and Josie were feline enough for me and Jack. Henry had left unhappy but had taken the cute ball of black fluff with him. I definitely did not want a repeat of that annoying episode.

Today's hours of outdoor manual labor had set my creative juices flowing, so I planned to write this afternoon and didn't want any two- or four-legged distractions. I had finally managed to scratch out fifty pages I thought were worthy and wanted to keep the momentum going. I'd even come up with a catchy title, "The Shower Floor Murders." Clever, eh? My Lieutenant Joe is still hot on the trail of the serial killer. I hadn't come up with a heroine yet, though a Sophie creation was still a possibility. Hopefully the perfect female protagonist will come to life soon.

One of my weed-pulling brainstorms was to add a human trafficking angle to the story, but I was unsure how to incorporate that. Maybe my serial killer could also be a human trafficker? Seemed like the two occupations don't really mix, especially for a killer whose primary concern was climate change. Still had to think on that, but since my water conservationist plot had started flowing right along again, my plan after scrubbing the sweat and dirt off was to write, write, write. Whoever was ringing my bell needed to go away quickly.

I cautiously approached the glass storm door, ready to drop behind the couch and pretend not to be home if the visitor was Henry. I always have a storm door installed as I don't like opening the front door when the bell rings and having nothing but air in between me and whoever is on the other side. Glass door installation had been one of the first projects Jimmy handled when I moved into the cottage.

Peeking carefully around a lampshade, I saw Danny Taylor's niece standing on the porch, backlit by sunshine and dust motes. Outside of the tailor shop, I'd only seen her in passing at the softball fields, so I was surprised to see her at my door and couldn't imagine why she was here. Besides not having any clothes being repaired at the tailor's, Danny didn't offer delivery service. Brenda looked upset and like she'd been crying though, so I quickly unlocked the door and waved her inside. "Brenda, honey, what is it?"

The perfectly weighted door shut softly behind us as I ushered her to the couch. "Sit down, sit down. Can I get you a drink, a glass of water or a Coke or something?"

Brenda nodded yes, hiccupping out, "Maybe a Coke," and wiped tears from her face with her shirt sleeve. Handing her a box of tissues I said, "Here, blow your nose, I'll be right back."

Jilly and Josie peered at Brenda from their favorite spots on the comfy wingback chairs, debating whether or not to investigate this wet, sobbing human. Josie decided against, stalking tail high into the kitchen with me. Jilly voted for, dropping on her belly into attack mode and heading straight for the neatly tied shoelaces on Brenda's red tennis shoes.

As the refrigerator door spit ice cubes into a glass, I opened the other side, pulling out a can of frosty Coke. Hearing a soft click, like a door closing quietly, I took a quick peek through the back screen door to ensure Jack was still in the yard. Occasionally, he liked to practice his piloting skills and fly over the fence for a free-range run on the beach. But my sweet shepherd was still sniffing out the numerous scents that had materialized in the two hours since his last patrol.

Filling the glass almost to the brim with the bubbly beverage, I grabbed a bag of chocolate sandwich cookies from the pantry on my way back to the front room. As Aunt Lucy would say, "Sugar helps every crisis."

Crossing the threshold into my small living area, I was bewildered to find Brenda gone. In her place stood Danny Taylor, filling my little cottage's space, not appearing bashful or introverted or physically slight at all. Astonishingly, he almost matched my five-foot-eleven, and he was brazenly looking at me with an anticipative look on his face.

"Danny? Where's Brenda? What's going on?"

I set the Coke and cookies down on the end table, thinking furiously, trying to make sense of Danny Taylor in my living room. Danny watched me but didn't say a word.

"Danny, you're creeping me out. Talk to me or leave. Now."

Where I got this forceful voice from, I don't know; I was shaking in my flip-flops. Some primal part of my brain was flashing "Danger, danger!" but I couldn't figure out why. Despite my demand to know what he wanted, Danny stayed mum, eyes bright with an anticipation I didn't understand. Remembering the shower was running and knowing my handgun was in the bedroom, I said, "I've got to turn off the bath water and let Jack in; I'll be right back."

I ran into the bathroom to turn off the faucet, intending to grab my weapon from the nightstand then get Jack, not realizing my mistake. I should have let my faithful companion in first, he who possessed no fear and forty-two razor sharp teeth, because when I turned from the shower, Danny was right behind me. Before I realized what was happening, he knocked me to the floor with a vicious punch to my left temple. Crying out when I hit the tile floor of my beautiful walk-in shower, I heard Jack start to bark wildly, growling and jumping at the back door, ninety pounds of fury trying to get through a tightly closed barrier.

Turns out my observational skills really do suck, as Danny is not only tall, he's also strong. None of my self-defense moves were helping me get away from him. He had me pinned to the floor, straddling me at the hips so I couldn't roll him off no matter how I twisted and turned. I had fallen with my right arm trapped under my back, but I hit Danny as hard as I could with my left fist. He immediately grabbed my hand, snapping the wrist back, and I screamed like a banshee as the delicate bones cracked. From the back yard, Jack snarled and howled like a deranged wolf. Danny put his hands around my neck, choking me until I stopped moving, almost passed out.

Releasing my neck, he ripped my shirt down the middle, buttons popping in every direction, and crazily I thought, *boy I'm really going to need a tailor after this.* As I sucked in oxygen, Danny paused for just a second, staring at my exposed breasts. I screamed for Jack and help and God Almighty as my attacker reached for a small kit he had brought with him. He stuffed a washcloth in my mouth, putting an immediate end to my screams, kneeled on my left forearm, and pulled out the biggest sewing needle I had ever seen, along with a small gleaming knife. The needle was threaded with thick, dark red thread. The knife blade glinted sharp and shiny.

I took as big a breath around the washcloth as I could, and started kicking my legs, bucking my head, trying to break his nose with my forehead, throw him off me, anything to get free. He reacted by pummeling my mid-section repeatedly with both fists. The cracking sound of ribs breaking forced me to stop moving, intense pain taking away what little breath I had. I thought of my folks who would never understand, my sister, who would cry her heart out, and my Lieutenant Joe who would now never grace the printed page. I wondered who would take care of Jack and the girls.

As Danny sliced my abdomen several times with the blade, I gasped in agony, sucking the washcloth deeper into my mouth. Danny held the needle over my face for a moment, looked me in the eyes, then began his work on the knife cuts. I didn't understand what he was doing, only knew whatever it was hurt like hell. I was drifting into blackness when a deafening splintering sound filled the house. Seconds later, Jack came streaking through the bathroom door, eerily silent. As he launched that gorgeous black and tan body at Danny, my world went mercifully dark.

CHAPTER 48

JOE

Terry ran the Crown Vic with both lights and siren at full speed through the traffic, something they rarely did as detectives. Knowing Joe was distracted, he had grabbed the car keys from his partner's hand and jumped in the driver's seat. As they raced through town, Joe was quiet, his mind on the strange messenger and his upcoming meeting with Diane. He would need to be extra careful in case it was some type of setup. *What could Diane have gotten herself into that required meeting so clandestinely?* Deep in thought, Joe started when Terry sharply called his name. He looked up to find they were stopped in front of a pretty beach cottage surrounded by emergency vehicles with lights flashing.

"Guess this is it." Joe said. "You ready?"

Terry looked his friend squarely in the eyes. "The question is, are you ready? We think we're about to arrest our serial killer. Are you focused? Because if you're thinking about Diane, go on back to the office and I'll bring Taylor in without you. We'll hitch a ride back with a uniform."

Knowing Terry was right, Joe shook his head. "Nope, I'm good. I swear. We've got to get this guy now. Let's go do it."

Terry didn't argue. Joe was a good cop, a consummate professional with an unwavering ability to put away emotion and compartmentalize when the situation required. Terry knew now that Joe's head was in the game, nothing would distract him. The two men stepped out of the vehicle and surveyed the hectic scene.

Two EMTs were bringing a sheeted body out on a stretcher. As Joe headed across the lawn to speak with the lead EMT, she waved him off. "Gotta go, sir, the patient's in critical condition. You'll have to catch up with her at the hospital. She can't talk right now, anyway. She's unconscious and been choked almost to death. Probably be a day or so before she can speak, assuming she comes back around."

Joe nodded, looking grimly at Terry. Loud barking emanated from the house as both men moved toward the door. Joe had been to chaotic crime scenes before, but not many. Typically his scenes were quiet, the victims dead or already transported to the hospital, the suspect long gone. In this little oasis by the sea where untoward violence had occurred, a large German Shepherd was alternating between barking down the hallway toward the bedrooms, lunging in the direction of the stretcher carrying the victim, and quieting down to take a treat from a uniformed officer who was trying to lure him outside. Then the dog would start the sequence over again.

Underneath the canine's commentary, a string of continuous cuss words issued from the back of the house. Walking down the hallway toward the voice, Joe and Terry arrived at the master bathroom door to find Danny Taylor on the floor being tended to by

EMTs, bleeding profusely from his thigh, and cursing like the sailor he used to be.

"That damn dog," seemed to be Taylor's refrain for the day.

✳ ✳ ✳

While Joe and Terry had been racing to the beach in search of Danny Taylor, a car had crept slowly up the Morgans' drive. Belle cocked her head at the sound of the engine, rose from her warm bed, and padded softly to the front window, hoping their visitor was the postman with a treat to pop through their mail slot.

Peering through the pane, she saw three men in a large white vehicle, which came to a stop, motor running, while the occupants studied the house. A couple of minutes passed, then a small, blonde-headed man exited. He cautiously approached the front door. Belle had never seen him before, but she didn't like his looks or his smell. Growling low in her throat, she moved to her guard position behind the oak door. When the doorbell rang, she started barking ferociously, repeatedly lunging seventy pounds of solid muscle at the door. Despite the thick barrier between man and beast, Surfer Dude jumped back, almost falling down the steps, and ran to the car. The vehicle began backing out of the drive before the passenger door shut completely. Belle remained vigilant until the sound of the engine faded at the edge of Joe and Diane's woods.

✳ ✳ ✳

Back at the station, Taylor, bandaged up and sitting in the interview room, wasn't talking. He had lawyered up the moment of his arrest and had stayed almost mum since. He refused to acknowledge his real home country or admit to knowing any of the victims or anything about the murders. The only time he spoke, in a perfect American accent, was when Terry questioned him about the attack on Phoebe Evans, presumably speaking because he'd been caught red-handed in the middle of the assault. Taylor simply said the afternoon was a date gone wrong. She had invited him to her house and they were having rough consensual sex, which "that damn dog" misinterpreted. The knife foreplay was Phoebe's idea.

Terry snorted in disbelief, shooting a look at Joe through the two-way mirror. "You're telling me Miss Evans wanted you to cut her five times on her abdomen with a knife? Then use a needle and thread to outline the cuts? And she wanted you to break her wrist and two ribs? And choke her half to death? That's your story?"

"Hey, no accounting for crazy women, is there? Some of 'em like the pain. Now, I said I want my lawyer and I got nothing else to say until my guy gets here. And I need some painkillers, man. That damn dog tore out a chunk of my flesh."

Terry sighed, picked up his pen, notebook, and folder, and walked out of the interview room, shaking his head. Entering the small room behind the two-way, Terry threw down his notebook in disgust. "Can you believe this guy? He's got some damn balls."

Joe sympathized with his partner, as he was ready to mutilate and strangle the tailor himself. Or better yet, let "that damn dog" interrogate him again. Instead, Joe said, "It's getting late. We can't question him until the attorney shows, so I'm going to head home. Need to change before meeting Diane. We can resume questioning Taylor tomorrow with his lawyer. Or you and Jeremy can tonight if the guy shows up." Before Terry could broach the topic of Joe going to the woods alone, Joe stopped him. "I know what you're going to say. The answer is still no, Terry. I'm doing this alone. You wait for Taylor's attorney or head home to your kids and prep questions for this jerk for tomorrow. You can help me out by briefing the chief before you leave. I told her we'd stop by and fill her in on whatever we got from Taylor."

Terry nodded and said he'd get a uniform to take the presumed murderer back to his holding cell. Joe picked up his jacket, shrugged it on, and held the door for his partner.

✯ ✯ ✯

A few minutes before seven, Joe grabbed the department-issued shotgun from the rack in the Ford and stepped out of the vehicle, senses on full alert, his spirit eye awake and echolocating, pulsing the air for threats. The woods resonated with a multitude of nature's sounds. Clouds bounced fading light through the foliage, haunting images appearing and disappearing as a slight wind ruffled leaves. When he stepped into the clearing, Joe immediately spotted Diane underneath the tree where they had spent so many love-filled hours.

Diane's gorgeous hair was chopped off in a ragged cut. As best Joe could tell in the flickering light, she looked worn, aged, sad. He wanted to rush to her, pick her up and crush her to him. Instead, he walked towards her slowly, deliberately, as though trying not to spook a wounded animal. Diane held up a hand to stop him when he was about five feet away.

"Di, what's going on? Where have you been? Why all this secretiveness?"

"Wait, Joe, we haven't got much time. I'll tell you the whole story, but later. There's a little girl, Joe, in a motel off the highway. I need you to help her. She needs a doctor."

"A girl? Diane, what is going on? Whatever trouble you're in, come home, let's talk about it and figure out what to do together. Like we've always done."

"Joe, I want to come home, I do. But first we have to save this girl. We need backup, as many cops as we can get, Joe, we need more, we need, we need . . ."

Diane faltered, sagging with fatigue. Joe was processing her words when gunfire suddenly erupted throughout the clearing. As pistol shots reverberated in the night air, Diane dropped like a stone. Joe fell to the ground, crawling rapidly to cover his wife, bullets flying over their heads. A lull in the fire allowed Joe to rise. He saw movement in the bush to their left and blasted the shotgun, then dropped immediately back down on top of Diane. A scream, more rounds speeding in their direction, then quiet.

Ten seconds later, a voice boomed. "This is the Saint Samuel Police Department. Put down your weapons and come out slowly with your hands in the air. We've got this area surrounded."

Joe didn't know what just happened or how the cops got there, but he was too worried about Diane to care. Rolling off her, he saw a red stain blossoming on her blouse. She was struggling to speak. ". . . the girl, Joe, in the mo . . . motel, exit three, the Red . . . Red Wheel. Keep . . . keep safe."

"Hush now, honey, you can tell me later. I love you, Di. Stay with me now. Ambulance will be here soon, honey."

Joe's voice trailed off as he saw the life leave Diane's eyes. She was gone. He had just gotten her back and she was gone, slipping away right in his arms. He had failed. He had failed his duty as a husband, a law enforcement officer, a man, to protect his wife. Crumpling over his longtime love, he drew her warm body close and held on, not speaking, not crying, and trying not to feel.

✸ ✸ ✸

"Joe?" Terry's tentative voice came from behind him. "Joe, the ambulance is here."

Holding on for a last embrace, Joe finally released Diane down to the leaf-strewn earth and struggled to his feet. Two medics moved in and bent down, uselessly checking for signs of life. Joe watched for a moment, then turned away. Several St. Samuel police officers and Frances County sheriff's deputies had converged on the clearing, searching the bushes and trees for the shooters.

"What are you all doing here?" Joe looked at his partner bleakly.

"Did you really think I was going to let you come here without backup? You know better. I put a team on standby and got here early. If I'd just seen Diane, then fine, I would have melted away into the night. But when I reconned the area, I found fresh boot prints from three people. Looked big enough to be men's, not women's. Then I saw Diane. She didn't look like she was aware she had company, so I went ahead and called in the team. Then you showed up."

Terry was interrupted by a Frances County detective. Dale Curtiss, the county's longest-serving law enforcement officer, had worked with Joe and Terry on several cases in the past. Terry was glad to have Dale in charge of the scene and he knew when Joe came out of his daze, he would be, too. Dale looked sympathetically at Joe, then focused on Terry as he said, "Joe, if you want to head home, Terry can fill me in. I'll catch up with you tomorrow. Go home and get some rest. You've got some long days ahead."

Joe looked at Dale, eyes dull. Without speaking, he turned on his heel and walked slowly back to his car. Terry watched until his partner stepped into the vehicle, then turned to Dale. "We need to find out who's behind this before he does."

"Yes, we do. What's been happening since Diane disappeared? I know we spent weeks helping you guys try to find her when she first went missing."

Terry told Dale nothing had happened in the interim until Joe was handed the mysterious note earlier that day. They still had no idea where Diane had been for the past five months. Or what she'd been doing or why she had returned to St. Samuel. Neither he nor Joe had ever seen the guy who delivered the note. Terry couldn't fathom what Diane had gotten into that would have resulted in a gunfight in the woods and he doubted Joe could, either.

"Alright," Dale said. "Let's see what the techs find, and maybe that will shed some light on this mess. You go take care of Joe. I'll be in touch with both of you tomorrow."

Terry shook the investigator's hand and with a final, despairing look at Diane's body, he left the woods to find his partner.

CHAPTER 49

PHOEBE

I could hear voices, but I didn't want to open my eyes. I was cold, and every part of my body hurt. The thought "I should have died" kept popping up in my mind, but my brain was so foggy I couldn't remember why I should have died. My left wrist was encased in something hard. I suspected if I did open my eyes, I would see a cast. My neck felt odd, like I was wearing a turtleneck that was too tight for my throat. Pain radiated from somewhere in my abdomen.

Reaching up with my right hand, I gingerly felt around my neck. Wherever I touched, pain flashed like the lights in a pinball machine. My hand, as though searching for the source of all this agony, fluttered down to my stomach, finding and tracing five sets of stitches to the right of my belly button. My stomach roiled as I suddenly remembered why I was engulfed in pain. Danny Taylor. But these seemed to be professional physician stitches, not psychopath Danny Taylor stitches. I vaguely recalled the madman hadn't finished his job because Jack finally chewed through the back door and raced to the bathroom to save me.

I was unconscious during Jack's huge hero moment, but apparently my boy grabbed Danny by the back of his thigh, pulled him to the floor, and stood with his jaws clamped around the would-be-murderer's neck, snarling and daring him to move. A couple of vacationers walking on the beach heard the commotion and bravely came to investigate. Finding a ninety-pound German Shepherd pinning a large man to the floor via his carotid artery and an unconscious woman lying beside the pair spurred the couple to action. They called 911 but wisely left Jack to his mission, although they did inch quietly and carefully up to me to see if I had a pulse. Which I did, but just barely.

Turns out Danny Taylor was a serial killer I hadn't been aware we had in our midst. Obviously, I really need to start watching the news again. His modus operandi followed the same four-step pattern with each victim. Initially he would throttle a woman until she almost blacked out. While she was gasping to get air back in her lungs, he would perform his weird buttonhole ritual. Then he would rape her. Finally, he strangled her to death with his hands. Lucky for me, Jack's jaws of steel chewed through the door before the final parts of Danny's ritual were carried out.

Yeah, Danny Taylor, the tailor. Can you believe it? As I eventually discovered, Danny was wanted in Australia for the exact same type of attacks that occurred over a decade ago. He terrorized women on the Australian coast for years and the authorities Down Under believe he killed at least twenty young women. He slipped out of the country when law enforcement finally caught on to him and immigrated illegally to the United States.

Unbeknownst to anyone in St. Samuel, the man had a lovely Australian accent, spoke three languages, and both lusted after and hated women. In addition to all that, his niece wasn't really his niece, just a fellow criminal he'd met on the run whom he paid well to corroborate his made-up life in the States. How he came to settle in St. Samuel was still being investigated. Danny had laid low since moving here, keeping his urges at bay, with what I don't know, maybe his fancy buttonholes. The cops assumed something triggered him to begin killing again but they hadn't figured out what yet.

I learned all this from one of the two lead detectives at St. Samuel PD, Lieutenant Terry Hampton. And guess who he turned out to be? Yep, the same detective I dealt with in Atlanta after the Anna incident. Small world, eh? He remembered me immediately, kindly asking if I had recovered from that event and inquiring how I came to be in St. Samuel. He used the same tactics interviewing me this time as he had before, making small talk until I was comfortable, chatting about the weather and asking about Jack. He was compassionate and kind. He said his partner would ordinarily be with him but was temporarily out for a family emergency, something about a disappeared wife. I don't know, didn't really pay attention. My throat was on fire, my buttonhole wounds were screaming, and my whole psyche just wanted sleep, blissful, oblivious sleep. And more morphine.

To Lieutenant Hampton's credit, he recognized my distress and said he would come back, hopefully with his partner, the next day. I guess being the only living victim of a murderous rampage earns a person sympathy with the local po-po, especially when that victim's canine actually caught the perpetrator. The police just showed up with handcuffs and spouted Miranda warnings. Jack did all the hard work.

My sweet boy didn't get too badly hurt saving my behind, but he endured enough wounds for an eight-hundred-dollar vet bill.

After the cops managed to inveigle him off Danny Taylor (copious amounts of Slim Jims were involved, from what I understand), one of the young patrol officers, who fortuitously happened to be a former military working dog handler, took Jack to the vet because blood was dripping from my pup's mouth and nose. His mouth had several small cuts and abrasions, which did not prevent him from sucking down all those delicious bribes, and his soft snout was cut in several places, too. The source of most of the bleeding was Jack's lacerated tongue, which will heal, but the poor guy will have a tough time enjoying dry kibble for a while. My hero didn't fracture any teeth in his efforts to eat a hole through the door, but his paw pads sustained multiple tiny cuts that should heal quickly.

The techs at our vet are all female and they all love Jack, who always charms the treats right out of their pockets. A dose of antibiotics, soft food for a while, lots of rest, and Jack should be right as rain soon. He's staying with Gram and Pop-Pop while I recuperate in the hospital. If I know my mom, he's getting homemade bacon milkshakes three times a day. What Jilly and Josie were doing during the attack will always be a mystery. I suspect they were hiding deep in the closet, but who knows? Maybe they jumped on Danny's toes the same time Jack grabbed his leg. At any rate, they are also with Gram and Pop-Pop, being spoiled right along with their brother who, as soon as his mouth heals, will be getting ribeye steak and mashed potatoes every night for dinner, with doggie ice cream for dessert.

For the record, if I ever get the chance, I'll rip Danny Taylor's fingernails out one by one to pay him back for Jack's injuries. Then I'll stab him, and then I'll sew his lips together with the biggest needle I can find, and then I'll...well, you get the idea. Hurt me if you must, but don't touch my dog.

✹ ✹ ✹

When I opened my eyes, Mom was at my bedside, where she'd been since shortly after the ambulance brought me in. Sophie was on her way down from Boston, and Dad was at the farm, tending the crops and animals, trying to make sense of a world in which his older daughter could almost be killed by a monster.

Mom had a lengthy conversation with Lieutenant Hampton while I drifted in and out. She got most of the scoop from him, which she later relayed to me. The lieutenant told her Brenda had stalked all the women Danny killed so she could learn their routines for him. Brenda, whose real name wasn't Brenda, was paid handsomely to be an accomplice, even making friends with a couple of the victims.

Although our teams never played each other, I had seen Brenda a few times at the softball field. She'd been friendly enough there and whenever I came into the alteration shop. While my mom told me what the police had discovered so far, I thought of the woman standing on the beach watching my house not too long ago and wondered if that had been Brenda scoping out my place. She had been picked up as soon as the detectives discovered Danny was more than likely their man. A patrol officer found her crossing the street from the tailor shop to one of the less appealing bars in town. There being no honor among thieves, or murderers either, Brenda had quickly made a deal with the cops and gave up everything she knew about her phony uncle.

The schoolteacher, Jillian Finn, Danny Taylor's second victim, was one of the women Brenda had befriended. On the night she was murdered, Jillian was supposed to have drinks with Brenda and a couple of other friends. When Jillian cancelled because she was sick, Brenda sent Danny a text to alert him the woman was home alone. She knew Jillian's routine well enough to tell him she would probably be showering around nine.

The pair would go together to local bars or the mall or the grocery store, wherever young women might be. Brenda had even joined the softball league specifically to meet potential candidates for her fake uncle. Danny would make his selection, then Brenda would attempt to strike up a friendship with the chosen woman. If she was able to form a relationship, Brenda would find out everything she could about her. Brenda even obtained house keys for three of the victims. May Ellen had needed someone to water plants and get the mail when she went on vacation for a week. Brenda had eagerly offered her services, conveniently never returning the spare key. Thanks to Brenda's sticky fingers, Jillian Finn "lost" her house key. Roxanne Richardson had a coded lock but no situational awareness, so Brenda was able to learn the code by watching Roxanne's uncovered fingers each time she opened the door. And Eleanor Connelly simply left her door unlocked most of the time, even when she was home.

Why Danny decided to use Brenda as a decoy to get into my house rather than have her befriend me to learn my schedule, I have no idea. If Brenda knows why, she hasn't told the cops yet. Danny had to know Jack would be home and would be a problem. You'd think he wouldn't have wanted to chance getting a thigh full of Jack's bared teeth. Finding me ready to take a shower was just a coincidence as even I didn't know I'd be bathing at that hour of the day. Next time I shower, I guarantee Jack will be in the bathroom with me when I step in.

When my mom expressed her thanks to Lieutenant Hampton for their efforts in finding the town's killer and my almost killer, the lieutenant blushed and said an hour or so would have prevented Danny's attack on me. He wished they had gotten confirmation of Danny's background just a little earlier. Apparently, he and his partner had been getting ready to go back to Taylor's known haunts when they learned about the incident at my house. Right after, a follow-up call came in from their immigration contact, all but confirming Taylor was their killer. The ICE agent had told them the agency had no record of a Danny Taylor arriving anywhere in America from Australia or any other country in the timeframe Danny would have migrated, and that he was wanted for questioning in the disappearance of multiple women in Australia. The lieutenants had lingered at the office just long enough to tell one of the younger detectives to get search warrants for Taylor's house and business, then headed to the beach.

CHAPTER 50

JOE

Joe sat numbly at his kitchen table. Belle, sensing something was terribly wrong, sat at Joe's knee, repeatedly nosing his hand onto her head. Every time he took his hand away, she stuck her snout under his palm and pushed the limp appendage back up to her ears.

"She's not coming home, Belle. She's never coming home again."

Belle cocked her head at his words, whimpering quietly, unsure how to help. At the sound of a car door slamming, Belle growled slightly and turned to the door. She poked her nose behind the window curtain, did a little happy dance, ran to Joe with a big doggy smile, and ran back to the door, looking over her shoulder at Joe expectantly. Joe didn't move, staring at the table as though the secrets to the universe were burned into the oak.

A brief knock coincided with the door's opening. Terry appeared, backlit by the porchlight. Belle danced around, thrilled to see their good friend. Terry bent over, rubbing the black beast's head, planting a big kiss between her eyes and whispering words of sympathy he couldn't yet bring himself to speak to Joe. Condolences complete, Terry silently walked to the cabinet to the right of the sink, took out two whiskey glasses and set them on the table, then pulled their familiar friend, Jack Daniels, from the liquor cabinet.

Terry was as comfortable in Joe's house as he was his own, having spent a multitude of hours in this kitchen discussing cases or enjoying rowdy dinners with the Morgans and his kids. Diane and Joe had always treated his family as their own and Terry wasn't sure how he was going to tell his children Aunt Diane was dead. They had been worried enough over her disappearance; this news would devastate them.

Pouring a generous amount of whiskey into each glass, Terry leaned back in the wooden chair, watching Joe, who had yet to meet his friend's eyes. Finally, Terry said, "Diane's with the coroner. He moved her ahead of a couple he has waiting. Hopes to have her complete by tomorrow afternoon."

Joe cringed and slumped lower in his chair. The image of his beautiful wife under the autopsy lights was more than he could bear to think about. After a few more minutes of silence, Terry told Joe that they'd found a dead man in the bushes and a wounded guy crawling down the access road.

At that, Joe looked up. "Were they hit with a shotgun? I shot into the bushes at some point."

"Yes, the dead guy was. One of the Frances County deputies shot the injured one. He's probably going to pull through. Undergoing surgery now or Dale would be talking to him. We stationed Petit as the hospital guard. The SOB will be lucky if Chuck allows the docs in to check on him when he gets to the recovery room. The bastard will be luckier still if young Chuck himself doesn't send him to the great beyond."

Charles J. Petit, aka young Chuck, was a patrol officer who had previously worked at the Saddle County Sheriff's Office with Diane. Diane had been his first partner when he was a rookie and he adored her. He had seemed so enamored with her, Joe had wondered a time or two if the young man was in love with his wife. When Joe asked if he should be worried, Diane had laughed and laughed.

"Nope, I'm pretty sure young Chuck is gay, he just doesn't know it yet."

Given that "young Chuck" was about ten years younger than Joe and had the kind of looks that belong on the cover of GQ magazine, after the young sheriff's deputy jumped ship to St. Samuel PD, Joe made a point to introduce himself as Diane's husband, standing tall and flexing his muscles as best he could during their first handshake. Terry had laughed at him later.

"Good, Petit will do the job well. Did you find any other shotguns at the scene?"

"We recovered your shotgun and are checking the ballistic matches now. No other shotguns. We found bullet casings from two different forty cals. The wounded guy had a Ruger nine mil. We recovered his wallet. Name is Neil Coffey, Miami address. Dead guy is a Casey Miller, also a Miami address. Young. Lot of muscles. Looks like a surfer. Checking databases for them both now.

"While I was driving over here, Dale called and said the team found two cars at the outskirts of the woods. One vehicle belongs to some twenty-year-old male down in Camden County, lives in Kingsland. We're thinking Diane drove that one to meet you but have no idea how she got it. They're dusting it for prints; Maxwell and Hoffman have gone to round him up for an interview. The other vehicle is a white Chevy Suburban, registered in Miami to a corporation. Fingerprinting that one, too, and digging into the ownership. We figure that one belongs to the men.

"The odd thing is we haven't found a third person, even though the techs found three different sets of shoe prints around the SUV. I saw three sets in the woods, too. The missing guy either didn't have the car keys or he couldn't get back to the vehicle before we were around it. Must have escaped on foot. We're still canvassing the area."

Joe offered no response to this information, seeming to retreat into himself, head down, drink still not touched. Terry waited for a few minutes, then offered, "I think I'll stay here tonight. Seems like you and Belle could use the company."

Joe looked up, grief aging his face. "No, Terry, I appreciate it but go on home to your kids. They'll be upset about Diane, too. Belle and I will manage. And before you ask, no, I'm not alright, I don't know if I'll ever be alright again, but the reality is, there's nothing you can do to help. I'll be in touch tomorrow. Go on home."

Terry considered these comments while he finished his drink, wanting to disagree but knowing he couldn't. As he moved to the door, Terry looked at his childhood friend and said, "Look, Joe. You know the kids and I loved Di, and I'm so, so, sorr . . ."

Terry choked, wiping away the tears before they could stream down his face. Joe stood up heavily, put an arm around his friend, squeezed hard, then turned to the living room, Belle glued to his side.

✳ ✳ ✳

Joe flipped out his badge. "I'm her husband, and I'm a cop, and I have reason to believe a crime has been committed. I need the key."

The clerk—Joshua, according to his nametag—gave Joe a wide-eyed look and started tapping the keys on his computer. "I'm sorry, sir, no one is registered under Diane Morgan."

"Any Morgans or Dianes at all?"

"No, sir, no Morgans, but I can't search by first names only, so there may be some Dianes; it will take me a few minutes to go through the files manually." Joshua glanced at his watch, clearly hoping the time required for that task would make Joe leave.

"Do it and do it quickly, please. While you're looking can you tell me if you saw a woman with short auburn hair and a young girl check in sometime in the last day or so?"

Joe felt as though he was grasping at straws and was shocked when Joshua looked up at him and said, "A pretty woman with a blonde-headed kid?"

"Yeah, maybe. I'm not sure what the child looks like."

"Well, we're kind of slow right now so it's not hard to remember who checks in, especially when they stand out like that woman. She was so pretty, but her hair was all messed up. And she was dirty, her face and her clothes. Looked like she hadn't slept in days. The little girl wouldn't let go of her arm, clung to her like a cocklebur. The whole thing was off. I mean, we're not a five-star hotel or anything, but we get a calm type of crowd here, usually no roughnecks or troublemakers. Just people kinda down on their luck. This lady stood out, too, because she paid in cash. We don't get much cash these days. I felt sorry for her, she seemed kinda desperate or in trouble or something."

Joe pulled out his phone and showed Joshua an old photo of Diane. The clerk said, "Yep, that's the lady but her hair's short now. Let me see, let me see."

His fingers moved across the keyboard. "I remember she checked in yesterday afternoon, and oh yeah, here she is. Becky Finnegan, Room 202."

Joe didn't bother saying thanks as he snatched the key from the clerk and ran out the door, Belle at his heels. Becky Finnegan had been Diane's best friend in high school, so Joe was sure 202 was the correct room. A quick check of the closest room number signs indicated a left turn and up the stairs. The room he sought was second from the end. Joe paused in front of the door, settling himself. If a little girl was inside, he didn't want to scare her. The child was why he had brought Belle along. Belle always knew exactly what people needed and she loved children.

Joe knocked quietly, three raps. No answer. Joe reasoned the young girl may be sound asleep. The sun was just now rising; a little kid would not likely be awake yet. When no one answered his second series of knocks, Belle assisting by woofing softly, Joe called out.

"This is the police. I'm going to open the door. I have a key. Please stand away from the door."

Joe pulled his .38 from his ankle holster and inserted the plastic card into the lock. He carefully pushed the door open, keeping Belle behind him and standing well back just in case the third bad guy from the woods was also in the room. Reaching a hand around the frame, he flipped the light switch by the door, observing two empty queen beds, the covers mussed in the one furthest from the door. His eyes swiftly swept the room, and landed on not one, but two blonde-headed girls, arms wrapped around each other, scrunched up under the sink in the back of the room. Huge gray eyes stared at Joe, faces filled with fear.

Joe stepped into the room, followed by Belle, who sniffed her way back to the girls, then sat quietly in front of them. They shrank back at first, but as Belle sat patiently while Joe silently checked the bathroom and under the beds before holstering his weapon and slipping to the floor beside the trio, the oldest one reached out a hand to stroke Belle's side. In the soft voice he reserved for traumatized victims and witnesses, Joe told them Belle's name and that she loved to be scratched on her tummy. When he told Belle to roll over and she complied with a happy grin on her face, both girls smiled just a little, reaching out a tiny bit farther to pet the proffered belly.

Joe told the girls who he was, that they were safe now, and he would get them home just as soon as he could. What could they tell him about home?

At that, the oldest started to cry and the youngest asked where Diane was. Not knowing what to say and trying not to tear up himself, Joe told them Diane had gone away for a while, but she had asked him to take care of them for the time being, he would tell them the story later. Right now, he needed to know more about them. Had anyone else besides Diane been in the room with them? Joe sighed with relief when both blonde heads shook sideways.

"You guys keep Belle company while I make a couple of phone calls, okay?"

Slight nods and more belly patting followed. Joe rose from the floor, checked the bathroom and under the beds once more, then went outside to call Terry and social services.

✫ ✫ ✫

While the crime scene techs worked the motel room, Joe and Belle rode in an ambulance with the girls to the hospital. After they had finally crawled out from under the sink, Joe could hear Lorelei's ragged breathing and saw the way she held her side protectively. Both girls were covered in bruises and scrapes. Getting permission for him and Belle to accompany the girls in the ambulance had taken all of Joe's persuasive skills and law enforcement credentials. The senior EMT had been adamant no dogs were allowed in the vehicle, but Joe was fierce in his determination to keep the girls in his sight. After prevailing in the argument, he and Belle scrunched together on the front passenger seat, Belle's massive head poking between the seats into the back, her butt on Joe's lap, a hand from each girl reached up and tousled in the dog's fur.

Waiting for the doctor in the emergency room, after another battle to keep Belle at the children's side, Joe finally took a moment to ask the girls their names. They looked confused, exchanging glances but not saying anything.

Joe said, "Belle told you her name. She wants to know yours."

After a long look at each other, the oldest said Petunia, the youngest followed with Rose. Then Petunia burst out, "But not really. Our names in Montana were Trixie and Katie. But our names in Alabama were Libby and Lorelei."

Joe could think of no response to this unexpected statement other than, "Okay, lots of people have different names. What would you like me and Belle to call you?"

"Libby and Lorelei, please. We want our mom. When can we see her?"

✢ ✢ ✢

Four hours later, the girls were released, and Joe took them to the station. Except for the bruising and small wounds which would heal in time, and the emotional trauma, which might or might not ever resolve, Libby was deemed healthy. As Joe suspected, Lorelei suffered from a broken rib, but luckily her lung wasn't punctured, and she hadn't developed pneumonia. The ER doc combatted her dehydration and weakness with an intravenous bag of fluid, prescribed ice for the wounded rib, lots of rest, and extra helpings of vanilla ice cream.

Now sitting in an interview room, the girls were comfortably fed after sharing small bits of grilled cheese sandwiches and French fries with a drooling Belle. The big Schnauzer was keeping a careful eye on two large chocolate chip cookies when the social service worker arrived. Joe had asked for a child welfare veteran he'd worked with many times before, a woman named Dean Sterling. Dean was rarely shocked by the human adult's capacity to harm children and maintained a calm manner young people found soothing, no matter how traumatized they were. Terry took Dean into their office to brief her. She exited the room with angry eyes, fully prepared to take the children to an undisclosed location for a few days. Not yet being sure if any bad guys were still hanging around and not knowing who they were or what their interest in the girls may be, Joe was taking no chances.

The Livingston, Montana, police were currently trying to locate the mom. The girls didn't know their Montana address, but they did know their Montana last name, so Joe hoped the locals could find the woman quickly. The kids would improve immeasurably if they could at least talk with their mother by phone. Their story was chilling, and Joe was determined to keep them safe. Diane had given her life for them. If he never accomplished anything else on this earth, Joe would reunite the little girls with their mom.

As Libby and Lorelei had haltingly relayed what they could remember of their saga, Joe's anger grew. He hated human traffickers more than he hated any other criminal. To sell children or vulnerable adults into slavery was something Joe could not abide. He could understand why Diane helped the girls, but he couldn't figure out how she encountered them initially or why she didn't simply call law enforcement the moment she realized they were victims of a human trafficking ring. The girls weren't sure where they were when Diane came to their motel room door although they agreed they were somewhere in Florida, the state where Mickey Mouse lived. Without a city name, or a phone or credit card trail, Joe doubted he would ever be able to trace Diane's movements before she arrived at the motel where she connected with the girls.

When Libby reached the part of their story about the traffickers giving Diane a choice to leave or stay, Joe went perfectly still, staring resolutely out the window. Terry, who was sitting out of eyesight of both girls, had let Joe carry the interview, sensing his desperate need to understand Diane's involvement and fulfill her dying wish. Assuming this next revelation would be excruciatingly painful, Terry moved slightly forward, ready to intercede if Joe needed him. Belle, also sensing her dad's distress, left her position by the girls and walked over to put her head on Joe's knee, looking up at him anxiously. The girls hesitated, intuiting but not understanding the new tension, then continued reluctantly, telling them the man called Oscar had told Diane she could do one of two things. She could stay with their group of five and earn money with them. If she did that, and if they all brought in enough money, the bad men would let Diane stay with the girls in their room. Or Diane could be taken to another man for some reason the sisters hadn't understood. Diane had chosen to stay at the warehouse, a decision the five girls had been thankful for.

Just as Joe was forming the words to ask how the girls were required to earn money, a question to which he was confident he already knew the answer, the front desk sergeant stuck her head in the door to tell him an investigator from the state had arrived. The GBI had a large human trafficking unit with well-trained officers experienced in breaking up trafficking rings. Agent Dalton had requested their support as soon as Joe walked in with the children. Joe motioned to Terry to stay with the girls, then walked out to greet Special Agent Tim Dillon, who was waiting in the lobby with a diminutive woman by his side. Joe and Tim had worked two previous cases together, quickly forming a collaborative relationship and full respect for one another.

Joe filled Tim in on the case with what he knew so far. When he got to the part about Diane in the woods, Tim grasped Joe's shoulder but didn't speak, knowing nothing he could say would help or comfort his colleague. Thankful, Joe concluded his brief by repeating the last few moments of his interview with the girls. Tim nodded thoughtfully, then glanced at the woman beside him. He introduced Joe to Special Agent Mary Louise Hall, one of the GBI's officers who specialized in adolescent interviews. Since Joe and Belle had established a rapport with the sisters he didn't want to disrupt, Tim suggested Mary Louise sit in the room and observe without asking questions at first. Joe agreed, shook hands with Hall, and led the agents to the girls.

Belle greeted the newcomers with a tail wag and a smile, the girls with wide gray eyes and exhausted faces. Joe introduced Lorelei and Libby to the agents, then sat on the floor beside Belle. The girls giggled, then hopped from their chairs and joined the duo, leaning against Joe and snuggling as close to Belle as they could get. The giant dog sighed, laid her head on Joe's thigh, and closed her eyes, purely content with the little hands stroking her belly.

Quietly, Joe continued with his questions until the social worker, who had left to stock the safe house for several days' stay, returned.

"Lieutenant Morgan, I really need to get these young ladies squared away. They need baths and a good night's sleep. And possibly a big dish of ice cream."

Smiling, the veteran child welfare advocate held out her hands to the girls. Lorelei and Libby looked at Joe who explained they were to go with Miss Dean. He promised to come see them the next day. "You'll see Belle tomorrow, too. I'll bring her to the house you're staying in. Thank you for talking so long with me today. You've both been really brave."

Before he could stand, Libby hugged Joe fiercely around the neck and whispered, "Thank you for rescuing us. Tell Diane we want to see her soon."

Joe winced at the innocent words while he rose from the floor with the little blonde wrapped around his waist like a monkey. Lorelei grabbed his thigh in a one-armed hug, then silently took Dean's outstretched hand. Not wishing to let go of Joe but following her sister's lead, Libby reluctantly climbed down and took Sterling's other hand.

Joe looked at the GBI agents and Terry, shaking his head. The girls had told them about their father's debt, their months of captivity, their narrow escape through the gate, the scary overnight in the bushes, the truck rides to the Red Wheel Inn, and seeing their kidnappers in the white SUV. Joe's anger grew when he recalled seeing a white SUV drift slowly past the station twice the day Diane died. When Joe had asked about the other girls who had been held with the group, neither Libby nor Lorelei would talk for several minutes. They had sat with their heads down, limp blonde hair covering their faces, tears streaming down their cheeks, small hands furiously stroking Belle's fur. Seeing their additional distress, Special Agent Hall had tapped Joe on the shoulder, indicating her desire to take over. Joe nodded and moved to make room for the investigator to join the foursome on the floor.

After some softly spoken, well-worded questions from the female agent, Libby had finally said they didn't know what happened to Lily, just that she didn't make it through the gate. Maria had squeezed through the opening with them but fell down just as the gate closed. Diane had told the girls to run, which they did, but they couldn't go fast because of Lorelei's rib, and they were too frightened to run too far away from Diane, anyway. She had stopped to help Maria, so the sisters had waited a little way down the road. When Diane caught up with them a few minutes later, blood stained her shirt. She only said Maria would be staying behind. The girls figured Maria was dead, and Lily was too. They had heard the gunfire but had been too scared to ask.

Watching the girls carefully, Joe mouthed "Elizabeth" to Agent Hall, who nodded but paused her questioning to ask the girls if they wanted some water. Both girls mumbled no. Before the agent could form a question about Elizabeth, Lorelei blurted out, "We left Elizabeth, too. We didn't want to leave her, but they took her, and we didn't know where she was. She got all upset one night and went sort of crazy and they took her away from us. We didn't want to leave her, we didn't!"

This declaration had resulted in more furious fur stroking, with Belle licking tears off the girls' faces as fast as the fat drops rolled down the thin cheeks.

✯ ✯ ✯

DEATH WRITES ITSELF

By the next day, the Livingston police had tracked down the girls' mother and put her on a plane to Georgia at GBI expense. She was expected to arrive late afternoon. Ali and her daughters would stay in the safe house until Tim Dillon and his team had gotten all the information they could from the reunited family. Tim had called in the FBI, knowing the Feds had been on the hunt for the girls' father, Sean Templeton, almost as long as they'd been looking for Frank Levy. With the information about Oscar, the warehouse, and the compound the girls could provide, the government agency's chances of busting the national crime syndicate and capturing two individuals on their "Most Wanted" list increased exponentially. Tim had also reached out to the United States Marshals Service to get Ali and her daughters into the Federal Witness Security Program. Tim knew Levy and Oscar would never stop looking for the young girls, even if the criminals were arrested and jailed. Aside from seeking revenge for Levy's son, the girls could testify against the criminal organization. The witness protection program would keep the family safe from Levy's widespread syndicate, as well as from Sean Templeton.

As promised, Joe took Belle to visit the girls later that day. He stayed until Ali arrived from the airport, then slipped out quietly as the little trio reunited. With the girls safe in federal hands, he could now turn his attention completely to closing out his murder cases…which would keep him from thinking of Diane's death and the life he faced without her.

✫ ✫ ✫

As Terry and Joe worked to close their part of the Danny Taylor case, they were surprised at how many people they interviewed gave similar, inaccurate descriptions of the tailor. All had characterized him as physically small and abnormally introverted. The man had been an Oscar-winning performer because, as all his victims had discovered, he was tall, muscular, and not shy at all. The introverted persona had enabled him to fade from people's awareness quickly—perfect cover for a serial killer.

The Darwin police were thrilled to hear their man had been caught and had already started extradition proceedings. Extradition wouldn't happen until Taylor had his day in the Georgia courts and became intimately acquainted with the Georgia penitentiary system. Or with luck, Joe thought, a fancy chair decorated with specialized electrical equipment.

Because Taylor's fake niece had squealed like a pig, Joe and Terry finally had several answers about their four cases. A search of Taylor's home produced five pairs of women's underwear. According to Brenda, Taylor took the underwear hoping to direct police focus to Kurt Von Schuster, since Kurt's arrests for his undergarment thievery had been widely covered in the local news. Maxwell and Hoffman begrudgingly gave the guy kudos for that tactic, but Joe and Terry refused to credit the killer with anything. Brenda couldn't explain the buttonholes except to say Taylor was proud of his sewing talents and really was a good tailor.

After their final interview with Brenda, Joe suggested they go to the hospital to attempt another interview with Phoebe Evans. She had been in and out of a painkiller-created haze both times Terry had been to see her previously. The hospital doctor had said today might finally be worth a third attempt.

Terry looked at Joe, saw the fatigue lining his face, and said, "Let's go see her tomorrow morning, first thing. We've got our killer in custody, so waiting one more day won't hurt. I've got a parent-teacher conference for Devlin this afternoon, anyway, and Ellen's little library friend is coming over for supper tonight."

For the first time since Diane's death, Terry saw the semblance of a grin emerge on Joe's face.

"Oh yeah? Aren't you the enlightened dad. Make sure you put your guns in the safe as soon as you get home. What are you feeding the punk? Poison mushrooms?"

Terry happily took the ribbing from his grief-stricken friend. "Yeah, yeah, I hear you. Pizza, no mushrooms. And I think Ellen is making cupcakes. The boys are under strict orders to behave. Not sure how that's going to work out. I've told Devlin no pranks or he'll lose his phone for a year. Wanna come? I could use the backup."

Joe laughed a little, but declined. "Let's not scare the appetite out of the poor kid. One dad at the table is enough. I'll head over to the hospital. You've been pulling my weight for a while now, let me get back in the game. Take care of your family. I'll call you later and let you know what Ms. Evans has to say."

CHAPTER 51

PHOEBE

Joe arrived at Phoebe's hospital room door just as an orderly was removing a mostly uneaten tray of food. The detective took a moment to shake images of Diane from his brain and gather his thoughts about his living victim. Then he rapped on the steel frame.

"Ms. Evans?"

At the sound of her name, Phoebe looked up from her book to see a tall, handsome man who looked considerably like a young Tommy Lee Jones standing in the doorway.

"I'm Lieutenant Joe Morgan with the Saint Samuel Police Department. Homicide Division. I'm investigating the murders of several women in the area as well as the recent attack on you.

"May I come in?"

ACKNOWLEDGMENTS

The accomplishment of a mission is only achieved through teamwork. I was blessed to have a lot of great teammates on this journey. Besides the folks listed here, I also have a super group of friends too numerous to name who encouraged me along the way.

Early editor and friend Terri Barnes, author of *Military Spouse Calls.*

Four-time Pulitzer Prize finalist, exceptional journalist, and author, Tony Bartelme.

Long-time friend and pilot extraordinaire, David Corts.

The most excellent nurse practitioner and friend, Marilyn Dippold.

Scott Garrett for finding me the perfect word when I needed one.

Captain Johnny Guy, St. Marys, Georgia Police Department.

Brad Mallett, owner of Coastal Coffee Roasters, for letting me borrow the name Carolina Morning.

Lt. Andy Martin, Dorchester County Sheriff's Office, Summerville South Carolina.

The best Marine Corps helo pilot ever, Major Sam Myers (USMC, retired), for information about MCAS New River.

James M. Scott, Pulitzer Prize finalist and author of *Black Snow, Rampage,* and *Target Tokyo.*

Genius veterinarian Dr. Sheri Wagner-Green.

For superb advice on writing and publishing, cozy mystery and romance author Dorothy St. James (aka Dorothy McFalls), along with Jonathan Haupt, literary arts leader and executive director of the Pat Conroy Literary Center, Beaufort South Carolina. Also, for her publishing advice, Shari Stauch, owner of Main Street Reads, Summerville South Carolina.

Early readers, cheerleaders, and encouragers include: the best big sisters a girl could have, Ramona and Rhonda; dear friends Charlotte Branum, Christie Baird, Marie Bilotta, Larry Borland, Tanisha Brown, and Marybeth Wishart (award-winning author of *Parker the Purple Penguin*).

Many thanks to Publish Pros editor Mary Hall, whose fine work made my story infinitely better, and Rich Carnahan, the owner of Publish Pros, who developed an amazing cover and, along with

HUMAN TRAFFICKING RESOURCES

Human traffickers use force, fraud, or coercion to recruit, harbor, transport, or control a person and place them in involuntary servitude for labor (domestic, agricultural, retail, etc.) or commercial sex purposes. Persons of all ages, genders, races, religions, and countries are trafficked around the globe daily.

If you are a victim or believe you know someone who is, call 911 (in the United States) or reach out to one of the organizations listed below.

National Human Trafficking Hotline (operated by the Polaris Project)
polarisproject.org
Live Chat: humantraffickinghotline.org
Call: 1-888-373-7888
Text: 233733 (Text HELP or INFO)

A21
a21.org

Coalition to Abolish Slavery and Trafficking
Hotline: 888-KEY-2-FREE (888-539-2373)
info@castla.org

Freedom Network USA
freedomnetworkusa.org

National Center for Missing and Exploited Children
Hotline: 1-800-THE-LOST (1-800-843-5678)
missingkids.org

Modern day slavery is present in every community, every town, every city, every state, every nation. I encourage you to become educated about human trafficking, learn the signs, and get involved to help eradicate this global scourge.

www.ingramcontent.com/pod-product-compliance
Lightning Source LLC
LaVergne TN
LVHW020731151224
799042LV00025BA/376/J